TAKING HIS LORDSHIP IN HAND

The infuriatingly self-assured Earl of Dambroke had set himself up not only as Catheryn Westering's sponsor in London society but as her stiflingly protective guardian and stern taskmaster as well.

Clearly Dambroke had much to learn.

He had to be convinced that he was driving his sister Tiffany into the arms of a fortune-hunter scoundrel.

He had to be shown that he was being unjustly cruel to his occasionally wayward young brother, Teddy.

And above all, Catheryn had to teach him that she was not a flighty young female who had to be kept caged—but a woman who had to be wooed and won by a proud lord who badly needed to be humbled....

THE FUGITIVE HEIRESS

SIGNET Regency Romances You'll Enjoy

☐ **THE INNOCENT DECEIVER** by Vanessa Gray.
(#E9463—$1.75)*
☐ **THE LONELY EARL** by Vanessa Gray. (#E7922—$1.75)
☐ **THE MASKED HEIRESS** by Vanessa Gray. (#E9331—$1.75)
☐ **THE DUTIFUL DAUGHTER** by Vanessa Gray.
(#E9017—$1.75)*
☐ **THE WICKED GUARDIAN** by Vanessa Gray. (#E8390—$1.75)
☐ **THE WAYWARD GOVERNESS** by Vanessa Gray.
(#E8696—$1.75)*
☐ **THE GOLDEN SONG BIRD** by Sheila Walsh.
(#E8155—$1.75)†
☐ **LORD GILMORE'S BRIDE** by Sheila Walsh. (#E8600—$1.75)*
☐ **THE SERGEANT MAJOR'S DAUGHTER** by Sheila Walsh.
(#E8220—$1.75)
☐ **THE INCOMPARABLE MISS BRADY** by Sheila Walsh.
(#E9245—$1.75)*
☐ **MADALENA** by Sheila Walsh. (#E9332—$1.75)
☐ **THE REBEL BRIDE** by Catherine Coulter. (#J9630—$1.95)
☐ **THE AUTUMN COUNTESS** by Catherine Coulter.
(#E8463—$1.75)*
☐ **LORD DEVERILL'S HEIR** by Catherine Coulter.
(#E9200—$1.75)*
☐ **LORD RIVINGTON'S LADY** by Eileen Jackson.
(#E9408—$1.75)*
☐ **BORROWED PLUMES** by Roseleen Milne. (#E8113—$1.75)†

* Price slightly higher in Canada
† Not available in Canada

Buy them at your local bookstore or use this convenient coupon for ordering.

THE NEW AMERICAN LIBRARY, INC.,
P.O. Box 999, Bergenfield, New Jersey 07621

Please send me the SIGNET BOOKS I have checked above. I am enclosing
$_____ (please add $1.00 to this order to cover postage and handling)
Send check or money order—no cash or C.O.D.'s. Prices and numbers are subject to change without notice.

Name _____

Address _____

City _____ State _____ Zip Code _____
Allow 4-6 weeks for delivery.
This offer is subject to withdrawal without notice

The Fugitive Heiress

by
AMANDA SCOTT

A SIGNET BOOK
NEW AMERICAN LIBRARY
TIMES MIRROR

NAL BOOKS ARE AVAILABLE AT QUANTITY DISCOUNTS
WHEN USED TO PROMOTE PRODUCTS OF SERVICES, FOR
INFORMATION PLEASE WRITE TO PREMIUM MARKETING DIVISION,
THE NEW AMERICAN LIBRARY, INC., 1633 BROADWAY,
NEW YORK, NEW YORK 10019.

Copyright © 1981 by Lynne Scott-Drennan

All rights reserved

SIGNET TRADEMARK REG. U.S. PAT. OFF. AND FOREIGN COUNTRIES
REGISTERED TRADEMARK—MARCA REGISTRADA
HECHO EN CHICAGO, U.S.A.

SIGNET, SIGNET CLASSICS, MENTOR, PLUME, MERIDIAN AND NAL
BOOKS are published by The New American Library, Inc.,
1633 Broadway, New York, New York 10019

First Printing, August, 1981

1 2 3 4 5 6 7 8 9

PRINTED IN THE UNITED STATES OF AMERICA

PUBLISHER'S NOTE

This novel is a work of fiction. Names, characters, places, and incidents are either the product of the author's imagination or are used fictitiously, and any resemblance to actual persons, living or dead, events, or locales is entirely coincidental.

I

When one is running away from home, thought Miss Catheryn Westering idly, one ought to suffer at least a twinge of guilt. One certainly had no right to expect such delicious thrills of adventure and excitement as she was presently experiencing. To be sure, there had been that brief moment of doubt back at the posting house near Maidenhead where they had stopped for lunch, when it had suddenly occurred to her that the Earl of Dambroke might not be in London at all, that he might just as well be at his country seat in Hertfordshire instead. But her driver-companion, Bert Ditchling, had reassured her.

"There now, Miss Catheryn, don't fret yourself," he had said affectionately in his gravely baritone. "His lordship will be in London right enough. Where else would he be this time of year? Use your head, lass. Why, the social season's just beginning. All the smarts'll be in town." It was true enough, and Catheryn remembered as well that Dambroke's sister, the Lady Tiffany, would probably be out this year. Indeed, except for the youngest, a mere schoolboy, the whole family should be in town.

She settled back now against the squabs and surveyed the passing countryside. She and Bert had left Caston Manor during the small hours and, though excitement kept her awake for a while, she had slept most of the way as they rolled through the towns and villages nestled at the foot of the Berkshire Downs. Dear Bert had been scolding off and on all day, of course, first about being dragged from his bed in the dead of night and then about dining alone with her in a private parlor. He thought her journey a purely impulsive start and an altogether improper one at that.

"Traveling the Bath Road in a shabby carriage with

none but a groom to look after you!" he had sputtered at one point. "And you call yourself a gentlewoman!"

Well, she was a gentlewoman. And if the chaise was shabby, at least it was her own. The chaise and pair, her grandmother's emerald necklace, and about a hundred pounds were all that remained once her grandfather's debts had been settled after his death the previous year. As for Bert Ditchling, he was certainly more than a common groom, for Catheryn had known and depended upon him all her life. It had seemed perfectly natural that he follow when she went to live at Caston Manor with her aunt and uncle. That thought caused her to wonder what the Castons might be doing now. Sir Horace had had business that took him to Bath the day before, but surely he had returned to the manor by now and had heard of Catheryn's departure. He would be worried and angry and probably think her ungrateful.

"Which I'm not," she muttered aloud. "Not a bit." After all, the Castons had offered her a home when her grandfather died and had treated her as kindly as though she had been their own daughter. But they also clearly approved of their son Edmund's intention to marry her, and Catheryn had no wish to marry Edmund. She had explained her feelings carefully, but to no avail. Her Aunt Agatha, placid as always, had simply folded plump hands at plump waist, smiled, and told her not to be a goose.

"For you will not wish to be left forever upon the shelf, my dear Catheryn. And no man in these parts is looking about for a twenty-one-year-old female who has spent her formative years dashing about the countryside on horseback and who knows less than nothing about keeping house. I myself," she added with a certain loftiness, "would oppose the match were Edmund not so set upon it; for, despite the training I have endeavored to impart this past year, I do not consider you a suitable bride for him. However, that is as may be. Dear Edmund has said he will marry you, so marry you he shall."

As for Edmund himself, Catheryn liked him well enough, but even his friends referred to him as the "estimable Edmund," and "estimable" was an excellent description. He had done well at Harrow and Cambridge and had never been sent down from either school for misbehavior, a fact that did not impress his cousin

Catheryn. She would have preferred to see some spirit in him. Nowadays, he spent his time learning about the estates which would one day be his, was always tastefully if conservatively attired, had excellent manners, and was, in fact, a dead bore. For some reason, beyond Catheryn's understanding, he had chosen to fall head over ears in love with her most unworthy self. Constant discouragement seemed to make little impact, but she had never really doubted her ability to deal successfully with his suit, even if life at the manor should become a trifle difficult in the meantime. The matter of Uncle Daniel's money proved to be another matter altogether.

Daniel Westering, her grandfather's younger brother, had died in India three years before. Having never met him, Catheryn did not think much about it at the time, so when Edmund had inadvertently mentioned the previous afternoon that Uncle Daniel had left her ten thousand pounds, she had been astounded.

"Why was I never told of this?" she had cried.

Edmund explained simply that her grandfather, a joint trustee with Sir Horace for the money, had not wished Catheryn to know of her fortune, lest she insist that some of the money be used to restore Westering. He preferred that it be saved for her dowry. "When he died," Edmund had gone on rather condescendingly, "we never thought about informing you, what with one thing and another, and later there seemed no reason. After all, your coming of age made no difference to the trust, and females know nothing of money matters. My father handled everything, as he will continue to do."

"Of all the muttonheaded, idiotish, high-handed, infamous, *damnable* things to do!" Catheryn had exploded. "How could you be so unnatural, so . . . so deceitful! Do you mean to tell me that all the time we scraped and pinched to put food on the table and keep Grandpapa comfortable, ten thousand pounds were just idling away in some stupid banking house!"

Edmund calmly pointed out that the money had been drawing interest and hardly sitting idle, but Catheryn was unimpressed. She demanded to know where the money was located and how she could get her hands upon it so that she might leave Caston Manor at the earliest opportunity. Her cousin had been amused.

"The money is in trust until you are twenty-five, Catheryn, or until our wedding, of course, since you are of age. Come now, and be sensible. We would have told you perhaps had it crossed our minds to do so. It just never did."

That had been the final straw. Furious, Catheryn had restrained herself, knowing it would be useless to argue further with him. It was bad enough that they expected to marry her to Edmund at all, but to think they had meant to do so without informing her that she carried a dowry of ten thousand pounds was outside of enough. She had known that neither her uncle nor her aunt would support her feelings in the matter. Uncle Horace would agree with Edmund about females and money, and Aunt Agatha would tell her that she must consider her good fortune and not bother her head about the details.

Who, she had wondered, would support her? It was then that she bethought herself of Richard, seventh Earl of Dambroke, the head of her family. Her grandfather and his, according to the family Bible, had been first cousins. Obviously, that meant she and the earl were also cousins, though to what degree Catheryn was uncertain, having never understood the difference between a second cousin and a first cousin once removed, let alone anything more complicated. The remote kinship and the fact that the family was large made it more than likely that Dambroke was unaware of her very existence, but could she not, with all propriety, apply to him for aid? Of course she could.

She was not perfectly certain how trusteeships worked, but surely Dambroke could at least advise her as to the best course, and he would be bound to help keep her from being forced into an unwanted marriage. On the other hand, might he not consign a letter from an unknown female relation to the nearest fire? After brief consideration, she had rejected the thought. He might think about the fire, but his duty would require that he return some sort of answer. It was much more likely that he would simply order her to trust the judgment of her aunt and uncle and obey their wishes in the matter.

Having convinced herself that a letter would be a waste of time, she determined to confront him in person and took advantage of her uncle's absence to act upon the impulse at once. When she woke Bert, she told him only that she was leaving in order to escape Edmund's undesirable attentions and that she hoped Dambroke would support her cause. Despite his grumbling, Bert had asked no questions, but she could not delude herself that the earl would be so accommodating. Indeed, it would not surprise her if he demanded her immediate return to Caston Manor. With a confidence born of experience, she hoped she might depend upon her own resourcefulness to avoid that end.

Smiling, she straightened, stretched herself much as a cat does, and settled back with these thoughts for company to admire the view. When they had passed through Heyword Village, Bert shouted back that it would not be long now, and the excitement welled up within her again. Eventually a house flashed by and then another, and the carriage wheels clattered on cobblestones. They were in London. Bert slowed the horses to a walk and soon pulled into the flagway to hail a passing pedestrian for direction to Grosvenor Square. Her long journey was coming to an end.

It did not occur to her until the chaise actually turned into the lovely square with its enclosed garden and tall, imposing homes that her initial meeting with the earl might be a trifle awkward. Her aunt would thoroughly disapprove of calling upon a gentleman without benefit of chaperone, regardless of his being the head of her family; and, though Catheryn was not perfectly certain what the proprieties were in a case like this, she had an odd notion that she was not living up to them. Briefly, on the front step, she considered asking for the countess instead of the earl before rejecting the notion as a mere waste of time. Only the earl could help her.

A very proper butler answered the door and, to her relief, did not turn a hair when Miss Westering requested speech with his master. He merely bowed his head a fraction and ushered her into a pretty saloon, furnished with elegant taste and no apparent regard for cost. Catheryn declined to sit and, perceiving a mirror over the fireplace, stepped toward it with fluid grace. Removing her cloak and gloves, she straightened her hair and white muslin tucker and smoothed the skirt of her pomona-green morning frock, then paused to gaze directly at her reflection.

The face in the mirror was not beautiful, being heart-shaped rather than fashionably oval and much too brown. Since Cathyryn stayed indoors only when it was impossible for her to be outdoors and rarely wore a hat, her blond curls had been streaked nearly white by the sun, but her charcoal-gray eyes were set wide apart with long, dark lashes and were wont to sparkle irrepressibly with merriment or mischief. They narrowed now as she grimaced. Very likely, the great and powerful earl will feel exactly as Sir Horace and Edmund do about females handling money and will refuse to help you at all, my girl, she told herself. She shook her head and the grin peeped out again. One could only try one's best.

She wondered what Dambroke would be like. Her grandfather had spoken little of his family and had written the young earl off as a "damned Corinthian." Catheryn had attended an occasional assembly in Bath and knew a Corinthian to be an elegant gentleman more interested in sport than in dancing attendance upon simpering belles at fashionable squeezes. Some had a tendency toward foppishness, which she despised; many of them were fond of deep play, and she herself had seen more than one strolling down Milsom Street in the company of dashing ladies of questionable repute. On one such occasion, when she had been with her aunt, that redoubtable lady had insisted upon crossing the street in order to avoid meeting such a couple. Just as she was smiling at the memory and wondering if Dambroke would prove to be the type of gentleman disapproved of by Lady Caston, the doors were flung open and, in sonorous tones, the butler announced his lordship.

Dambroke paused on the threshold and lifted his quizzing glass. Thus, her attention was drawn first to the deep-set ultramarine eyes, then to the firmly chiseled features and sun-darkened skin; but, from the top of his carefully disordered locks to the tips of his glossy Hessian boots more than six feet below, the earl was a fine figure of elegant masculinity. There was not a wrinkle or loose thread to be seen. His snowy cravat was stiffly starched but simply tied, his collar points were of moderate height, his dark blue coat fit snugly across broad shoulders, and buff stockinette breeches complemented every rippling muscle in his legs when he moved. His jewelry included only a gold watchchain with a single fob and the Dambroke signet worn on the third finger of his right hand. She knew him to be twenty-seven and, despite the quizzing glass, Catheryn decided approvingly that this man was no fop.

She did not move from her place near the mantle, nor did she take her eyes from him. If he expected to stare her out of countenance with that chilly, rather aloof gaze, he would be disappointed, for she was made of sterner stuff than that. Dambroke seemed to recall himself and turned sharply to his patently interested butler, letting the glass fall. "Refreshments, Paulson," he ordered in a pleasantly deep voice. "Uh . . . ratafia and biscuits, I think."

Catheryn chuckled, interrupting the butler's dismissal. The earl turned quickly enough to catch sight of the decided twinkle in her eye as well as her still twitching lips. His eyebrows lifted in silent query, and she made a sterner attempt to control herself. "Forgive me, my lord," she said, "but you do not seem the sort of gentleman who would relish ratafia. I am certain you would prefer Madeira or port, and I myself should much prefer a glass of lemonade."

His own lips twitched responsively, so perhaps the gentleman possessed a sense of humor. He stifled it, however, and moved toward her, speaking over his shoulder. "See to it, Paulson." The door shut softly and Catheryn sank into a belated curtsey. "Shall we be seated, Miss Westering?" The words were uttered crisply, more like a command than a suggestion, as he led her to a comfortable chair in the window and seated himself in its twin. A low buhl table stood between them. "Paulson must have told you that my mother is expected momentarily, but perhaps, in the meantime, I may be of service."

A slight frown disturbed her features at this subtle insistence, despite her specific request to the butler, that she must have come to see his mother. "My business is with you, my lord, though I should be pleased to meet her ladyship, of course. However, perhaps I impose altogether. I'm certain you don't even know who I am."

He smiled faintly. "On the contrary. I believe you are

the granddaughter of Sir Cedric Westering, my grandfather's late cousin, and that you have come to London from somewhere in the neighborhood of Bath." Catheryn was amazed till he went on blandly, "I am head of the family, Miss Westering. It behooves me to know its various members." Her eyes narrowed as amazement shifted to suspicion. "Have I said something wrong?"

Demurely, she gazed at her folded hands. "No, sir. Only, you're doing it much too brown—as my grandfather would say." She peeped at him from under her lashes.

This time the smile was rueful but warmer than before. "You are perceptive. I'm forced to admit that Mr. Ashley, my excellent secretary, was present when Paulson brought word of your arrival. I have him to thank for my knowledge."

Catheryn smoothed her skirt carefully, grateful for the pause made necessary by the arrival of their refreshments. She could usually size people up quickly, but the earl presented something of an enigma. Though he seemed to maintain an aloof dignity, there had been those brief, encouraging flickers of humor. Paulson set a tray containing glasses of lemonade and Madeira as well as a plate of small, delicious-looking cakes on the table, effectively breaking her train of thought. He then executed a bow rather deeper than the one with which he had greeted her and inquired whether there would be anything further. Dambroke waved him away.

Catheryn took a small sip of her lemonade. Then, drawing a resolute breath and setting the glass down, she looked directly into the blue eyes opposite her own. "Lord Dambroke, I must thank you for your kindness in acknowledging a relationship that is distant at best, for, quite frankly, I have come here hoping to take advantage of it." She paused, looking away, seeking words. "Oh dear, I knew this would be difficult. Perhaps, after all, it would be easier to present my case to your mother."

"Is your case so desperate then?" he asked gently.

"Not . . . not desperate. Only uncomfortable. I'm afraid I've run away from home." Seeing that he looked shocked and not a little severe, she felt herself plunging into unknown waters. "I know I ought to have written first, my lord, but I was afraid you'd misunderstand and insist I let myself be guided by my aunt and uncle."

"Are you not afraid I will say the same thing now, Miss Westering? I must tell you," he added sternly when she stared down at her hands once more, "that my first reaction is to hear no more of this but to send you packing instead. My butler informed me that you brought no maidservant. Am I to infer then that you traveled alone all the way from Somerset?" She nodded, still looking at her hands. "Good gracious, child! 'Tis most unseemly! What were your relatives about to allow it!"

She looked up gravely. "I believe I explained, sir, that they did not exactly allow it. And I could not bring my maid, for she is actually in my aunt's employ and would have apprised her of my plan. It was difficult enough to rouse Bert. I am not a schoolgirl, my lord."

"And who, if you please, is Bert?"

Catheryn smiled. "His name is Bert Ditchling, sir, and he was my grandfather's estate manager. He's been my groom since we removed to Caston Manor. I know such a change of position must seem strange, but it is not. Bert was raised at Westering. When Grandpapa gambled away the better part of his lands and fortune and had to release most of his servants, Bert refused to go. For several years before his death, Grandpapa suffered from the gout and was unable to leave his bed except to sit sometimes in a chair, and he came to depend entirely upon Bert. After he died, Bert refused to abandon me—his words, sir—and my uncle was kind enough to allow him to accompany me to the manor. I might add that Bert agrees with you wholeheartedly on the subject of my journey to London. I have been forced to endure his scolds all day."

"Knowledge of where my duty lies gives me the feeling that you should endure mine as well, Miss Westering." She looked at him anxiously, and he added more mildly that he would endeavor to restrain himself. "You speak kindly of your uncle. I confess a curiosity to know what necessitated this flight."

She blushed. "It was not entirely my uncle, sir, but also his son, who believes himself in love with me. I don't know what ails the man, but it's rather wearing."

Though she had hoped to provoke it, his laughter was

nonetheless surprising, softening the stern countenance and bringing the glimmer of a twinkle to his eye. "I beg your pardon," he said, hurriedly recovering himself, "but you look so woebegone. I've never seen a woman react in such a way to the admission of a man's love for her. Pray forgive me."

The color in her face became more pronounced, but she smiled. "Not very becoming of me, is it. I'm afraid I am not as conscious as I should be of the honor Edmund does me, my lord. It seems quite ridiculous. I cannot love him and have no wish to spend my life buried in the country. But that is not all, sir. There is more." He raised his brows again, and she proceeded to explain the matter of Uncle Daniel's money. When she finished, Dambroke was broodingly silent for some time.

"The matter interests me," he said finally, "but I do not understand precisely what you expect me to do."

Catheryn took a deep breath, cakes and lemonade forgotten for the moment. "I am not certain exactly how matters stand, sir, but Edmund said the money must stay in trust until I am twenty-five or until I marry, with my uncle as trustee. As I said, I have no wish to marry Edmund, but with my uncle holding the purse strings, I shall have little opportunity to meet anyone else; and, eventually they may wear me to the point that I shall accept Edmund against my better judgment. I need someone to support my case, and I hoped you might oblige. I should like very much to set up housekeeping in London for a time, to see the sights and, perhaps, to partake of some of the pleasures. I should be perfectly willing to accept your guidance in order to go about the thing properly, and I do not necessarily aspire to the heights. But I should like to experience life beyond the West Country and perhaps have a chance to meet someone suitable to marry. If my uncle could be persuaded to loosen his hold on my fortune at least to the point of granting me an allowance, I'm certain I could contrive to live within it. You wield a good deal of power, my lord, or so I have heard. If anyone could convince him, it would be yourself. I could never hope to do so unaided."

She waited expectantly, hoping she had struck the right note by appealing to him as a man of power, encouraged by the fact that he did not instantly refuse her.

When he spoke, he seemed to choose his words with care. "You tell me you are no longer a schoolgirl, Miss Westering, and yet your behavior indicates that you are not very old. No doubt you have acted in haste and without forethought. Since you admit that your relatives treat you kindly, it would be improper of me to do anything other than restore you to their care. Whatever else I decide, they must certainly be informed at once of your whereabouts."

Inwardly burning at his rebuke, Catheryn reminded herself that true resourcefulness meant not giving up at the first sign of defeat. There were always other notes to strike. She straightened her shoulders, shedding the demure for the self-sufficient. "My lord, I am of age. Perhaps I have not behaved with all due propriety, but I am determined upon my course. Since you can do nothing to help me, I should be very grateful if you will recommend a reliable man of affairs who would at least look into the details of the trust for me."

"You misunderstand me, Miss Westering," he countered smoothly. "I am not casting you off. I will certainly do all I can to help you protect yourself against an unwanted marriage and to see that your fortune is not used as a weapon against you. I'm not entirely convinced, however, that your uncle has any such intention. You cannot speak of his kindness on the one hand and accuse him on the other, you know. The matter must be properly investigated. You may trust me to see to it. As for allowing you to set up housekeeping in London, I shall certainly do nothing to further such a scheme. In that, you must be guided by your relatives."

Though grateful for the half loaf, she would have debated the last point had not the sound of voices in the hall arrested his attention. "I believe you are about to meet my mother, Miss Westering."

The doors flung wide and Elizabeth, Dowager Countess of Dambroke, hurried into the room with silk skirts rustling. She ignored her son, who had risen to his feet, and passed straight on to Catheryn. The countess was small and round and, though nearing the middle forties, still very pretty. Dressed in yellow with pale blue ribbons, she carried a light shawl over her arm and wore a frivolous lace cap with matching ribbons perched upon her soft brown curls. The cap ribbons fluttered as she approached, and the total effect was charming. Though rather awed by her ladyship's entrance, Catheryn had stood up automatically when Dambroke did and now proceeded to make her graceful curtsey. Immediately the countess's two soft hands stretched out to her.

"Come, come, child! Stand up and let me look at you. I am Lady Dambroke, you know." She raised Catheryn to her feet and, gazing straight into the dark eyes, demanded, "But who are you, my dear? My servants informed me only that Dambroke has been closeted for more than half an hour with an unknown girl. I had quite given up hope of his ever falling in love, I must tell you. And here he is inviting you to visit with never a word of it to me!"

II

Catheryn blushed fiery red and the earl interrupted hastily. "Mama, this is Miss Catheryn Westering, granddaughter of the late Sir Cedric Westering, my grandfather's cousin."

"Yes, yes, Dambroke, but how did you meet her and why have you never mentioned her to me before?"

The humor of the situation struck Catheryn as she watched the earl try to bring things into focus for his parent. "I met her here today, Mama. She has run away from home."

"How shocking!" The countess surveyed Catheryn more closely. "But how fortunate that she should choose to run here and at this particular moment!" Catheryn stared at the pair of them. Her ladyship seemed to be attempting a sort of silent communication with her son. He only looked grim. "Surely," she insisted, "it's the very thing! But come, child—Miss Westering, did you say?" Catheryn nodded, smiling shyly, too bemused to speak. She found her hands clasped tightly, and two bright blue eyes twinkled into her own. "You must come with me at once and tell me about yourself."

"Mama! Miss Westering belongs with her relatives. I have already explained to her that she must return at once."

But her ladyship seemed not a bit cast down by his harsh tone. "Nonsense, my dear. She cannot leave at once. How absurd! Order a bedchamber prepared for her immediately. She certainly cannot leave before morning, and perhaps we shall contrive to keep her for a short visit." Noting his stern look and rigid jaw, her ladyship was moved to entreaty. "You must see, dear, that she is the answer to a prayer." It was clear that he did not see. "Dambroke, only consider Tiffany!"

"I have considered Tiffany more than enough for one

day, madam. Where is she, by the way? I thought her to be with you."

"Oh no. She does not like Letty Mearing, you know. She was upstairs when I left, rather indisposed, poor dear."

"Sulking in her room, you mean," retorted Dambroke in exasperated tones.

"Very likely." Her ladyship was unconcerned. "Nevertheless, she is quite cast down and needs a distraction. Miss Westering may be the very thing."

Catheryn felt a little like the ball at a tennis match but was fascinated by the dialogue and waited anxiously for his lordship's response. He glanced in her direction and then looked straight into her eyes, his expression thoughtful. At last, he looked back at the countess.

"There is a certain matter concerning Miss Westering that I should like Ashley to look into, and she did express a wish to remain in town for a while. She wishes to set up housekeeping on her own, however."

"But that would never do," protested the countess. She smiled at Catheryn. "Really, my dear, it would not answer. You will be much more comfortable here with us. You will be excellent company for my daughter, and she will be delighted to show you just how to go on."

Catheryn liked the sprightly countess. "I should be pleased to stay, my lady, if his lordship will permit it."

Dambroke shrugged. "Very well," he agreed. "Perhaps your relatives may be induced to allow you to remain here a short while as our guest. But do not look so overjoyed," he added sternly. "I have not entirely capitulated, you know. Despite my mother's confidence, I don't know that it will answer her purpose. However, if you can distract my sister from what she feels to be the ills of her situation, I will thank you most sincerely. I shall use the time to look into the other matter, but you must write your aunt and uncle at once. You may tell them that my mother invites you to stay for a week or two. That should allay their anxiety, and if they agree, you are welcome." He smiled faintly. "Perhaps a separation from your cousin will help you see his suit in a new light, too. Absence, the heart, and all that."

But Catheryn refused to think of Edmund at all. Her eyes were sparkling as she thanked Dambroke and agreed to write the letter. Lady Caston stood in awe of any title and would never refuse an invitation for her to visit a countess.

Lady Dambroke spoke up. "I shall send a note of my own as well, Miss Westering." She shot a look of triumph at her son. "Now, Richard, order a bedchamber for her, if you please, and tell Paulson that we shall want tea in the drawing room in twenty minutes. I shall send for Tiffany to come to us there." She put her arm around Catheryn's waist. "You shall tell us all your adventures, child. What a nice surprise you are, to be sure."

When they reached the drawing room, she sent a footman off to inform the Lady Tiffany that her presence was required. Catheryn appreciated the brief respite. Things had moved at whirlwind pace since her ladyship's arrival, and she needed a chance to catch her breath.

The drawing room was magnificent. It occupied much of the front half of the first floor and, despite the formality of yellow velvet curtains and gold-inlaid furnishings, the room had an atmosphere of cheerful warmth. Lady Dambroke's workbasket and tambour frame sat beside one chair and a fire had been laid, ready to light, in the fireplace. Catheryn's gaze came to rest upon the mantle clock, an exquisite creation by Godin of Paris, dated 1742. She learned later that it was one of the countess's favorite pieces, to be found wherever she chanced to be at home. The face was supported by a flower-bedecked ormolu branch under which stood two porcelain Oriental figures, the taller draped in flowing Mandarin robes and the other, short and round, dressed in the trousers and loose-roped shirt of a peddler, a bulging pack slung jauntily over his shoulder. Both men seemed to be sharing some joke or other, their merriment so vividly expressed that anyone looking upon them found cause at least to smile. Catheryn chuckled just as the countess turned from dismissing her footman upon his errand.

"Amusing, are they not?" she smiled. "But now, my dear, tell me about yourself. I declare I've not had such a diversion in an age." She settled upon a sofa and patted the cushion invitingly.

Laughing, Catheryn sat and, in less than ten minutes, had put her in possession of the pertinent facts of her recent history. When she came to the point of her arrival at Dambroke House, the countess interrupted.

"Never mind the rest, my dear." Her eyes sparkled. "I can well imagine Dambroke's reaction to your tale. Just like his father before him, he can be most punctilious with regard to the women of his family and must always look first to the proprieties. I daresay he lectured you about your lack of a proper attendant."

"Yes, my lady, he did, and I know it was very wrong."

"Well, there's no need to refine too much upon it," Lady Dambroke remarked comfortably. "I quite understand why you felt you must leave Caston Manor and, though I cannot applaud your methods, I shall contrive to overlook them." She patted Catheryn's knee. "It is not as bad as it might be. At least you had the sense to complete the journey in a single day. A night spent on the road would alter the thing considerably. But that is as may be and no use discussing further. You are most welcome here, my dear. I should like to keep you a good long time, but Dambroke must be made to think it his own idea, and that will take a bit of scheming." She paused, brows knit, affording Catheryn the opportunity to point out that Sir Horace Caston must likewise be convinced.

"I've no wish to hang on your sleeve or to become a bone of contention between you and his lordship, ma'am. I am certain he would object strenuously to my making a visit of indeterminate length without my uncle's full support. Besides, what would you do with me?"

"Do with you! Why, you foolish child, I shall present you!" When Catheryn stared in amazement, she went on, "Yes, introduce you to everyone! The best way to avoid marriage to your Edmund is to contract it with another. In order to do that, you must meet other men. I can certainly arrange that. Of course, I cannot promise a brilliant match," she cautioned, "but there must be any number of suitable young men in London."

Catheryn was sitting bolt upright by this time, her eyes wide with astonishment. "But, my lady, I've not a feather to fly with unless Lord Dambroke can pry some of my fortune away from Sir Horace!"

The countess waved the objection away with an airy gesture. " 'Tis of no consequence. We shall contrive."

Feeling that her wildest dreams were in a fair way to coming true, Catheryn nevertheless won a battle with her baser instincts and forced words of expostulation. "My dear ma'am, you cannot wish to saddle yourself with me in such a course. It would cut up all your peace. And the expense! The clothes I have are unfashionable beyond belief, and even if Uncle Horace were to allow me access to my money, I doubt I could afford all I should need. There is your own daughter to be considered as well. What would she think?"

"I can do nothing with Tiffany, my dear. Dambroke is her guardian and said only today that he will not allow her to marry yet a while. Besides, I don't much like her, and I think I like you very well." Catheryn's shock was evident, and the countess continued hastily, "Please don't think I do not love all my children. I do, truly. Only, Tiffany has become excessively spoiled of late and makes me uncomfortable. She was used to be such a cheerful, sprightly child until she inherited a prodigious fortune from her godmother and began to think herself a great heiress who can do as she pleases. She and Dambroke come to cuffs all the time. He is very strict with her, you see, and she flouts his authority constantly. When I consider how upset I was to discover that my husband had named Richard guardian, instead of myself, I can scarce believe it now. That was five years ago," she added with a sigh.

"But he must have been very young for so much responsibility!" Catheryn exclaimed.

"Indeed, and it shows. He used to laugh so easily and liked a lark as much as any of his friends. But he found the responsibility a heavy burden, I'm afraid, and has changed a good deal. He laughs less, seems much more rigid, even perhaps a bit arrogant at times, though I should not say so." She sighed again. "If only Tiffany would take a liking to you, it would give her someone to think of besides herself. I assure you that, if that happens, it may be enough to convince Dambroke to let you stay indefinitely!"

Catheryn was spared the necessity of commenting by the entrance of two footmen with the tea service. She noted with approval that the countess believed in doing the thing lavishly. There were little sandwiches filled with crabmeat, or ham and cucumber, and colorfully iced cakes. She sighed with pleasure. "Shall I pour out for you, my lady?"

"Thank you, dear." The countess turned to the footman who had answered her bell earlier. "Morris, did you convey my message to Lady Tiffany?"

"Yes, my lady. Her abigail informed me that her ladyship is indisposed but that she would attempt——"

"Drat the girl! Still sulking, I make no doubt. Go and say that she is to compose herself at once and come down to meet her cousin. If she still seems recalcitrant, you may hint that his lordship will not approve such rag manners. Do you understand me, Morris?" His face carefully blank, the footman bowed and left the room.

When they were alone again, Catheryn said, "If she is out of sorts, my lady, perhaps it would be kinder to put off our meeting." What she had heard so far left her with little desire to meet Lady Tiffany. Surely, it could wait till she finished this lovely tea!

"Nonsense, Miss Westering. My daughter is merely indulging in a fit of sulks. She and Dambroke had an altercation this morning, and I fear she was sadly worsted. I wasn't present, of course. I find such scenes excessively unpleasant. I do know she fled the library in tears, however—certainly not a sign that she came off very well, do you not agree?"

"To be sure, my lady. Would it be impertinent of me to ask what caused the altercation?"

"Of course not, Miss Westering—oh, how silly! Here I am treating you as quite one of the family and still calling you Miss Westering. You will not mind if I call you Catheryn, will you, my dear?" Catheryn shook her head, smiling. "Good. And let me hear no more miladies from you. You shall call me Aunt Elizabeth!"

"But you are not my aunt, ma'am. I am only distantly related to your husband, a slight connection to you at best."

"I promise I shall not regard it. Perhaps it would be more appropriate for you to call me Cousin Elizabeth, but that would make me think of Cousin Lucy—down at Dambroke Park, you know—and she is quite old. I prefer to be called aunt."

Catheryn's ready sense of humor was nearly her undoing, but the laughter went no further than her eyes. "I will be happy to do as you ask, ma'am. It would be churlish to do otherwise. Besides," she added frankly, "I should like very much to have you for my aunt."

"Wonderful!" applauded the countess. She took a dainty bite from her crabmeat sandwich and wrinkled her brow. "Where was I? Oh, of course, Tiffany. I am afraid Dambroke found it necessary to reprimand her for her extravagance. She has been wasting the ready, as Teddy would say."

"Teddy?"

"My younger son. He's away at school—Eton, of course." Catheryn nodded, allowing her to dismiss Teddy. "At any rate, she has been spending too freely of late, and I know Dambroke has tried to be patient, but he was prodigiously angry this morning. I found him sitting at the library desk behind a pile of her bills. The foolish girl had run through her allowance and then ordered the rest of the reckoning sent to him. He was exceedingly displeased, I assure you."

"I can believe it, ma'am, but she must have known he would not like it." Catheryn remembered the stern blue eyes and wondered at Lady Tiffany's temerity.

"My daughter considers no one's wishes save her own. As I mentioned before, she flouts him at every turn. Why, at Christmas he refused to let her attend a country house party. She was not yet out, you know, and it would have been most improper. She threatened to starve herself, but fortunately Jean-Pierre prepared a *crème brûlée* for dinner that night, so it came to nothing." The countess sighed deeply, then gave herself a little shake and touched her cap as though to be sure it was on straight. With a glance at the closed door, she observed that she could not imagine what was keeping her daughter.

Catheryn had been wondering if the afflicted damsel would put in an appearance at all. Having managed a hearty meal during the countess's discourse, she now eyed the nearly empty tea tray with misgiving but salved her conscience with the thought that, should Lady Tiffany prove to be hungry, the tray could be replenished. Helping herself to another cake, she noted that the countess seemed to have fallen into a brown study and returned to her own reflections.

Her conversation with the earl had left her with the impression that he was a fair-minded, intelligent man who would not easily be influenced by anyone. His air of command was almost awe-inspiring. Clearly, he expected instant obedience from his household and would not long tolerate such behavior as his sister seemed capable of displaying. He was cold, aloof, exacting, probably arrogant, certainly challenging, elegant, suave, vastly intriguing—and quite above your touch, my girl, she told herself sternly.

Forcing her thoughts into a new direction, she considered the countess, who was everything her Aunt Agatha was not. Lady Caston—tall, thick-waisted, horse-faced, and crisp-voiced—displayed an air of the *grande dame* that was totally lacking in the countess. Making the latter's acquaintance was truly a novel experience. Her impulsive generosity was captivating, and Catheryn felt, without understanding the feeling, that she had known her for many years. Clearly, Lady Dambroke had little if any sense of duty to her children and was primarily interested in her own comfort and pleasure. Some of the things she had said were downright shocking, but Catheryn found her delightfully charming nonetheless and willingly overlooked them. At this point her thoughts were interrupted by the sound of the door opening. She raised her eyes and nearly exclaimed aloud at the vision they encountered.

Lady Tiffany Dambroke stood on the threshold, her hand resting lightly on the door handle. Her slimness made her appear taller than she actually was, and the raven curls piled high atop her exquisitely shaped little head added to the illusion. She was attired in an elegant afternoon gown of rose twilled sarcenet, cut simply and caught in high above the waist with a white silk ribbon, the ends of which trailed to the hem. The dress was cut low at the bosom, and a rope of seed pearls was wrapped twice around her lovely throat. The color of the gown seemed to be reflected in her glorious complexion and also, Catheryn thought stupidly, in her eyes. This thought and the realization that she was staring rudely brought Miss Westering to her senses. She dragged her gaze back to her hostess.

"I'm pleased you decided to join us, Tiffany dear," that lady was saying mildly. "Allow me to make Miss Westering known to you." Tiffany let the door swing to behind her and advanced into the room. "My daughter, Lady Tiffany, Catheryn. Pay no heed to her attitudes, if you please. She merely puts on airs to be interesting."

Nothing daunted by this stricture, Tiffany held out a beautifully manicured hand and made a slight bow. Catheryn wondered briefly if she was expected to kiss the hand. Mentally shaking herself, she arose with her customary grace, politely offered two fingers, and returned the curtsey. Barely allowing their fingers to touch, Tiffany moved to the tea tray and poured out a cup for herself.

"I collect, Miss Westering," she said loftily, seating herself on a small gilt and velvet chair opposite the sofa, "that you are in some manner related to us. I don't believe I've heard your name mentioned before this day, however."

Before Catheryn could gather her wits to answer this haughty speech, the countess interposed, "For heaven's sake, Tiffany! Do try for a little conduct, or Catheryn will think you raised in a cow byre. I declare you put me to the blush."

Recognizing a light of battle in the red-rimmed eyes, Catheryn attempted diversionary tactics. "Dear ma'am, pray do not scold her. She is quite right to question my presence. It must seem that I have thrust myself upon you all and that it is I, rather than she, who is sadly wanting in conduct. Why, you know yourself that Lord Dambroke was displeased with me," she added sweetly.

The countess stiffened beside her, but the calculated speech had had the desired effect. Lady Tiffany visibly abandoned her supercilious attitude. As Catheryn had hoped, where his lordship condemned, she would empathize. "Was my brother angry with you for coming to us, Miss Westering? Whyever for?" The countess relaxed and moved to refill her own teacup, while Catheryn summoned a rueful smile.

"I'm afraid he was shocked by the fact that I have run away," she said. "He simply could not understand my feelings."

The countess turned in astonishment, unable to let such a statement pass. "Really, my dear, you exaggerate!"

But before she could continue, her daughter interrupted. "Oh, Mama! Must you always defend him? He is positively Gothic. You know he is. I can just imagine the sort of Turkish treatment he accorded poor Miss Westering. You are not shocked by her conduct or you'd not have presented her to me. And if you are not, then why should he be? It is outside of enough!"

"Tiffany dear, to speak of your brother in such a way is not seemly."

"Piffle!" replied her undutiful daughter. "Why, I can see just how it was. Heaven knows I've my own experience of his distempered freaks and that, let me tell you, puts me in great sympathy with Miss Westering. I wonder she does not fall into strong hysterics just thinking of the interview she must have had with him."

Judging by Lady Dambroke's rigid countenance that it was time to turn the conversation into more acceptable channels, Catheryn spoke up hastily. "Yes, but I promise I shall do no such thing, my lady, for your mother kindly came to my rescue and invited me to stay with her whilst his lordship looks into some trifling matters for me. She has also promised to help me make all right and tight with my aunt and uncle, which is no easy task, believe me."

"That's kind of Mama, I'm sure," Tiffany said, "but who are you, Miss Westering? Are you truly related to us?"

So Catheryn explained the relationship and then, not wanting to go into all the details again just then, turned the conversation to Lady Dambroke's promise to sponsor her, adding that she was very grateful.

"There's no need to thank me, child," said the countess. "It is the only sensible course, so that you may accompany us to the balls and parties we are forever attending. I daresay," she added in an aside to her daughter, "that with a little effort I may even procure vouchers to Almack's for her. Emily Cowper will oblige me, I think."

"Splendid," Tiffany approved. "And she must be included in our own ball, of course. That is, if Dambroke doesn't disapprove of her staying with us until then."

"Leave Dambroke to me," advised the little countess with airy unconcern. "Now, Tiffany shall take you upstairs, Catheryn, and I shall send Fowler, my dresser, to you half an hour before dinner to help you make ready. Mind you do not chatter long, Tiffany," she went on, "for Catheryn was up before the birds and will want to rest before dinner. You should do so, too, my love," she added kindly. "Your eyes are quite red, you know, from weeping. Not at all attractive." She followed them to the door. "Please do not neglect that letter to your aunt, Catheryn. You will find materials with the standish in your room. Dambroke will be sure to ask if you have obeyed his instructions and will not be pleased, I'm afraid, if you have not."

"I'll do my best," Catheryn said with a chuckle, "though I'm sure I don't know what I shall say, for she will be amazingly angry. I must rely upon your note to calm her."

"Well, I don't know," her ladyship said doubtfully. "After all, I am not acquainted with Lady Caston, though I daresay that after being in a worry, she will be grateful to know that you are safe here with me. I shall beg her to let you stay a good long time, too, and perhaps just mention that I shall introduce you to my friends. She will recognize that as an excellent opportunity for you, I make no doubt. We must just hope it will answer the purpose."

III

When Tiffany pushed open the door to a second-floor bedchamber Catheryn exclaimed with pleasure, mentally comparing its serene luxury to the decayed grandeur of Westering and the austerity of the chamber she had occupied at Caston Manor. The tranquil atmosphere was enhanced by well-executed woodland scenes decking white-paneled walls, pale green curtains framing a view of the rear gardens, and late afternoon sun spilling a bright golden path across the green carpet. Catheryn's meager belongings had been unpacked, and Tiffany moved at once to examine a pair of miniatures on the nightstand, asking if they were of Catheryn's parents. When Catheryn nodded, she exclaimed, "But how beautiful your mother was!"

Catheryn agreed. "Yes, was she not? Much prettier than I can ever hope to be."

Instead of refuting the statement, Tiffany stared at her thoughtfully. "Yes, very likely. But you have a great deal of countenance, Cousin, and I daresay could make much of yourself if you would but try. That dress is sadly out of date and ill-fitting, and you have allowed your complexion to get too brown. That will fade if you have a care of it. You are too short to be really elegant and have too sturdy a figure to be described as exquisite or delicate, but your eyes are very fine and your hair is lovely. If we put our heads together, I believe we can turn you out in style. The critics shall applaud you as a taking little thing."

Somewhat taken aback by this candid assessment, Catheryn smiled doubtfully but replied in agreeable tones, "I shall place myself in your hands, my lady."

"Very well, though you must call me Tiffany, you know, if we are to be cousins. But now, tell me all about yourself."

Catheryn complied willingly enough and soon decided, despite her first impression, that she could easily come to like the girl. There was warmth in the ready laughter following her unflattering description of Edmund Caston revealing a naive friendliness under that sophisticated veneer. She knew, too, that she would welcome Tiffany's experience and good taste when it came time to select her new wardrobe. Nevertheless, when Tiffany left, Catheryn breathed a sigh of relief and turned her attention to composing a brief note to Lady Caston. Once it was addressed and sealed with one of the wafers provided for the purpose, she removed her dress, curled up on the bed under a soft quilt, and soon fell fast asleep.

A gentle touch some time later caused her to stretch like a kitten and turn to her other side. A hand grasped her shoulder firmly, jogging her until she opened one sleepy eye and then the other. Suddenly remembering where she was, she came wide awake, sat up, and pushed her hair out of her face. A gaunt, middle-aged woman in a simple blue armazine gown stood beside the bed.

"You must be Fowler!" Catheryn exclaimed, impulsively holding out a hand. The woman hesitated but finally extended her own. Catheryn squeezed it warmly. "How kind of you to offer your services," she said, slipping off the bed. She sensed that Fowler did not approve of her and probably condemned her easy manners, so she summoned her most appealing smile. "It is quite a compliment to her ladyship that you have agreed to help me, for it cannot be a normal part of your duties to wait upon impecunious young relatives, and that's precisely what I am at the moment. I shall not be a credit to you either, for the only evening dress I have is an old white muslin. I shall look a perfect drab." She paused to light the candles on the dressing table, watching Fowler's expression reflected in the mirror for signs of a thaw. The woman remained silent, her lips pursed, but she seemed to be studying her with a rather professional eye. Hoping the look signified interest in her predicament, Catheryn spoke almost shyly. "Do you think you can help me?"

Fowler pulled herself together. "As to that, miss, there's no saying what might be accomplished with a little imagination. Their ladyships, having canceled their engagements for the evening, have decided not to change for dinner. My lord will wear evening dress, but that need not concern us, since he is going to one of his clubs after. Just you fetch that muslin, and we'll see what can be done."

Catheryn obeyed with alacrity, delighted that Fowler seemed willing to put forth a good effort on her behalf. Pulling the gown from the French garderobe, she laid it out on the bed, where the dresser eyed it askance. It certainly was a rather shabby garment, adorned with a faded pink ribbon that added nothing to its appeal.

"It's rather awful, isn't it."

"That it is, miss, but if it's all you've got, we'll make do. 'Tis a mercy it's simple and not one of them frilly embroidered things such as was the style some years back. Like as not, the threads and ruffles would all be frayed."

"It has been darned a few times."

"So it has, but that can't be helped," Fowler answered crisply. Ringing for a chambermaid, she sent her to ask if the Lady Tiffany would kindly lend Miss Westering the lilac ribbons purchased the previous week at the Pantheon Bazaar. The girl bobbed a curtsey and fled to return moments later with the ribbons.

"With the Lady Tiffany's compliments, Miss Fowler, and she begs Miss will keep them if she likes."

Fowler nodded approvingly. "Saw they didn't match the dress," she said with cryptic satisfaction. "Told her so at the time." She nodded to Catheryn. "We'll replace that sash with the long one and thread the narrow one through your hair." She motioned to the maid, still hovering inquisitively in the doorway. "Come you in, Mary, and shut that door. You may tend to the sash. Now, sit you down, Miss Westering, and we'll see what's to be done with your hair."

Catheryn watched the mirror in fascinated silence while the skillful fingers twisted and curled. Weaving lilac ribbon with one hand, Fowler arranged curls into a seemingly artless jumble with the other. Catheryn readily agreed that the style became her very well and complimented her skill.

Fowler deigned to smile. "Thank you, miss. 'Tis a

pleasure. You've got lovely hair, I must say." Catheryn blushed and began to mumble something by way of a thank-you, but Fowler brushed her words aside, commanding her to get into the dress that Mary now held ready. By the time her toilette was completed to Fowler's satisfaction, Catheryn had decided she liked the dresser very much, and Fowler had begun to address her as Miss Catheryn, a high compliment. Despite Fowler's lofty position, Catheryn learned quickly that she took her lead from her mistress and was not at all high in the instep, except below stairs, where it was quite naturally expected of her.

Confident that she looked as well as she could, Catheryn picked up the note to Lady Caston and sallied forth to the yellow drawing room where she found the rest of the family gathered to await dinner. The earl was deep in conversation with a strange gentleman who stood with his back to the fire, while Lady Dambroke and Tiffany occupied the sofa and gilt chair respectively. It was evidently the first time Tiffany had encountered Dambroke since their confrontation, for she was looking rather sullen. Nonetheless, she jumped up and went quickly to meet Catheryn who, surprised by the presence of another guest, had hesitated in the doorway.

"How pretty!" the younger girl exclaimed, effectively interrupting the gentlemen's conversation. "Fowler has worked a miracle indeed! Mama, do but see how nice Catheryn looks."

With a bemused smile, Catheryn allowed herself to be nearly dragged across the room, albeit wondering what possessed her sophisticated cousin to behave in such a manner. Tiffany's hand trembling in hers gave her the necessary clue. Clearly a case of nerves, she thought, as they approached the countess.

Lady Dambroke spoke in a more placid manner. "You look charmingly, my dear. Is that your note to Lady Caston? Just give it to Dambroke and he will frank it for you. Oh, first let me make you known to Lord Thomas Colby. Dambroke's cousin, Miss Westering from Somerset, my lord. Lord Thomas is a friend of Dambroke's, Catheryn, and has agreed to take potluck with us." Miss Westering and Lord Thomas bowed and murmured appropriate commonplaces. Catheryn gave Dambroke her note.

Lord Thomas Colby was tall, rather thin, and dressed with elegant taste in pale yellow pantaloons, a striped waistcoat, and a well-cut coat of rich brown velvet. His shirt points were just high enough to impede free movement of his head, and his neckcloth was intricately arranged in a style he called the Colby Twist. Nevertheless, broad shoulders, well-developed thigh muscles, and a certain athletic grace kept Catheryn from mistaking him for a dandy. She suspected instead that, like Dambroke, he was a member of the Corinthian set.

The gentlemen returned to their conversation as she took her seat beside the countess. "Thank you for lending Fowler to me, Aunt Elizabeth. She is remarkable."

The countess smiled. "I am happy she was of service, dear. We shall have to see about getting you some decent clothes. Perhaps we can visit the shops tomorrow."

"That would be wonderful, ma'am, but I'm afraid I am putting you to a great deal of trouble."

"Nonsense. It will amuse me."

Catheryn hesitated to accept the countess's generosity without word from her uncle regarding future access to her own fortune, but she decided it would be unworthy of her to argue against the proposed shopping expedition when her hostess showed such enthusiasm. Perhaps once his lordship spoke to Sir Horace, arrangements could be made to repay her. She noticed that Tiffany was still observing the gentlemen from under lowered lashes and decided to bring her into the conversation.

"Lady Tiffany will accompany us, will she not, ma'am? She has promised to help me achieve a creditable appearance."

Startled, Tiffany turned to them. "I beg your pardon? Oh, of course! Tomorrow?" A flush crept up her cheeks when she realized she was speaking too loudly. Both gentlemen stopped talking and looked at her, one rather grimly and the other with the conscious expression a gentleman dons when he believes a lady is attempting to command his attention.

Colby stepped forward and executed a graceful bow to the countess. "I beg your pardon, my lady, for our atrocious manners. We were discussing a horse we saw at Tatt's, and I fear we've been guilty of neglecting you. Pray forgive us."

Waving him to a seat, the countess informed both men that they were forgiven. "For you know, Lord Thomas, that when one takes potluck, one is not expected to do the polite. We are *en famille*, my dear, and wish you to be comfortable."

He smiled. "Thank you, my lady. Did I hear you planning an expedition?" he inquired with a hopeful look.

It was Tiffany who answered, curtly, "Only shopping, Colby. Nothing to interest you." A gasp from her mother must have brought her to her senses, if the look of warning in her brother's eye did not. The flush deepened. She spread her hands. "Now it seems it is I who must apologize, my lord. I have been a trifle out of sorts today and have the headache a little, but I should not have spoken as I did. We, that is, my mother and I, are taking Catheryn to visit the shops. She has been in the country and must replenish her wardrobe."

"I see. I'm sorry you are not feeling quite the thing, my lady, but a good night's rest will perk you up. If you are at all like my sisters, you'll enjoy your shopping tremendously and use Miss Westering's needs as an excuse to make some outrageous purchases of your own." He laughed at his little joke and, since Paulson chose that moment to announce dinner, quite failed to notice that he laughed alone.

Conversation at the table was general, topics ranging from the weather to the war in the Peninsula to the activities of Parliament and the controversial Prime Minister, Spenser Perceval. Lady Tiffany seemed to have recovered her poise and carried her part in the discussions easily.

Catheryn enjoyed the dinner. Realizing that she could safely leave the bulk of conversation to the others, she managed to look interested in the various topics presented while, at the same time, indulging herself in private thought. She decided that the contretemps between the earl and his willful sister must indeed have been a serious one. Certainly, she had noted tension in the drawing room even before Lord Thomas's unfortunate remark. She wondered also about Lord Thomas.

That he was interested in Lady Tiffany was clear, as clear as her ladyship's indifference to him. Would Dambroke support a match despite his sister's opposition? Perhaps there was scope for her talents here. Encouraged as he must be by his mother's attitudes and his sister's behavior, the earl certainly seemed capable of developing tyrannical tendencies, if he had not done so already. Unchecked, he would become quite the king of his castle! And Catheryn had not dealt with a cantankerous grandfather all those years to no purpose. Perhaps this visit, though not exactly what she had sought, would prove to be very interesting after all.

With the last course removed, the countess signaled that it was time to leave the two gentlemen to their port and adjourned to the yellow drawing room. "I was pleased to see you in better spirits, my love," she said to her daughter as they seated themselves in their customary places.

"I was afraid Richard would send me from the table if I was rude again," Tiffany answered frankly. "I think he nearly sent me away before!"

"Well, I should not have been surprised. Such a way to speak to Lord Thomas, my dear!"

Tiffany tossed her head. "I apologized for that. Besides, he is forever pressing his company upon us. If Richard thinks to marry me off to that odious man...."

"Surely not," the countess laughed. "Oh, Tiffany, Lord Thomas is a charming lad but a gazetted fortune hunter as well. He will inherit very little from his father, you know. Unless, of course, something happens to his brother, which you must admit is unlikely. And six sisters to be provided for, you know. A drain upon any fortune." Noting Catheryn's bewilderment, she explained, "Lord Thomas is the younger son of the Duke of Clairdon. The estates are entailed, of course, so he must marry an heiress. But not you, Tiffany dear. Dambroke has said he will not allow you to marry anyone until——" She caught her tongue. "Well, not for some time yet," she ended lamely.

"He probably said not till I learn conduct and economy, or some such nonsense," Tiffany stated bitterly. Since there seemed to be no acceptable reply to this observation, they sat in silence for some moments before Tiffany, with another shake of her curls, asked, "How can Richard encourage Lord Thomas to haunt the place, when he makes such a fuss about poor Mr. Lawrence being a fortune hunter? And how could Colby make such a remark after all Richard said this morning!"

"Mr. Lawrence is a particular friend of Tiffany's," the countess explained in an aside to Catheryn. "Lord Thomas hardly haunts the place, Tiffany. We have not seen him in more than a fortnight. And his birth must always recommend him, where Mr. Lawrence's does not. Mr. Lawrence, after all, is a younger son of a younger son of nobody in particular and has very little to recommend him." Tiffany looked mutinous, but the countess pressed on. "As for Colby's unfortunate remark, he knows nothing of your interview with Dambroke and cannot be blamed on that score. I do not precisely understand myself why his remark unsettled you so."

"Unsettled me! I should think so! Teasing me about outrageous purchases when Richard has practically forbidden me to do any shopping at all!"

The countess laughed. "Come, come, Tiffany, surely you exaggerate. In his worst temper, Dambroke would never do such a thing."

"Oh no! He sent back everything I purchased today and said I must live on twenty-five pounds a month, which amounts to the same thing, I assure you. And that is no laughing matter, Miss Westering!"

Indeed, Catheryn was unsuccessfully trying to stifle her ready laughter. Taking a deep breath, she looked ruefully at her indignant cousin and begged her pardon, explaining that twenty-five pounds a month seemed a large sum to her.

"Well, it will not seem so once you have visited Bond Street. This gown cost nearly eighty pounds, and it is only a simple afternoon dress, after all!"

Catheryn gasped in dismay and turned to Lady Dambroke. "Surely not, ma'am! It is unthinkable that you should spend so much on me. I had no idea!"

"It is quite unnecessary to upset yourself, child. I explained your need for proper clothes to Dambroke, and he has agreed to stand the nonsense himself. It will cost me nothing but my time, which I give most willingly."

"But I cannot allow him to pay my bills!" Catheryn cried. "That would be unseemly of me indeed."

"Don't be silly, my dear. You have cast yourself on his protection, and he has agreed to give it. This is mere quibbling, but if it will make you feel better, they are my bills he will be paying, not yours." Lady Dambroke dismissed the subject a bit impatiently and turned back to her daughter. "Are you certain he said you are to have no more than twenty-five pounds, Tiffany? It seems very harsh. He knows you cannot keep up your appearance on such a paltry sum."

Tiffany bit her lower lip. "Well, he said I should come to him if I need anything, and he will discuss it with me. I suppose he looks upon the twenty-five pounds as pin money. But it is unfair and humiliating!"

"There, I knew it!" declared Lady Dambroke. "You are simply out of charity with him. If you are sensible and use a little tact, you will not find him ungenerous."

"Piffle!" Tiffany scorned. "He only said we would discuss things. You know how he likes to exert his authority! He was even more outrageous about James Lawrence."

"But how on earth did Mr. Lawrence come into it?"

Tiffany bit her lip again and looked as though she wished she had not mentioned Mr. Lawrence. But the countess seemed prepared to await her answer. "Oh, very well, it was a bill from Madame Louise for a domino."

"And what, may I ask, did you need with a domino?"

"There is a masqued ball at Vauxhall tonight and——"

"A *public* masquerade at Vauxhall Gardens! Oh, my dear, how could you! And with Mr. Lawrence, of all people!"

"Please, Mama, I have heard all I wish to hear about it, I assure you. As you see, I did not go. Richard sent a note—probably a rude note—to Mr. Lawrence."

The countess sighed and turned back to Catheryn. "I am afraid this cannot interest you, my dear." Catheryn only blinked, thinking it would be impolite to contradict her. "Tell me, Catheryn, do you ride?"

"Of course, ma'am. I enjoy it very much."

"Splendid! I do not care for the exercise myself, but Tiffany often takes early rides in Hyde Park. Her groom accompanies her, of course, but I should be easier in my mind if she had you with her as well."

"But, Mama, there is no other lady's mount in our stables. Richard must send to the Park for one."

"Nonsense, dear. Teddy's horse will take a sidesaddle, I'm sure. You are not planning to race, after all. You will make Catheryn think you do not desire her company." Having surprised a look of dismay on the younger girl's face when the suggestion was first made, Catheryn had already drawn that conclusion for herself.

"Not at all!" Tiffany protested hastily. "Please don't think me so rag-mannered as that, Catheryn. I should enjoy your company. Truly!" And there the matter was allowed to rest as conversation drifted to more general topics.

IV

Early next morning Catheryn bounced out of bed like a child looking forward to a treat, dressed quickly in her old brown velvet habit, and hurried downstairs where, with the help of a friendly housemaid, she found her cousin in the breakfast parlor. Elegantly attired in a deep red habit perfectly molded to her figure, Tiffany sat munching an apple she had not bothered to slice. She smiled.

"Good morning, Catheryn. Help yourself. Breakfast won't be served until later, but I like a bite before I go."

Catheryn took an orange. She would have preferred to have her breakfast but was determined to encourage Tiffany's present mood. Judging her impatient to be off, Catheryn ate quickly and was therefore surprised when Tiffany led the way to the rear of the house. "Does not your groom bring your mount round to the front, Cousin?" she inquired.

"Why, of course, Catheryn, in the normal way of things," Tiffany called back over her shoulder. "But I had a notion to please you, and so we go to the stables."

"I beg your pardon!"

Tiffany laughed ruefully. "That did not come out quite right. But you'll see." They crossed the garden to the high wall, and Tiffany pushed open a gate leading into the mews. A few moments later she pointed out Teddy's horse, and Catheryn gazed with something approaching awe at the ancient nag.

"A fine gentle animal, miss," stated the stableman. "Shall I be saddling 'im along o' yer Angel, my lady?" Catheryn's attention was thus diverted to another stall where a stableboy was placing a sidesaddle on a dainty white Arabian.

"Oh, Tiffany! Is she yours?"

"Yes. Isn't she lovely?"

"Beautiful." Catheryn walked over and held out her hand to the mare, who nuzzled it gently.

"Catheryn, do you ride very well?"

Catheryn chuckled. "Well enough to manage that slug! He must be all of fifteen years."

"Sixteen," Tiffany answered absently. "But I'm serious. I mean, do you ride *really* well?"

Puzzled, Catheryn answered, "Well, I suppose I do. I've sat my grandfather's hunters and racers since I could walk."

Tiffany nodded and turned decisively to the stableman. "Place a sidesaddle on Chieftain, Hobbs. My cousin has no wish to ride Old Cloud." The man hesitated. "Don't dawdle, man. Miss Westering is an excellent rider and we are late already."

"I doubt he will take a lady's saddle, my lady."

"Nonsense. Dambroke proved not long since that he would. For a wager," she added.

Catheryn interrupted quickly. "Tiffany, you cannot mean for me to ride Lord Dambroke's horse! I'm certain he would never allow it!"

"Piffle! Richard will not care." Ignoring Hobbs's look of consternation, she continued, "You would only plod along on Old Cloud, and Chieftain is well-behaved. I wouldn't let you ride Blaze, of course." She indicated a huge black stallion tossing his head in a corner stall. "Even Richard has difficulties with him in town."

Catheryn protested weakly but allowed herself to be persuaded. Hesitant as she was to ride his lordship's horse, she knew the old gelding would offer no sport at all; nevertheless, she nearly had second thoughts when she was helped into the saddle. Big and well-muscled, Chieftain showed a decided aversion to skirts, and she had no time to arrange hers before he made his first effort to unseat her. Hobbs and the stableboy leaped to her aid. By grasping the reins and cocking her leg securely, Catheryn managed to settle herself properly, then called to the men to stand back. Chieftain danced and skittered nervously but made no serious attempt to dislodge her and, at last, stood docilely.

"You'll do, miss," Hobbs stated approvingly.

"Yes, I believe I shall," she replied with a smile. He seems to mind me well enough. Where is Bert?"

He emerged at that moment from the stable leading a short-legged bay lent him by one of the grooms. Tiffany's man helped her to mount and they were soon trotting toward the gates of Hyde Park. It was a glorious morning, so Catheryn was not surprised to see a number of persons riding sedately up and down the rows, nor to see the few elegant carriages that stopped now and again to enable their occupants to converse with one another or with the horsemen; however, having had several occasions in the city streets to realize that Chieftain might prove difficult should he take it into his head to defy the rein, she eyed the traffic doubtfully. Tiffany merely agreed that, although it was not the fashionable hour to be seen in the Park, the weather very likely accounted for the fairly heavy turn-out.

"Gracious!" she exclaimed suddenly. "There's Maggie, and she's seen us!" She directed Catheryn's attention to a vivacious young blonde waving from a nearby carriage, explaining with some asperity that Lady Margaret Varling, daughter of the Earl of Stanthorpe, was a dear friend but a chatterbox as well. Returning the wave with a charming smile, she added, "She will probably tell Richard she has seen us."

"Why would it matter if she did?" inquired Catheryn.

Tiffany evaded the question. "Maggie will probably be the next Countess of Dambroke," she stated. "Richard has just spent the best part of a fortnight jauntering back and forth between London and her home in Sussex." Catheryn's curiosity was piqued. It would be interesting to see what sort of female appealed to the earl's taste.

"Tiffany, by all that's wonderful!" Maggie exclaimed. "I declare, I never expected to see you this morning. Oh, and this," indicating the plump, gray-haired lady beside her, "is my Aunt Augusta, Lady Trevaris."

Tiffany made Catheryn known to the two ladies, then added, "I am surprised to see you out so early, Maggie. I didn't even know you had returned to town."

Lady Margaret giggled behind a daintily gloved hand. "Lud, Tiff, I shouldn't have left my bedchamber yet, were it not for Aunt dragging me out. For air, she said." The older woman smiled, rather grimly, Catheryn thought, steadying Chieftain. "She has set us all by the ears," Maggie added.

"Really?"

"Indeed, Tiff. You must know we have been down at Stanthorpe this past fortnight. Aunt stayed with us to help look after Tony—my brother, Miss Westering—and she came to town to relax and do the shops."

Tiffany interrupted before Maggie could continue, showing more animation than Catheryn had yet seen. "Is Captain Varling home then?"

Maggie looked surprised. "Of course he is! Didn't Dambroke tell you? Or Lord Thomas? Mama and Papa swore them to secrecy, of course, on account of not wanting lots of visitors before he was recuperated, but I should have expected Dambroke to mention it to you and her ladyship," she added naively.

"Well, he certainly should have mentioned it," Tiffany stated flatly. "Of all the ramshackle things!"

"Nonsense, Tiffany." Catheryn steadied Chieftain again and smiled at both girls. "Neither of you would expect his lordship to break his word."

"And what she could have done about it if he had," Lady Trevaris interposed with more candor than tact, "I should like to know."

Since the comment was clearly rhetorical, Catheryn ignored Tiffany's indignant and unladylike glare. "Has your brother been ill, Lady Margaret?"

"He was wounded!" Maggie answered with dramatic fervor. "He nearly lost his leg entirely!"

"Pack of butchers," Lady Trevaris stated. "Rather cut it off than tend it properly." Noting Catheryn's astonishment, she deigned to elucidate. "Boy was wounded at Cuidad Rodrigo." Catheryn opened her mouth to protest, but Lady Trevaris waved her impatiently to silence. "Yes, yes, I know that was January. Poor boy's been bounced from hospital to hospital for three months. Had to get to Brussels before he found a doctor who didn't want to cut the leg off. Weak as a kitten when he finally came home. Where he belonged," she added tartly.

Maggie smiled fondly at her aunt but her eyes twinkled when she spoke to the others. "Aunt Augusta is certain her ministrations are the sole reason for Tony's rapid recuperation. She knows perfectly well that, because of his major's knowing the doctor personally, Tony was got quite quickly to Brussels. All the same, it must have been horrid for him to think he might lose his leg."

"That's as may be." Lady Trevaris clearly intended to have the last word. "But Anthony made up his mind not to lose the leg and, easy-mannered though he may be, he generally gets what he sets his mind to. Miss Westering, that horse of yours fidgets!"

The others laughed, but Catheryn admitted that Chieftain was not best pleased to stand still while other horses trotted past him. She and Tiffany made their adieux, promising to call at Stanthorpe House quite soon. When they had left the Varling carriage behind, Tiffany, who had been looking about as though in search of a particular face, suggested that Catheryn take Bert and find a spot where she could exercise Chieftain properly.

"For he is fidgeting dreadfully, Catheryn, and I intend just to walk Angel along the row, stopping now and again, you know, to speak to my particular friends. I'm afraid Chieftain won't appreciate anything so tame as that."

Aware as she was that she was being manipulated, Catheryn nevertheless agreed. She was uncertain how much longer she would be able to control her powerful mount and, with relief, turned him toward an invitingly empty stretch of greensward where she could let him have his head. As she neared the open space, she turned in her saddle and was unsurprised to observe that Tiffany had been joined by a fair-haired gentleman on horseback and that Tiffany's groom had obligingly dropped some distance behind. Mentally shrugging her shoulders, she spoke to Chieftain.

"Now, my fine fellow, you shall have your run. Then, perhaps you will contrive to behave yourself. Stay with us, if you are able," she called to Bert.

"Aye, miss," was the gruff reply. Catheryn chuckled as she dug her heel into the horse's flank. Chieftain needed no further urging but was off, ears pricked forward and tail like a banner, his long easy stride making him a joy to ride. Catheryn felt the thrill of a long-denied pleasure. Lady Caston disapproved of what she called neck-or-nothing riding for females. It never occurred to Catheryn that members of the Beau Monde might likewise disapprove. The half-mile of greensward was soon behind her, and she had no difficulty slowing Chieftain for the turn before she gave him his head again. Bert had already turned his slower mount and she waved gaily when she passed him. He managed a smile in return.

Drawing near to the end of the green, she was startled to recognize the large black stallion with the white blaze whose rider, also recognizable and scowling besides, seemed to be waiting for her. Tiffany was nowhere in sight.

"Good morning, Lord Dambroke!" she called as she pulled Chieftain up before him. She patted the horse, pleased that he now seemed willing to behave and not missing the small gleam of reluctant admiration in his lordship's eye. Bert tactfully reined in some distance behind.

Dispensing with amenities, Dambroke snapped, "Are you such a madcap then, Miss Westering, that you must needs flout all the conventions?"

Catheryn blinked, taken aback more by his words than by his anger. "Not intentionally, my lord. Though I suppose," she added as the thought occurred to her, "it was not quite the thing for me to gallop headlong through Hyde Park." She sighed. "I did so enjoy it, too."

"You'll not get vouchers to Almack's by enjoying yourself in that manner, however."

"Almack's!" She had thought it was a mere pipe dream that she might actually visit the famous and very exclusive assembly rooms in Pall Mall. She stared at him, pushing windblown hair from her face. "Your mother mentioned it, of course, but I didn't think it possible. Does she truly intend me to fly so high?"

His expression relaxed. "She cannot wish for you to remain quietly at home on Wednesday evenings, you know."

"Heavens, how exciting! I am indeed sorry if I have done anything to overset such plans."

"Well, perhaps it is not so bad as that. My mother's friend Emily Cowper, one of the august patronesses, is possibly amiable enough to overlook this escapade." He frowned again. "You ride well, but Chieftain is not a suitable mount for you."

Catheryn chuckled. "I wonder if it will put you off

your stride, sir, if I admit that you are quite right." She peeped up through innocently lowered lashes.

"Of course it will not! I know I am right. Chieftain could toss you off at any moment had he a mind to do so."

Catheryn snapped her head up indignantly. "I daresay I should be less likely to put you into a rage if I were to agree with that ridiculous statement as well, my lord," she said steadily, "but if you consider the matter, you must know that could he have done so, he would have put me off in the stableyard. And so Mr. Hobbs must have informed you. Chieftain might run away with me, but he will not throw me."

Dambroke turned Blaze toward the gate, smiling at last. "A point to you, Miss Westering, though I hope we shall not haggle over details. The fact remains that you should not have ridden him."

"Yes, sir, I expect that is the crux of the matter," Catheryn answered sweetly, as she guided Chieftain in beside the stallion. "The fact is that you are in a miff, not because you worried about my safety, but because I rode your horse. I should not have done so, however, without your permission."

The contrite expression accompanying the final statement was belied by the twinkle in her eye, but if she expected a rise to her lure, she soon found she had mistaken her opponent. "I suppose I am, at that," he answered after reflecting for a moment. "However, I do know who is to blame for this. I have already sent my sister home with a flea in her ear and a promise that she will hear more when we return."

Having intended to draw his anger in order to shield Tiffany, Catheryn realized that she had underestimated his acuity. She watched with approval as he checked the stallion's aversion to an urchin who darted suddenly from the flagway. Chieftain had settled down admirably after his brief run, but Blaze seemed to become increasingly nervous as they encountered heavier traffic.

"You handle him well, my lord." He grinned and Catheryn was surprised by her reaction to it. She had not noticed before, but the blasted man was capable of charm. Oddly flustered, she added with more bluntness than she had intended, "He does not belong in the city, however!"

He sent her a quizzical look. "Getting your own back, Cousin? No, no!" he laughed when she tossed her head, a stormy glint in her eye. "I cry pardon. You are right. I had hoped to civilize him, but he is definitely a country horse. I intend to send him down to the Park. I shall have a suitable mount brought up to town for your use at the same time. You are not to ride Chieftain again."

"No, sir, I should not have taken him at all." She was contrite again, but genuinely so this time.

"I daresay Tiffany assured you that I should not mind," he answered grimly.

"Please, my lord, it was my fault. My grandfather would have flogged me had I dared to ride a new horse without his permission, and this is much the same thing."

"Nonsense!" he retorted. "My sister knows perfectly well that I allow no one to ride Blaze or Chieftain. She merely wanted an excuse to get you out of the way while she kept her assignation with that damned Lawrence fellow!"

So that was Lawrence. "Well, of course she did. Your mother practically forced me upon her in the first place."

"My compliments to my mother," he muttered.

"Oh, don't be so muttonheaded!" Catheryn protested, exasperated. "It seems to me, my lord, that you have been doing your best to make your bird-witted sister see herself in the role of star-crossed lover, and that damned Lawrence fellow, as you so snidely refer to him, would have to be every bit as muttonheaded himself not to take advantage of it." She stopped short, aghast at her effrontery, and stared at the back of Chieftain's head, waiting for the explosion of wrath. It did not come.

"By God," he said slowly, "I never thought about it in that light. She's probably poured her heart out to that scoundrel. He certainly encourages every excess, even agreed to take her to a masquerade at Vauxhall."

"Just so, my lord. And you put a stop to it, did you not?"

"Of course I did. Vauxhall's no place for a respectable female. But I see what you mean," he added. "Yes, I do see what you mean." He lapsed into meditation, and

Catheryn would have let the matter drop, but he spoke again. "Nevertheless, I shall speak to her about this morning's affair. Her conduct was both unmannerly and deceitful."

"Well, you need not," Catheryn stated flatly. "It would be a bacon-brained thing to do. And that's not funny," she added when he burst into laughter.

"I daresay," he answered when he could control himself. Meeting her accusing glare, he attempted to explain. "It's only that I have not been called muttonheaded or bacon-brained by a female since I was in short coats. Do you always use such colorful language, Catheryn?"

She blushed. "I beg your pardon. I know I should not do so, but when I get carried away, I forget. It comes of living so long with Grandpapa, I expect. And I have not given you leave to call me Catheryn, sir."

Ignoring the rider, he shook his head, eyes atwinkle. "Don't beg my pardon. I like it. This conversation makes me feel I've known you for years instead of just two short days."

She nodded. "Less than twenty-four hours, actually. But there is nothing like a quarrel for getting to know someone."

Dambroke laughed. "I never considered quarreling a means to friendship, but I believe you may be right once more. However, we are not quarreling now. I am as wax in your hands. If I must not take Tiffany to task, please, what am I to do instead?"

Regarding him solemnly as though to assure herself that he spoke in earnest, it occurred to her that she liked him very much in this mood. "You may not care for it, my lord." She paused, giving him a chance to demur, but he remained silent. "Very well. I think you must allow her to believe you hold me entirely responsible." His brows knitted. "You need say nothing," she added quickly. "Leave it to me. It is not impossible, I assure you. I could have stopped her, you know. I saw Hobbs's face when she said you would not mind." His frown deepened. "There, you see. You are becoming angry with me. I shall simply tell her that I have had a regular bear garden jaw and that you have nothing further to say to her."

"And what do you expect this to accomplish?"

She thought for a moment. "It seems to me," she began, "that if one knows oneself to be at fault for another's misfortune, one usually tries to make it up to that person in other ways. Even if she only believes me to be shielding her from your anger——"

"Which you are."

"Even so, she ought to be grateful and behave accordingly."

"Much you know."

Catheryn glanced at him uncertainly. "I believe it will turn the trick, my lord. Your mother said Tiffany needs to think about someone else for a change."

"True enough, but your plan comes from the twisted sort of thinking that passes for female logic. Tiffany is much more likely to take advantage of your good nature."

Catheryn smiled sweetly. "Not if you contrive to be out of charity with me a bit longer. She will take her lead from you, sir."

"Take her lead from me!" He stared at her and then grimaced. "I believe I take your meaning, Cousin. Did I say your logic was twisted? Upon reflection, I must correct the word to Machiavellian. My compliments."

"Never mind your compliments, sir. We are approaching Grosvenor Square. Scowl, if you please. Your sister is very likely on the watch for your arrival. Her bedchamber overlooks the square, you know."

V

Dambroke disappeared into his library, and Catheryn decided to have her breakfast before going in search of Lady Tiffany. By the time she had finished her second cup of tea, she had managed to learn from Morris, the footman, that her ladyship had refused breakfast, having come home, as he described it, "in a regular snit." Her ladyship still had not recovered when Catheryn found her a bit later in her bedchamber. Tiffany had changed to a becoming round gown of pale green sprigged muslin with a matching sash and was standing by her window gazing into the square. She turned, her expression sullen.

"Oh, it's you. I expected Richard." Catheryn was silent, radiating dejection. "Good gracious! Surely he has not been scolding you as well!"

Catheryn flung herself into a comfortable silk-covered chair. "I should never have ridden his stupid horse."

"Of all the odious, rag-mannered . . . he *knows* it was all my fault!"

Catheryn looked up wide-eyed. "But it was not your fault, Tiffany. I shouldn't have ridden his horse without permission. Besides, Dambroke was worried about my safety, and worry causes some people to become fearfully angry, you know."

"Piffle!" Tiffany snapped, coming from the window to sit in a most unladylike manner on the foot of her bed. "It was neither fear nor worry, but pure selfishness. He cannot bear anyone to ride or drive his horses. Or to use his guns, for that matter. He once gave our cousin, Jonathan, a trimming for taking a shotgun out without permission. And Jonathan, let me tell you, is a crack shot! Then, Maggie's brother, Captain Varling, just for a prank—he is a great jokester—once drove Richard's bays hitched to a farm wagon. Richard was livid!" She had been looking straight at Catheryn, but at this point she lowered her gaze to her hands, beginning to pick with the fingers of one at the nails of the other. "I know that is not qu-quite what I t-told you before, Catheryn, but I truly did not intend you to incur his displeasure. I should not purposely inflict that on anyone. I thought we would be home before he emerged from his bedchamber. He and Lord Thomas were out very late."

"I expect Hobbs had second thoughts and sent him a message," Catheryn replied.

"I-I never thought. Please, Catheryn, I only...."

"You only wanted me to be so occupied with Chieftain that I could not interfere with your assignation," Catheryn offered helpfully, when she hesitated.

"Yes ... I mean, no, of course not!" Looking into Catheryn's eyes, she encountered frank disbelief and hunched her shoulders. "Oh, very well. But please believe I never meant for you to suffer. I just wanted to speak with James—Mr. Lawrence, that is—and I did know that you would not like to ride old Cloud, so I ... well, I'm sorry."

Catheryn smiled gently. "I do believe you, Tiffany. But you must see that, with regard to Chieftain, I was as much to blame, for I do know better than to ride a gentleman's horse without his permission. Also, I am older than you. But I jumped at the opportunity and so have come by my just deserts. I only hope he won't pack me back to Caston Manor in disgrace."

"Well, he will not do anything so shabby," declared her ladyship. "He will still have much to say to me about meeting James, I daresay, but if he did not say at once that you must leave, he will not do so at all."

"Perhaps not. But why," Catheryn asked, deciding things were going very satisfactorily, "would he not merely assume that you had met Mr. Lawrence by chance?"

Willingly, Tiffany launched into a complete, though somewhat tangled history of her relationship with Mr. Lawrence. Punctuated though it was by animadversions upon her unfeeling and dictatorial brother and the lack of understanding by other such stuffy persons, the tale was easy enough for Catheryn to follow. According to Tiffany, Mr. Lawrence's family was a perfectly respectable one, and they had met at some party or other. They had discovered a mutual taste for early rides and often met at the Park where they carried on long and fascinating conversations. She described Lawrence as the epitome of all desirable masculine attributes, except of course in the matter of fortune. He was so kind, so good, so sympathetic, so understanding. He cared about her feelings in a manner of which others, unspecified, were incapable. She wasn't by any means certain as yet, but she thought she might very likely be falling in love with him. Dambroke, of course, would do all possible to rend them asunder. It was dastardly that she and James could see so little of each other just because he wasn't odiously rich. Indeed, Dambroke had insulted him, had called him a damned fortune hunter, which anyone with sense must know was perfectly ridiculous.

"I expect Dambroke is right, you know."

"I beg your pardon!"

Unruffled, though certain she had just joined the ranks of the unfeeling, Catheryn continued, "Don't fly into the boughs, Tiffany. I merely voiced an opinion. Probably I know nothing at all, but Dambroke strikes me as a fair man, a man of sense. I have little else upon which to base an opinion. You said, however, that Mr. Lawrence has no fortune of his own. I would think him odd if he did not make a push to acquire one through marriage—just like Lord Thomas, you know. But, of course, you know him. If you say he is no fortune hunter, I must listen." Tiffany regarded her doubtfully, and Catheryn chuckled. "Never mind. Even fortune hunters may fall in love. I daresay that is what has occurred here. After all, you are only seventeen. No fortune hunter worth his salt will want to wait four years or more for the fortune."

Tiffany, her expression suddenly thoughtful, opened her mouth to speak. At that moment, however, the door swung back on its hinges to admit the countess, charmingly garbed in russet. She exclaimed aloud at the sight of them.

"Why, what is this? Catheryn, you cannot go shopping in your riding habit! Surely, you have something more suitable, child. And Tiffany, that dress is much too thin. You will catch your death." They stared at her. Catheryn came to her senses first.

"Good heavens, ma'am, I quite forgot!" She started up from the chair and hurried toward the door. "Pray forgive me. Back in the twinkling of a bedpost, I assure you." She rushed to her bedchamber and, ringing for Mary, rapidly changed to a simple cambric frock. When she returned to Tiffany's room, the first voice she heard was that of the countess.

"He don't want to speak to you now, whatever you might think. He's gone to White's." She spied Catheryn in the doorway. "Let's bustle about, girls, I mean to finish this business this morning, so that we may call upon Emily Cowper this afternoon. I should like to stop at Stanthorpe House as well, now they have returned to town. Get your pelisse, Tiffany. I don't know why you should think Dambroke would wish to speak with you anyway." Tiffany obeyed slowly, still seeming to doubt that she might escape her brother's promised tongue-lashing. It was not until they were safely in the landaulet that she relaxed.

All three ladies enjoyed themselves. The fashionable modiste who delighted in the countess's patronage was only too happy to take Miss Westering's measurements and offer advice about materials, styles, and trims. Catheryn was awed by the number of garments deemed necessary for a young lady of fashion, but she placed herself in her cousin's hands and offered no demur. She was pleased to discover that several gowns, ready-made, could, with slight alteration, be delivered that very afternoon. Unused to London fashions, she was a bit shocked by the flimsy materials but, following Tiffany's advice, she ordered several frocks for day wear, three evening gowns, a fawn velvet pelisse trimmed with swansdown, and a dashing riding habit of lavender, ornamented down the front and at the cuffs *à la militaire* with black silk braid.

The rest of the morning was spent purchasing such necessary items as bonnets and hats, reticules, footwear, gloves, silk scarves, handkerchieves, and undergarments. In the Pantheon Bazaar Catheryn came upon an exquisite Norwich shawl that she thought would be nice to drape over her shoulders on chilly days, but Tiffany vetoed the purchase.

"You are too short, Catheryn. It would turn you into an absolute dowdy," she stated flatly. "The silk scarves will do nicely to add a touch of color to your pelisse, but anything like that shawl draped around you would only detract from the line of your gown."

"Very true, dear," agreed the countess vaguely. "Now, I think we have done for the present, but you must begin to be thinking about what you mean to wear to Lady Heathcote's dress party as well as to our own ball."

"Yes, indeed," put in Tiffany. "We must look through my copies of *Belle Assemblée* and *Beau Monde* for ideas."

As they climbed into the carriage, Miss Westering's eyes were sparkling with anticipation. The countess seemed to take it for granted that she would still be in London for the ball, still several weeks away. Catheryn was tempted to pinch herself but refrained, thinking that if it were only a dream it would be a shame to wake herself. She had given up thinking about the expense, but it did cross her mind briefly to wonder whether Dambroke, whom Tiffany declared to be odiously pinch-pennied, might not object to the number of her purchases.

Much to the surprise of his mother and the consternation of his sister, he greeted them in the hall, having, as he explained, observed their arrival from the library. Bestowing a cool nod upon sister and cousin, he kissed his mother's cheek. "Been wasting the ready, Mama?"

"Yes, indeed," she twinkled. "We have had a lovely morning. Dear Catheryn will be fitted out in no time. But I thought you had gone to your club!"

"So I had," he drawled, still ignoring the two girls. "White's was somewhat thin of company, so I returned and have been letting young Ashley plague me with matters of business. I think he must be overworked. With quarter day past, I thought he would have time to relax, but he tells me he has received instructions from my various bailiffs and agents desiring him to harass me with plans of improvements here and experimentation there. I am quite worn out with it and have ordered him off to lunch. I shall escape before he returns, I promise you." Tiffany looked relieved.

Lady Dambroke, unaware of anything out of the ordinary, laughed merrily. "I suppose you are off to Jackson's then," she said, referring to the great Gentleman Jackson's boxing saloon. "Of course, you will take a bite with us first."

"I think not," he replied curtly, casting a scowl in Catheryn's direction. Really, she thought, he needn't lay it on so thick.

Lady Dambroke was astonished and looked from one face to another, seeking an explanation. Catheryn looked conscious, Tiffany embarrassed, and the earl saturnine. "Richard, whatever is the matter?" the countess demanded.

"It is nothing important, Mama."

"That's not so," Tiffany argued. "Richard is at outs with poor Catheryn, Mama, and indeed he should not be, for it was quite my fault!"

Fearing that Dambroke would ruin all by agreeing, Catheryn broke into hasty speech. "Oh, no! Please, my lady, you must not!" She gazed imploringly first at Tiffany and then, with slightly more intent, at his lordship. "Indeed, it was my own selfish stupidity. He is right to be angry with me." Disconcerted by a gleam of wicked amusement in Dambroke's eye, she dropped her gaze to his shining Hessians and continued, "I-I have told him I am s-sorry. I had hoped the affair was ended."

The countess whisked to Catheryn's side, putting a protective arm around her before turning on her son. "Richard, I rarely interfere, as you well know, but Catheryn is my guest, and I'll not have her bullied. I do not know what she can have done in the short time she has been with us to incur your displeasure, but it cannot have been anything so dreadful. You must apologize at once." Then she quite ruined the effect of her uncharacteristic vehemence by adding, "Please, Richard?"

Catheryn, peeping from under her lashes at him, was much impressed by his iron control. The inner struggle with his sense of the ridiculous was not lost upon her. As it was, he was forced to brush a hand across his brow before answering. "I do apologize, Miss Westering. Though I must say that for me to worry when you are so foolish as to take one of my high-spirited mounts to Hyde Park without my knowledge or approval is no odd thing. However, I did not intend that my few words of well-deserved censure should overset you." Catheryn shot him a speaking look and encountered one filled with mockery that as much as told her she was being served with her own sauce. The countess's arm dropped.

"Oh, Catheryn," she gasped, "you didn't!" Her words effectively silenced her daughter who, for a split second at least, had looked ready to join battle in Catheryn's defense.

Catheryn, taking the sideplay in with an oblique glance, stepped forward and placed one demurely gloved hand in Dambroke's. Her lips twitched and she dared not look into his eyes, but she kept her soft voice under admirable control. "That is kind of you, my lord," she said. "I accept your generous apology and promise it shall not happen again." At this juncture, the earl, with a hasty mumble that Ashley would soon be upon him, turned rather precipitately and escaped out the front door.

Tiffany's face was a mixture of emotions. Guilt, hesitation, and determination all vied with one another. The countess still looked a bit shocked, and knowing it would only upset her to hear a more detailed account of the affair, Catheryn frowned Tiffany to silence before turning with a smile to her hostess. "Dear Aunt Elizabeth, do you suppose luncheon has been served? I confess I am exceedingly hungry."

With relief, Tiffany and her mother both agreed that if luncheon were not ready it ought to be. With that they retired to the dining room and subsequently to their bedchambers, where they spent a half-hour recuperating from the morning's exertions before setting out to pay calls.

The countess explained on the way to the Cowpers' great house in Berkeley Square that, along with Ladies Castlereagh, Sefton, and Jersey, Mrs. Drummond Burrell, Countess Lieven, and Princess Esterhazy, Emily Cowper was one of the patronesses of Almack's and that Catheryn must be on her best behavior. Lady Cowper condescended to be at home and, though she seemed an amiable shatterbrain, quickly saw through her principal guest's artless chatter and demanded to know if Elizabeth had not come seeking vouchers for Miss Westering. Lady Dambroke admitted it, whereupon their hostess turned her attention to Catheryn, asking a number of probing questions about her antecedents and fortune. She seemed to think the latter might better have been larger but laughingly added that breeding was what counted and that, after all, Elizabeth could not, in all courtesy, leave her guest at home on Wednesday evenings.

Catheryn nearly chuckled at this unconscious echo of Dambroke's words, but the thought brought another on its heels, and the next thing she knew she was making a clean breast of the morning's episode in Hyde Park while firmly ignoring Tiffany's guilt-ridden face and the agitated fluttering of Lady Dambroke's hands. Only Lady Cowper was unmoved, listening patiently until Catheryn had finished her confession and made a graceful apology. Then she smiled.

"It could have been worse, my dear," she said. "At least you did not choose the promenade hour. Of course, you must never do it again, but if anyone brings the matter to my attention, I shall simply say I know all about it and that your horse ran away with you. It is much better, you know, to have aspersions cast upon your horsemanship than upon your conduct."

When they climbed back into the carriage for the ride around the square to Stanthorpe House, Tiffany squeezed Catheryn's hand. "I thought you must be mad, Catheryn, but I see you knew exactly how to carry it off! Imagine if she had heard about it later! She would not have been so conciliating then."

Lady Dambroke agreed heartily and expressed gratitude to the Fates who had guided her to Lady Cowper for the vouchers and not, though she knew her quite as well, to the much haughtier Lady Jersey. She added that Catheryn would be the death of her if she meant to make a habit of confessing her crimes at such awkward moments. By the time Catheryn had apologized for giving her such a start, the carriage had drawn up at Stanthorpe House. The ladies were soon shown into a bright drawing room, where a regular party seemed to be in progress.

Gay laughter and chatter came to a momentary halt as the butler announced them, only to renew itself in merry greetings to the newcomers. Out of what seemed a mob of people, Catheryn recognized a few familiar faces. Lord Dambroke got up from a chair next to the settee upon which reclined a pale young man with blond hair and blue eyes, who seemed to be the focal point of the gathering. One of his legs was propped up, and a lazy apologetic smile lit his face when he saw them. Lord Thomas stood behind him, and Lady Margaret jumped up from a low stool in front of the settee to greet them.

Catheryn was soon introduced to the Countess Stanthorpe, a brisk, bright little bird of a woman who greeted the Dambroke ladies with great affection, reacquainted them with Lady Trevaris, and complimented them on their looks. Then she clasped Catheryn's hands warmly between her own and told the three girls that she knew they had no wish to sit gossiping with old women and to take themselves off.

It was easy to see how the Lady Margaret came by her vivacity, Catheryn thought, as she was borne off by that young lady to meet the others. Maggie laughed when she began the introductions, begging everyone's pardon in advance in case she should make a botch of it.

"First, there is Lord Thomas Colby and two of his sisters, Lady Prudence on the right," indicating a girl a year or two older than Catheryn with rather prim features and a more placid expression than any of the others, "and Lady Chastity, of all things, on the left," indicating a merry-eyed brunette who looked fresh from the schoolroom. "We call her Chatty," Maggie went on, "for reasons that will become obvious."

"Oh, Maggie, I do not chatter all the time," retorted the damsel in question with a giggle. Her sister smiled with a fondness that lightened the prim features and made Catheryn think she could come to like her very well.

"And you know Richard, of course, or I should have introduced him first." That gentleman bowed. "And these are my cousins, Tom and Cynthia Varling." A hand waved in the direction of a smiling blond youth with a pretty, if a bit rabbit-faced girl at his side. "Tom has been rusticated from Oxford and is in deep disgrace, as you can see," Maggie volunteered. General laughter followed this comment but did not seem to dismay young Varling in the least.

"Takes more than deep disgrace to ruffle our Tom," noted the gentleman on the settee. "What queers me is why he didn't manage to talk his way out of the whole shenanigan."

"Well, you see," Tom replied with a sweet smile, "it was the Bagwig's own nag." A shout of laughter caused Tiffany and Catheryn to look inquiringly at Maggie.

"Tom quite forgot to mention that bit before," she laughed. "He told us only that he and his friends had enticed a horse into the don's study with a rude note attached to his, that is, to the horse's tail. The don, oddly enough, took exception and reported them to the Bagwig, but this explains why the Bagwig was so out of reason cross about it!" She went off in another peal of laughter. "But wait, Catheryn," she gasped when she had herself nearly in hand. "You will let me call you Catheryn?" Catheryn nodded, still grinning. "Well, I thought you would, and I am Maggie, you know, and *this*," with a grand gesture, "is Tony, that is, Captain the Honorable Anthony Varling, late of Wellington's Army! You remember Tony, don't you, Tiffany?" she added while Catheryn smiled a greeting.

Tiffany nodded shyly. "Yes, indeed I do, though it has been some time since last we met. I was but a scrubby brat in the schoolroom, so he may not recall it himself."

Blue eyes twinkled up at her from the settee while the captain gallantly kissed her hand. "A schoolroom miss, perhaps, but never scrubby, my lady."

"A brat, however, Tony. That cannot be denied."

"Nay, Dickon," laughed Captain Varling, while Lady Tiffany glared at her brother. "I'll not allow even you to cast slurs on a guest in my father's house."

Catheryn was surprised to hear Dambroke called by a nickname, but she soon learned that the two and Lord Thomas had suffered the slings and arrows of Eton and Oxford together and had remained fast friends despite differing interests afterward. Dambroke had turned to his estates and Varling to the Army, while Lord Thomas was haphazardly hanging out for an heiress. Catheryn listened with amusement while they compared their own pranks with those of Tom and his cronies. Captain Varling quickly emerged as the erstwhile ringleader. He boasted, too, of more recent escapades, which had occurred before his unfortunate mishap. Catheryn realized she was seeing a new side of Dambroke. Relaxed and at his ease, he seemed to have cast off the burden of his responsibilities for a moment in the sheer pleasure of welcoming his friend back to town.

"You must have been out of reason bored in Sussex, Tony," declared young Tom suddenly.

A thin hand ruffled through already tousled blond curls. "I was that," he admitted. "If it hadn't been for Dickon's visits and Colby's and the governor having the papers sent down from town, I'd have been a candidate for Bedlam. As it was, I amused myself with the antics of Perceval and company."

"Didn't know you were a Conservative," Colby murmured.

"Not. Brought up in solid Whiggery, just like you. Thought like everyone else that old Wellesley would turn the trick and Perceval would be out when Prinny's year of restricted Regency expired in February."

"I thought you said the Marquess of Wellesley was a pompous prig," piped up Maggie from her stool.

Varling reached out and tweaked a curl. "So I did, my lady, but there's no need for you to repeat such things." When, to the general amusement of the others, she only wrinkled her nose at him, he went on, "Wellesley would be Prime Minister now, I think, were it not for his unfortunate personality. Even Bathurst, the only man in the Cabinet he could possibly claim for a friend, deserted him in the end."

"Cut from the same cloth, if you ask me," Colby said. "Bathurst disapproved of Wellesley's threat to resign, so he cut loose himself."

"Time was," Dambroke commented dryly, "when I thought you were rather fond of Wellesley, Tony."

Varling grinned. "You never thought any such thing. I approve his chief cause, but never the man himself."

"His cause, Captain Varling?" Tiffany spoke shyly.

"The war in the Peninsula, Lady Tiffany. His family's rather involved, you know. He was used to be our ambassador to Spain, where he's been replaced by his younger brother, Henry. Then of course, the new Earl of Wellington, our glorious commander, is also his brother. Wellesley's been pushing for more troops, weapons, and money for years, but he's got better support now than he did as Foreign Secretary."

"If he does, it's a bit of a personal victory for you, lad," Dambroke said gently. "Public opinion has swung a long way since the fall of Cuidad Rodrigo and Badajoz."

"So I rest on my laurels," quipped the hero.

Having drifted into serious channels, the conversation eventually turned from the war on the Continent to the potential for a new war in America and then to the smaller but no less economically damaging wars right there at home. The latter were caused by working class unrest and stirred by the notorious Luddites, who supposedly fought for full employment and higher wages while, in reality, they terrorized whole villages.

"To my way of thinking," Varling opined, "General Ludd is mythical, a rallying point and nothing more."

The statement might have opened a whole new debate, but by this time Lady Stanthorpe managed to surface long enough from her own conversation to notice the change in atmosphere. She jumped to her feet and demanded to know what was toward. "For I won't have you unsettling Tony's homecoming with a lot of gloomy talk," she assured them. "Nothing but cheer, you lot, or out you go!"

Coming as it did from such a small lady, her head thrust belligerently forward and her arms akimbo, the vehement threat caused a great deal of merriment. The gentlemen obligingly turned the conversation onto a more cheerful course, but it was not long before an unspoken signal from Dambroke, who had been keeping a close eye on his friend, urged a general departure. Catheryn, following closely behind the earl with his mother and sister as they moved to bid their hostess farewell, overheard Lady Stanthorpe's expressions of deep gratitude when she grasped Dambroke's outstretched hand.

He smiled down at the little countess. "It is my pleasure, ma'am," he replied. "He is doing very well, I think, but still must not overtax himself."

"Oh, I know, and the company has done him good,

but he insists he will dance at your mother's ball, my lord."

"He has great determination, ma'am. We'll just see he does nothing foolish in the meantime. I shall visit often to help keep him in line. Now, I am keeping you from your duties as hostess. Come, ladies." He held out his arm to Lady Dambroke. Tears of gratitude lingered in Lady Stanthorpe's eyes as she wished them good day. Catheryn noted them and smiled approvingly at Dambroke when he helped her into the carriage. He grinned back, clearly having forgotten that he was supposed to be out of charity with her.

VI

There were frequent visits to Stanthorpe House in the days ahead, while Captain Varling continued to recuperate. Tiffany went every day, often escorted by her brother, and Catheryn thought they seemed to be on excellent terms with each other for once. Though nothing was heard from Sir Horace regarding her fortune, she did receive a curt reply from her aunt, acknowledging receipt of her note, while Lady Dambroke received a more gracious approval of her invitation.

The earl sent Blaze down to Dambroke Park, and over the weekend a spirited bay mare called Psyche came up to town for Catheryn's use. Tiffany still accompanied her on morning rides but now seemed to do so more on Catheryn's account than on her own. They often met Mr. Lawrence. Catheryn found him rather intriguing and had no difficulty understanding Tiffany's attraction to the man. He was slim, above average in height, and possessed of a boyish face that belied his thirty years. She thought his boots might have been the better for a bit of polish, and he had an irritating habit of pushing his fingers through his thinning, sandy hair, but he knew the trick of charm and displayed flattering interest in every word that dropped from Tiffany's lips.

He seemed to credit Tiffany's rather casual attitude on these occasions to Catheryn's ubiquity and twice brought along his foppish friend, Lucas Markham, whose obvious purpose was to draw Catheryn away from Tiffany. Mr. Markham, sporting red silk boot-tops and an intricately tied pastel neckcloth, was just the sort of simpering beau Catheryn found most ridiculous. She turned a deaf ear to his more subtle hints and once, when he openly suggested that they drop behind the others, stared at him in such wide-eyed astonishment that the fop actually blushed. Mr. Lawrence became more visibly frustrated. It did not seem to occur to him that Tiffany made no move to abet his tactics, if she was even aware of them, but cheerfully included both Catheryn and Lucas Markham in her conversation.

There was only one small contretemps between Dambroke and his sister, and that occurred several days before Catheryn's debut at Almack's, when Tiffany announced that she would need a new gown for the occasion. Smiling, Dambroke informed her that she could manage very well with one of the many frocks already crowding her wardrobe. She looked mutinous, but he saved the situation by offering his escort to Stanthorpe House if she didn't dawdle.

When she accompanied them on these visits, Catheryn amused herself by observing the relationships of the company, one to the other. She noted that Tiffany had a decided interest in Captain Varling; but, since he treated her with the same teasing affection he bestowed upon his sister, she wasn't sure that he returned Tiffany's regard. As for the earl and Maggie, again Catheryn couldn't be sure, although she realized that Tiffany, not knowing of Captain Varling's return, had misinterpreted Dambroke's visits to Sussex. It was true that he flirted with Maggie, but Maggie divided her flirtations equally among all the males in the room, or in any room where Catheryn chanced to meet her. Lord Thomas seemed equally interested in Lady Margaret—also heiress to a tidy fortune—and in Tiffany.

Catheryn dismissed Tom Varling as too young to have a decided interest in females and didn't waste much thought on either of the younger girls, but Lady Prudence interested her. She had called the day following their first meeting, bringing her elder sister, Patience, Lady Easton, to meet Catheryn. Lady Dambroke had gone to a loo party, and Tiffany and his lordship were at Stanthorpe House, so Catheryn received the two visitors alone. Her expressive face gave away her thoughts when the introductions were made, and Lady Prudence's low, melodic chuckle broke out as she settled upon her chair.

"Isn't it absurd, Miss Westering? My mother has a fit of the dismals whenever she has to introduce us all at once. We are, in descending order, Patience, Prudence, Piety, Chastity, Honour and Promise." She laughed when Catheryn's eyes widened in dismay, and Lady Easton grinned broadly.

"Good gracious!" Catheryn exclaimed.

"It really is dreadful," Lady Easton confirmed. "My father's elder sister eloped to Gretna Green with a nobody at the age of sixteen. Her reputation was ruined, of course, and Papa decided his own daughters would not suffer the same fate if they were blessed with virtuous names. Mama held out against him, but to no avail. And none of us except Prue lives up to her name at all."

"Are you so prudent?" Catheryn asked with a twinkle. Prudence opened her mouth, but the older girl spoke first.

"Indeed she is! And as a result is practically on the shelf. No, Prue, don't interrupt. You know it's true. You've had offer upon offer, or did before you let Piety get married before you. Now you will just dwindle into an . . . an aunt!"

Lady Prudence smiled the slow smile that lit up her face. "Pay her no heed, Miss Westering. Patience simply cannot understand that the London beaux, so far at least, do not interest me. When the right man comes along, I shall know it, never fear. I'll not end my days as a spinster aunt."

Catheryn believed her and soon came to think of her as a good friend. She made others as she was whisked by her hostesses from one entertainment to another. Hardly a day passed without morning calls, evening parties, shopping, and promenades. She saw and met many members of London's Beau Monde and was amused by their idiosyncracies—Poodle Byng driving in Hyde Park with his dog up beside him; Lord Petersham, who refused to set foot outside his house till after six o'clock; Lady Caroline Lamb, notorious for her outrageous pursuit of the poet Lord Byron; and Lord Alvanley, who had removed his door knocker in an attempt to confound dunning creditors. The famous Beau Brummell, arbiter of fashion and manners, was out of town, but she heard a good deal about him, wherever she went. He complained about his gout because it attacked his favorite leg and broke off his engagement because the lady liked cabbage. Catheryn thought he must be a trifle odd. She enjoyed everything, but the highlight was yet to come.

Her second Wednesday in London dawned bright and clear, and she awoke with a grin of anticipation. Tonight she was going to Almack's, which, despite its many rules, was still the seventh heaven of the fashionable world. She spent the morning washing her hair and attending to final details of her dress; and, when Tiffany insisted, despite her protests, upon lending her a string of pearls, she agreed. They relaxed later with Mrs. Radcliffe's latest novel from the subscription library and joined Lady Dambroke for an early dinner. His lordship having engaged to dine at Stanthorpe House, it was assumed that he would remain there to bear Captain Varling company, since Lady Stanthorpe and Maggie also meant to attend the Assembly.

After dinner the three ladies retired to prepare for the evening. Mary helped, and Catheryn was soon ready. She wore a simple bright blue dress with a high waist, puffed sleeves, and a demitrain. The white spider gauze overskirt had a scalloped hem with knots of blue satin ribbon. The sash, its ends trailing into the train, was of matching ribbon, while yet another strip was threaded through curls piled artfully atop her head. She finished buttoning her long white gloves, asked Mary to be certain the pearl rosettes were fastened firmly to each blue satin slipper, took a final turn before the mirror, and declared herself ready.

Mary exclaimed that she would fair take the shine out of everyone, and Catheryn chuckled. But, draping her satin evening cloak over her arm, she proceeded downstairs feeling quite the grand lady. The front hall was empty except for Morris, who was lighting tapers in the wall sconces. He turned to watch as she descended the last few steps. Then he grinned and, taking the liberty of a wink, said, "Miss Catheryn, there won't be one to compare!"

She twinkled back at him. "I thank you, sir. I do so adore flattery." He grinned again, and then his face went properly blank as his mistress came down the stairs.

"Catheryn, how quick you are!" exclaimed the countess. "I quite intended to be before you, for I know how you young things tend to get the fidgets at times like this."

"Never mind, ma'am," Catheryn replied, smiling. "I'm

much too excited to be nervous. And anyway, I have been talking with Morris." That young man, his ears crimson, applied a flame to the last candle and effaced himself. The countess watched him go, her brows wrinkled in a frown.

"I do wish you would not be so familiar with the servants, my dear," she reproved. "It is not at all . . . good heavens!" she broke off. "Richard!"

Catheryn turned to see his lordship, complete to a shade in a black velvet coat, knee breeches, white clocked stockings, and black shoes, descending the stair. He looked very handsome, she thought, very debonair. He smiled, lifting a quizzical eyebrow. "Well, Mother?"

"But, Richard, this is wonderful!" she exclaimed. "So you intend to give us escort after all."

"As you see." He turned warmly to Catheryn. "My compliments, Miss Westering. That style becomes you. I shall be pleased to offer escort to three such charming . . . uh, there are three of you, are there not?" He raised his quizzing glass.

"Indeed there are," replied the countess. "Whatever is keeping your sister? Ah, here she is now," she added, sighting her daughter on the half-landing. "Come, Tiffany, we are ready. Dambroke has decided to bear us company, as you see."

Tiffany's color rose and a myriad of expressions played across her countenance, chief among which were dismay and annoyance, though Catheryn detected a hint of fear as well.

"I thought you were visiting Captain Varling," Tiffany muttered.

Dambroke, too, had been watching her, his brows knitted, but his voice was even. "We decided he should make an early night of it. I thought you would be glad of my escort."

"Well, of course we are," she asserted, but the sparkle in her eye robbed the words of truth. He gave her a steady look before turning to help Catheryn with her cloak. Lady Dambroke and Tiffany wore theirs already. The countess's, edged with swansdown and fastened with a jeweled clasp at the bosom, trailed to the floor from an inverted vee, while Tiffany's velvet military cape fastened down the front with a row of golden frogs.

Paulson appeared, opened the great doors, and watched them to the carriage. Catheryn, sitting next to Tiffany and across from Dambroke and the countess, was reminded by the latter to be on her best behavior, to mind her unruly tongue, and, above all, not to dance the waltz until she had been given the approval to do so by one of the patronesses. "For it is a hard and fast rule, my dear, and you will be thought fast if you do not attend to it."

Catheryn promised to be careful, admitting that she had learned the controversial dance in Bath before her grandfather's death but had not danced it since. Tiffany was noticeably quiet, and Catheryn thought once or twice that she actually shivered. The night was a bit chilly, but surely Tiffany's extraordinary cape was enough to protect her from the crisp air. She was about to ask if her cousin was feeling quite the thing when the carriage drew to a halt outside the brilliantly lighted windows of Almack's Assembly Rooms.

They were handed from the coach by obsequious footmen and made their way to the entry hall, where they were greeted by another minion ready to take the ladies' wraps. Catheryn and Lady Dambroke soon handed him theirs, but since it seemed Tiffany would be some time undoing all the fastenings of hers, he accepted her brother's offer to help her with it, while he bestowed the others. Tiffany's fingers twitched nervously as she slowly undid each frog. A suspicious glint leaped to the earl's eye, but he waited patiently. Her mother did not.

"Good gracious, Tiffany, don't be all night. It's chilly in this hall." Her words ended in a shriek as her daughter opened the cape and Dambroke began to lift it from her shoulders. "Tiffany!" The exclamation was followed by an exasperated moan. Catheryn thought her own eyes must be popping out of her head. Tiffany's rose muslin gown was cut so daringly low in the front that her breasts billowed like white apples above it. The thin skirt clung to her body in such a way that every lovely curve was blatantly revealed. Dambroke, standing behind her and lifting the cape, had missed the full effect, but at his mother's cry he lowered the wrap with whistling speed, took one good look, and whisked the cape back over her. She opened her mouth to protest.

"Not one word, if you value your skin, miss!" he snapped. His jaw was clenched and his words low-spoken, but the fury in his tone was unmistakable, frightening Tiffany to silence. She began, more nervously yet, to refasten the frogs. Dambroke spoke to the countess. "I'll return, ma'am. If anyone inquires, say she was taken ill. She may very well *be* ill before I've done with her," he added grimly.

"Richard!" Lady Dambroke reached out a hand, but he had turned away and, with a firm grip on her arm, was steering his sister out the door. "Oh, Catheryn!" The countess turned to her lone support. "Why did she do it? And when everything was going so well!" Aware that they were beginning to present a spectacle of their own to new arrivals, she did not wait for an answer but, drawing Catheryn's hand through her arm, made her way toward the main assembly room. "We mustn't stand like stocks, my dear." She managed an almost normal smile and nodded to a passing acquaintance. "I only hope Dambroke returns before eleven," she added in an undertone. "The Regent himself couldn't get through those doors after that hour. That wicked girl! I hope he gives her a scold she won't forget!"

Catheryn chuckled a little nervously. "By the look of him, Aunt Elizabeth, he is more like to beat her!"

"Oh, if only he would," her ladyship breathed wistfully, but her face fell as she added, "but he will not. I suggested it once, and he said that I should have attended to it years ago. But I never could, and her father never would, so there we are ... and, oh, how could she!"

Catheryn pulled her a little to one side, allowing others to pass. "Please, Aunt, what did she do to that dress? Surely, she never purchased it looking like that!"

"Of course she did not! I know that dress," Lady Dambroke retorted. "She pulled off the lace ruching and damped her petticoat—that is, if she was wearing one. She will catch her death. And she should have worn a white dress. I told her!" The countess was becoming more agitated by the minute. Catheryn touched her arm soothingly.

"My lady, you must calm yourself. It was very shocking conduct, to be sure, but it is done now. I don't believe anyone else even saw her."

Cheered by these words, Lady Dambroke was soon able to compose herself and attend to her duties as Catheryn's chaperone. The necessary introductions completed, Miss Westering was soon standing up for her first country dance with Lord Thomas Colby, who seemed to have been watching for their arrival. As soon as he could do so without being impolite, he asked where the Lady Tiffany was. Catheryn was asked the same question many times as the evening progressed by most of her various partners, including Mr. James Lawrence, and always gave the same reply. Her ladyship had been taken ill. No, it was not serious and, yes, she would be out and about in no time. She kept watch for the earl but was engaged in conversation with young Tom Varling and missed his entrance. Tom, with a guilty grin, explained that he hated dancing but that his mother had demanded his escort for herself and Cynthia, insisting that he should make himself useful since he had been so stupid as to be sent home. Catheryn was still laughing when she looked up to see Dambroke bearing down on her. His expression was grim.

"Cousin, I'd like this dance, if you please." The orchestra had begun a waltz, and he took her arm preparing to swing her into the dance. Catheryn dug in her heels.

"Dambroke!" she gasped, more in merriment than dismay. "Would you undo all my good behavior, you wretch?"

"What? Oh, the devil!" With a guilty grimace, he looked around for a moment, his eyes searching the gathering. Spotting the object of his search, he pulled Catheryn away from a grinning Tom Varling and wended his way across the floor. She was brought up breathless and protesting in front of Lady Jersey, whom she had met, briefly, upon her arrival. Her ladyship raised a haughty brow.

"Well, my lord?"

He had known her all his life and was not the least undone by her attitude. "Miss Westering says she cannot dance the waltz with me without approval from one of the patronesses," he said with a beguiling smile, much

Catheryn thought, in the manner of a cozening schoolboy. "All her other dances are taken, my lady, so will you please give your approval in order that I may dance with her?"

Lady Jersey tapped his arm with her silver fan. "Am I to understand that Miss Westering will not dance the waltz or will not dance with *you* without approval?" When he looked more than ready to enter into repartee on the subject, she laughed and said, "Very well, devil. I daresay you'd only drag her onto the floor willy-nilly and ruin her reputation for her if I denied you. My blessing, Miss Westering."

Catheryn thanked her and she waved them off. Dambroke swept Catheryn into the dance without further comment. She peeped up at him from under her lashes, following his lead without as much difficulty as she had expected and fully enjoying the feel of his arm about her waist. "Would you really, sir?"

He looked down at her. His face was stern again and his thoughts seemed distant. "Would I what?"

"Drag me willy-nilly?"

"Of course not," he scorned. "Lady Jersey is a foolish woman who likes her men to be rakes and devils, that's all." He frowned again and was silent. Deciding they were making no progress, Catheryn pushed to the heart of the matter.

"Have you murdered her?" she asked sweetly.

"Very nearly." The reply was stiff and Catheryn was suddenly fearful.

"Dambroke, you didn't ... you didn't beat her!"

The earl looked surprised, but then a smile crept to his lips. "No, Catheryn, I didn't beat her, though I think," he added with a reminiscent gleam, "I came as near to doing so as I ever shall, and she knew it."

Much relieved, Catheryn followed him carefully through an intricate step before asking what he had done.

"Gave her a trimming she won't forget in a hurry and ordered her off to bed." He sighed, relaxing. "But I didn't dance with you to talk about my misbegotten sister."

"Did you not? Then why?"

"Because I wasn't in a mood to be social and I had to

dance with someone, or some well-meaning tabby would have presented me with a partner. I'd forgot about the waltzing," he added apologetically.

"That's all right now." She was amused. "Tell me something, my lord. Are you at all successful with the fair sex?"

He choked. "I beg your pardon!"

"Granted."

He shook his head, laughing. "You know very well what I meant, Catheryn. Such questions are not at all proper."

"Well, I did wonder," she replied in a musing tone, "since your answer to my last question was not what I have been led to expect from a gentleman."

He thought back to what he had said. "Oh, did you take snuff at that? I do beg your pardon, then, for I never meant to offend you."

"One should never trifle with a lady's sensibilities, my lord," she advised primly, adding, "and you are very free with my name tonight, sir."

He laughed again. "Nonsense! And for your information, I am accounted an expert in my affairs with the gentle sex."

"Ah, yes," she returned sagely, "your bits of muslin, birds of paradise, opera dancers——"

"Catheryn!"

She dimpled at his warning tone, and he gave it up, changing the subject abruptly. When the music stopped he grinned, speaking in an undertone. "If it affords you any satisfaction, little witch, I accomplished all I'd hoped by dancing with you. I thank you most sincerely."

Lady Dambroke looked a bit flustered when he restored a glowing Catheryn to her side, but his easy smile reassured her. "I'm glad you were able to get back in time, Dambroke," she said with a searching look. "I have just been telling Letty," indicating the plump, bespangled matron at her side, "that poor Tiffany was taken ill and ... and...."

"And is devastated to miss the Assembly, ma'am," said his lordship, stepping into the breech with aplomb. "How do you do, Lady Mearing? She has taken to her bed, Mama, and should be much improved within a day or two." He soon took his leave, retiring after a dance or two more to the card room, where he lingered until Lady Dambroke sent to inform him that they were ready to leave.

Next morning Catheryn slept late and, by the time she had dressed, it was nearly noon. Mary informed her that Tiffany was still in her bedchamber and had just ordered breakfast, suggesting that she might enjoy Catheryn's company. Catheryn agreed with a sinking feeling, for she preferred her meals unaccompanied by tragedy scenes.

Tiffany was sitting on the bed with her knees tucked up when she entered, and eyed her a bit warily. "Have you come to scold me, too?" she asked with a sullen look. Her eyes were red from weeping and had deep purple circles under them.

"No, of course not," Catheryn replied cheerfully. "I've come to have breakfast with you."

"Oh."

This response not being particularly encouraging, Catheryn determined to get over the heavy ground as quickly as possible. She settled into the comfortable silk chair. "Whatever possessed you, Tiffany?"

"I knew you meant to scold."

"Don't be nonsensical. It's not my business to scold you. Besides, I'm sure Dambroke has done a thorough job of it."

"Oh, Catheryn, the things he said!" Tears welled up in her eyes. "He was furious. He said . . . he said I . . ." The tears spilled over as her voice broke.

Catheryn had come prepared and handed her a cambric handkerchief, saying practically, "Well, of course he was angry, Tiffany. What else could you expect?"

"I never meant him to know!" Tiffany wailed. "He was supposed to spend the evening with Tony—Captain Varling—and I only did it because I was angry that he wouldn't let me have the new gown. I knew Mama wouldn't tell him."

"But surely someone else would have done so!"

"They never did before." Catheryn's mouth dropped open with astonishment. "Oh, I never did it so much before, nor with such a neckline—only a bit here and there to make a skirt hang properly." Tiffany's words were punctuated with sobs and hiccoughs, but under

Catheryn's steady serenity and lack of overt sympathy, she began to control herself. "I suppose I overdid it last night, but I only damped the petticoat, not the dress itself. It was daring, I-I know, but it really wasn't so bad when we left. I was as amazed as anything when Richard m-made me look at myself in the long glass. It was ever so much worse than I thought!" She choked back another sob.

Catheryn chuckled. "What a peagoose you are, to be sure. By the time we reached Almack's, you idiotish child, the damp from your petticoat had soaked through the dress itself. Under that heavy cape it must have been like a Roman bath. It's no wonder you looked like, well like a...."

"Like a Haymarket d-doxy, is what R-Richard said. He hates me, Catheryn. He will never forgive m-me!"

"Oh, piffle, as you like to say," Catheryn retorted. "He should not have said that, but he will recover and so will you." She fell silent when two maidservants entered with breakfast trays, but once they had gone she offered a suggestion. "What you need is fresh air. Why do we not have Psyche and Angel out for a ride in the park?"

"I can't." The tone was bitter. "Richard ordered me to keep to my bedchamber, lest I inadvertently meet some caller and give the lie to that story he told about my being taken ill. Not," she added gruffly, "that anyone will believe it. We met Maggie and Lady Stanthorpe just before we reached the carriage. They could see how angry he was!"

"I don't know about that," Catheryn said thoughtfully. "It seems to me it would annoy a gentleman to discover his sister was hiding an illness just to go to a dance. Especially if she were overcome just as they arrived and he had to turn right around and take her home again. And I daresay it's not unusual for a girl in her first season to do just that sort of thing."

Tiffany seemed much struck by this line of reasoning. "Catheryn, that's very true. They might believe that."

"I think they might," Catheryn agreed, "however, as to staying inside, I'm afraid he's right. It would never do to be seen when you are supposed to be ill. Besides," she added in her blunt way, "you look wretched."

She was rewarded with a sardonic smile. "Thank you,

Cousin. I really don't mind staying here. I just wish I had something to do."

"Easy enough! I'll fetch Mrs. Radcliffe and we'll finish the tale together. I'm feeling rather lazy myself." So, when they finished breakfast, Catheryn whisked down to the drawing room to fetch the novel. She had just turned back upstairs when Michael, the youngest footman, hurried toward her with the information that his lordship wanted to see her in the library at once. She handed him the book, asking that he take it along with her apologies to the Lady Tiffany. Entering the library a few moments later, she stopped short in astonishment.

"Good afternoon, Cousin," said Edmund Caston.

VII

Catheryn returned Mr. Caston's cool greeting and seated herself in a small oval-backed chair, carefully ignoring Dambroke's look of lazy amusement. "What brings you to town, Edmund?" she inquired.

Caston sat near the fireplace. He seemed surprised by her question. "Why, I've come to fetch you home, of course. I've been explaining to his lordship." He nodded toward Dambroke, who was now leaning back in his desk chair, hands folded across his waistcoat. "Mother is much distressed by your hoydenish behavior, and Father absolutely refuses to frank this outrageous start of yours."

Dambroke flicked at a letter on the desk. "Your uncle's answer, Catheryn. It's rather brief but essentially it's just as Mr. Caston has told you. Sir Horace adds only that he would consider himself derelict in his duty as your trustee if he allowed you to squander your inheritance on frivolities."

"I see." Catheryn was still for a moment, stunned by the news. She had been nearly certain that, rather than have her financially beholden to the countess, Sir Horace would make her an adequate allowance. Instead, he seemed to have dug in his heels, expecting no doubt that by refusing his support he would compel her return to Somerset. She realized her hands were gripped in her lap so tightly that her knuckles were white, and forced herself to relax. Taking a deep breath, she spoke directly to Mr. Caston. "I'm sorry Aunt Agatha has been distressed, for I am fond of her, but she agreed that I might stay, and I shall not return with you, Edmund." She glanced at the earl, but his expression had not changed.

Mr. Caston, on the other hand, showed signs of a rising temper. Of medium height with a figure solidly muscled by years in the saddle, he was, at twenty-six, generally a placid man. At the moment, however, his fine light brown hair was disordered where he had shoved a frustrated hand through it, his jaw was rigid, his toffee-brown eyes flashed, and his voice was tight.

"Don't be fatuous, Catheryn. You have had nearly a fortnight in town, though you've no business to be here at all, and it's time to come home. No doubt, you are apprehensive of reprimand, and I cannot deny that my parents and I are displeased. However, that will pass, and now that you have seen the metropolis, perhaps you will be content in future to remain at home." He permitted himself a smile. "We are not buried there, after all. We often avail ourselves of the cultural advantages permitted by the proximity of Bath."

Dambroke blinked. Catheryn was used to Edmund's manner of speech and had been on the verge of losing her temper, but the earl's rather obvious reaction amused her and helped restore her self-control. She spoke evenly. "Edmund, Lady Dambroke has generously asked me to stay, and I've no immediate intention of leaving. I know you think me ungrateful, even wicked, but——"

"Nonsense," he interrupted. "You are not wicked, my dear, merely thoughtless and a bit flighty. Living with your grandfather so long with no proper female guidance . . . but we have been over this ground before, have we not? Besides, we impose upon his lordship. You will return post with me tomorrow, and I'll tolerate no further argument on the subject. If we depart before noon, we shall be only the one night on the road. I shall call for you at eleven." Clearly believing the interview ended, he began to rise from his chair. Catheryn opened her mouth in angry protest but shut it again when help came from an unexpected quarter.

"I think not, Mr. Caston." Dambroke's voice held a note of surprise. "It would be most improper, you know."

Edmund was on his feet and turned to the earl a bit stiffly. "There is nothing improper about it, my lord. Miss Westering and I are by way of being betrothed, and . . . and we shall have Ditchling as well, of course," he added hastily as Catheryn, outraged, leaped to her feet.

"How dare you, Edmund!" she cried. "We are not by

way or in any way betrothed, and we never shall be! You have no right to make such a statement, to tell such, such——"

"Sit down, Catheryn." The earl's voice cut easily into her diatribe, though he did not raise it. Glaring at him and still muttering under her breath, she obeyed. "If you have quite composed yourself, Miss Westering," he went on blandly, "we shall continue this discussion in a civilized manner." She cast him a speaking glance but subsided.

"Thank you, my lord." Caston allowed himself a brief, man-to-man smile and sank back to his own chair. "As you see, she is just as I described her—quick-tempered and impulsive. Her very flight to London is sufficient evidence of that, of course. Surely, you must concur that her proper place is in Somerset under my parents' protection."

"Tommyrot!" cried Catheryn before the earl could speak. "You make me sound mentally deficient. Your parents' protection indeed! Aunt Agatha would cheerfully be rid of me if you had not convinced her that you want me for your wife. I never understood why before, but of course Uncle Daniel's fortune is the reason. Between you, you and Uncle Horace conspired to keep it in the family. I should never even have known of it, had you not suffered a slip of the tongue!"

He was instantly indignant. "That's not true, Catheryn, and you know it! I've even had recent second thoughts regarding our marriage, but I decided to overlook this escapade, not because of any interest in your fortune, but because I thought that, with patience and understanding, you might still be brought to a sense of proper conduct."

Catheryn spluttered but was again forestalled by the earl, who leaned across his desk and spoke rather sharply. "I think this has gone far enough for the moment. No, Catheryn," as she began to protest, "you cannot discuss these matters in so heated a fashion. Not, at any rate, in my library. Mr. Caston, my mother means to keep Miss Westering here for the entire season, though it is possible that she did not make that clear when she wrote Lady Caston." Catheryn stared at Dambroke in amazement, but he pointedly ignored her. "I am sorry Sir Horace has not seen fit to release some of her funds to her own use," he went on, "but that need concern neither her nor you. She is welcome here and will want for nothing while she is my mother's guest. I see no reason at this point why she should return to Caston Manor and a number of reasons why she should not do so in your sole company."

"But, my lord!"

"Now," Dambroke continued as though there had been no interruption, "I have several things to say. First, Miss Westering." She looked up, biting her lip at his stern tone. "You will discuss this further with Mr. Caston at a more appropriate time. When you have thought matters over, I think you will come to respect the fact that, rather than conspiring against you, he and his father were merely conforming to your grandfather's wishes. And you, sir, will also give thought to the matter. I think you will see that Miss Westering, female or not, ought to have been informed of the trust, if not upon the occasion of her grandfather's death, then certainly when she came of age. If nothing else, telling her would have avoided the development of such suspicions as she now harbors. Where are you putting up in town?" he asked abruptly.

"At . . . at Grillon's, my lord, but——"

"Is there any reason for your immediate return home?"

"No, my lord, my father has things in hand, but——"

"In that case, I suggest you take some time to acquaint yourself with London. You may either continue at your hotel, which is a very good one, or you may have your gear brought here. We should be pleased to have you as our guest."

"Oh no, sir, I could not impose! If I remain, I shall certainly continue with Grillon's. However, I would much prefer to settle matters now. My parents expect——"

"Mr. Caston, use a modicum of sense," interrupted the earl sharply. "Miss Westering is of age. You cannot drag her back to Somerset against her will. You are not yet her husband, you know, and if the two of you persist in your present moods, you will end by not speaking to each other at all. I doubt if either of you wants that." He paused, letting his words take effect. Catheryn remained silent. Glancing first at her and then back at the earl, Mr. Caston let out a long breath.

"There is much in what you say, my lord." He rose to his feet. "I shall defer my departure for a few days at least." He took a step toward Catheryn. "Cousin, perhaps I have been peremptory. I had no wish to offend you."

She stood, speaking stiffly. "We have always come easily to cuffs, Edmund. Perhaps I, too, was hasty."

He turned to take his leave of the earl. "I thank you for the solicitude you have shown her, my lord."

"My pleasure. I have a suggestion, or rather an invitation, Mr. Caston." He smiled his lazy smile. "My mother gives a dress ball the end of next week. I know she would be pleased to have you as one of the company."

"As to that, I cannot say, my lord, though I'm much obliged and would be honored to attend should I still be in town. Thank you and good day."

When he had gone, Catheryn fixed a wary eye upon his lordship. He seemed amused. "Your Edmund," he said, "seems an excellent young man. He will make you a fine husband one day."

She flared up immediately. "Of all the crack-brained things to say! I suppose you believe him about the money, too!"

He raised a hand, laughing. "Don't start with me, you outrageous girl! This is none of my doing." He stopped suddenly, when tears welled over and down her cheeks. Striding forward, he took her gently by the shoulders. "Catheryn, what is it, child? I was but teasing."

"You think it's funny!" she accused, trying to stifle a sob. "You promised to help but have done nothing, and now you laugh at me and tell me I ought to marry Edmund! Why did you not just pack me off with him, if that's what you think I should do!" She began to sob in earnest, but Dambroke gripped her shoulders more firmly and began to shake her.

"Stop it!" he ordered. "Stop that noise at once, Catheryn, or, by God, I shall box your ears!" Shocked out of growing hysteria by the threat as well as by his bruising grip, Catheryn stared up into eyes fierce with anger. "Now, you listen to me, my girl," he commanded with another shake. "Ashley has checked into your trust thoroughly and there is no breaking it. Far from mismanaging it, your uncle has done an excellent job. There is now a good deal more than the original ten thousand. As for sending you home with Mr. Caston, let me tell you that I fully intended to do so when he arrived. I do not know exactly what caused me to alter my decision, but please bear in mind that I can alter it again." He relaxed his hold, and his next words came gently. "I shouldn't have teased you about having him for a husband. It was unmannerly. Besides, I don't think you would suit."

Catheryn sniffed in a childlike manner and brushed tears from her face with the back of her hand, comforted as much, oddly enough, by his fierceness as by his apology. "Oh, Dambroke, it's all so stupid. I beg your pardon. I never really believed they meant to cheat me. It was all that money and . . . and Grandpapa!" Tears streamed unchecked down her cheeks.

"Calm yourself, Catheryn," he said quietly. "Your grandfather would never have allowed a penny of your money to be spent on Westering. It would have been exceedingly difficult for anyone to get at it, in fact, before you came of age, and it would most likely have become a bone of contention between you. Now, dry your tears and let's hear no more about it." When she could not produce a handkerchief, he offered his own.

"Thank you, my lord. I gave mine to Tiffany. What a weepy day this has been, to be sure!" He stiffened at mention of his sister but said nothing until they reached the door.

"Everything works itself out in time," he said then, looking down at her with a cool smile and an expression in his eyes that made her feel a trifle giddy. "You should rest now."

She went upstairs, making a strong effort to compose herself and firmly repressing all thought of that unsettling look. She hoped she was no simpering romantic miss and that she had better sense than to dwell upon a fleeting expression simply because a man was handsome and possessed of a certain charm. Such behavior could only lead to embarrassment, and the whole thing was perfect nonsense anyway. She would do much better to follow his lordship's very sound advice instead and get some rest. Therefore, discovering Tiffany deeply engrossed in Mrs. Radcliffe's purple prose, she pleaded a headache and escaped to her own bedchamber, conscious of a feeling of gratitude that the younger girl had barely looked away from her book. The rest of the day passed quickly enough, but the following morning found both girls yearning for exercise. So it was that, despite gathering storm clouds, Mr. Lawrence was accorded the pleasure of meeting them in Hyde Park.

He doffed his hat, greeting them cheerfully, and inquired about Tiffany's recent illness. She blushed, but Catheryn engaged his attention until she had composed herself, and they rode together amicably for some time before the sight of two approaching horsemen caused Mr. Lawrence to halt an anecdote midsentence. Catheryn had also seen the riders, their high-bred mounts moving at an easy walk. Only Tiffany had failed to observe them. She looked at Lawrence, surprised at his sudden silence, then followed the direction of his gaze. She gasped when she recognized her brother and Captain Varling.

Lawrence spoke immediately and in an undertone. "I would not wish to be the cause of your brother's displeasure, my lady. I shall take my leave before they are upon us."

Tiffany nodded a vague agreement but hardly acknowledged his farewell as she turned anxiously to Catheryn. "Do you see that it is Captain Varling with Richard? Oh, Catheryn, I am persuaded that he ought not to be riding yet. He may do himself further injury."

Catheryn chuckled. "I make no doubt that Dambroke would not be with him if that were the case, Tiff. He would be more like to sit upon him to keep him from his horse."

Tiffany smiled at the sally but still looked worried. As the horses came together both girls exclaimed their pleasure at seeing Varling out and about, but Tiffany avoided her brother's eye. He, too, wished them good morning, and Catheryn was relieved to note that he looked perfectly normal and not at all as though she had played him a Cheltenham drama in his library the previous day. His expression was not at all unsettling now but quite clear and friendly. Feeling completely at ease, she answered his greeting with a twinkle.

"It seems that you and Chieftain have been dragged out at an early hour, my lord, and on a dreary morning, too."

He laughed. "Yes, Cousin, an irresistible force drew us. Tony was determined to get out and scorned the offer of a sedate carriage ride. He threatened to have his horse out for the promenade, so his long-suffering parents begged me to knock some sense into his head. We compromised."

Catheryn nodded meaningfully at Lady Tiffany, who was steadily observing Angel's mane. Dambroke was quick to catch the hint, but his tone was cool. "I am glad to see you recovered, Tiffany," he said.

"Th-thank you, my lord," she murmured. "I-I am feeling much more the thing this morning."

The captain glanced sharply from one to the other and then at Catheryn. "Here, Dickon!" he exclaimed. "We cannot ride this path four abreast! Do you and Miss Westering allow the two invalids to ride ahead. You may then keep guard over your respective charges without crowding us."

Dambroke agreed with a smile but warned his friend that he would break his good leg for him if he dared to push his nag above a walk. The captain tossed him a cocky grin before riding on with Tiffany. Dambroke let them get some distance ahead before he lifted his rein. "Was that not that damned Lawrence fellow riding with you?" he demanded.

"Yes, my lord."

"Do you continue to encourage that folly, Catheryn? She does not seem to lose interest." His tone was grave and Catheryn chuckled. "I see nothing to laugh about!"

She turned her head to look at him, her eyes still brimming with laughter. "Do you mean to scold me, sir?"

"I should do so," was the uncompromising reply.

"Well, you may, of course, with my good will. But you will come to be sorry for it, sir."

He gave her a puzzled look. "Why is that?"

"Because I believe she is losing interest, my lord. He cannot really be a fortune hunter anyway. He is thirty, you know, and cannot possibly want to wait so long for the money!"

Dambroke gave her an odd look. "Did you discuss this aspect of the situation with Tiffany?"

"I'm afraid I did," she confessed, and was amazed when he chuckled. "What is it, my lord?"

He shook his head. "I had wondered myself about his continued interest and decided he was clutching at last straws. Your mentioning the money reminded me of something. I believe Tiffany expects to have her fortune when she marries. I as much as told her she would."

"I beg your pardon!"

The guilty grin flashed across his face. "I was furious at the time, and when she accused me of wishing to retain control over her because of her fortune, I replied—in heat, of course—that I would cheer the day I could turn both her and her fortune over to a properly overbearing husband."

"I see." Catheryn gave him a straight look. "How does her trust actually stand, then?"

"It is a normal one, only slightly different from your own." He shrugged. "I am her guardian until she marries or turns twenty-one, and I control her fortune at my own discretion until she's twenty-five. The difference is that I could relinquish before she comes of age, had I a mind to, whereas your trustees were committed. I should never relinquish to a man of Lawrence's stamp, of course."

"And Tiffany is ignorant of these terms! Good God, Dambroke! You are quite as Gothic as Edmund and Sir Horace."

"It never occurred to me that I ought to explain the trust to her," he replied, nettled. "I am also trustee for my brother's fortune and have never discussed it with him."

Catheryn shot him a look of scorn. "That is scarcely comparable, my lord. Teddy is a boy of ten, while Tiffany is a young woman. She should certainly be told the truth."

He frowned thoughtfully. "I think I must disagree. Not that I shouldn't have told her before. But not now. Wittingly or not, I think you may have forced her to give serious thought to his true intentions. He is undoubtedly laboring under a misconception, poor lad, since she probably misled him herself. But it's all to the good. Better she should cut the connection on her own than be hurt when he learns the truth."

Catheryn wrinkled her nose. She wasn't at all certain that Lawrence would accept rebuff. She had seen his growing frustration and distrusted him. Watching the two riders ahead, she smiled to herself, for they were deep in conversation, riding close to each other. One could not take such things for granted, of course; but, if things went well, Tiffany would have plenty of protection against men like Lawrence. Dambroke soon announced that he had to keep an appointment with his secretary, and the men rode off together. The two girls continued their ride for another half hour or so, stopping now and again when they met an acquaintance. The sky began to clear, and the sun made insistent attempts to shine through the clouds. Tiffany seemed a bit withdrawn. Catheryn forbore to intrude upon her reflections until they reached the house; but, when they entered the hall, she reminded her that the countess expected them to accompany her on a number of errands.

"Oh no, Catheryn!" Tiffany exclaimed, startled out of her preoccupation. "You go, but tell Mama I've decided to visit Maggie instead." She looked hesitantly toward the library and Catheryn, thinking she meant to beg Dambroke's escort when he had finished his business with Mr. Ashley, agreed to carry her apologies to the countess and went upstairs.

VIII

The weekend passed peacefully, but Monday morning, charmingly attired in a green-and-white-striped muslin frock, Catheryn entered the breakfast parlor to find Dambroke alone, scowling at a letter on the table beside the remains of a hearty breakfast. Morris deftly began to remove the dishes while Paulson seated Catheryn.

"Good morning, my lord." Receiving a curt reply, she calmly began to butter toast and presently to apply herself to an excellent breakfast. She glanced at the earl several times while she ate but made no further attempt to engage him in conversation. He was drinking coffee and seemed to be concentrating upon some knotty mental problem. At last, however, he sighed, looked up, and caught her eye. A tiny smile quivered at the corner of his mouth.

"Wondering if I shall bite?"

She smiled. "No, sir. My grandfather was always in crotchets at breakfast, too. I promise I don't regard it."

The black eyebrows rose. "In crotchets! My dear girl, that is a limp description of my feelings. I've just had my plans for the day as well as my normal good temper—don't you dare laugh—destroyed by this devilish letter!" He smacked the article in question.

"I shan't laugh," she assured him, "but may I ask what has occurred? I shall understand if you don't want to tell me."

"I can't say that I particularly wish to discuss it, but you will know the whole soon enough, so I may as well tell you now. You have heard us speak of Edward, of course."

"Certainly. Your younger brother, Teddy." She had indeed heard much talk of "that young limb of Satan," as Mrs. Paulson, the housekeeper, called him. "He is at Eton, is he not?"

Dambroke grimaced. "I've been asked to rectify that."

"Rectify? You mean you must remove him? But why?"

"According to this letter from Dr. Keate, the headmaster, they can no longer accommodate him. He cites unacceptable behavior, inattention to lessons . . . in short, the boy is being expelled, and they request his immediate removal. I shall have to drive down today." He looked at his watch. "As a matter of fact, I must leave very shortly."

"But what has he done? Surely, they have dealt with recalcitrance successfully in the past. Even I have heard of Dr. Keate, and Teddy is only ten, after all."

"Nothing seems to do the trick," Dambroke said heavily. "You see, this is not the first time there's been trouble. I've made spur-of-the-moment trips down there before—once when he ran away to avoid a flogging and another time when I simply thought I might make my feelings clearer in person than in a letter. But now, Keate leaves me no choice. He must come home." Since the look in his eye boded no good for the hapless Teddy, Catheryn took courage in hand.

"I think a drive to Windsor would be delightful," she said brightly. "It's a glorious day, and I had no plans of importance. If you are in a hurry, I'll just collect my pelisse and meet you in the hall."

"Catheryn, you are not going with me!"

She cocked her head, blond curls flashing golden in an errant ray of sunlight. "Did not your nanny teach you, sir, never to contradict a lady?"

He sputtered. "It would not be conduct becoming a *lady* to travel out of the city with only my escort, miss!"

"How thoughtful, my lord," she retorted sweetly. "Lady Tiffany will be glad of the diversion. I'll tell her to make haste, and we can all have luncheon in Windsor." She arose and headed for the door. The anticipated explosion came before she reached it.

"This is not a pleasure jaunt, Miss Westering! I am going to collect my brother from a school which doesn't want him, and it will *not* be amusing. It will be damned unpleasant, certainly for Edward. He will not want you! Besides, I shall take my curricle," he added lamely. "There won't be room."

Catheryn had stood facing the door during this tirade. Without moving, she spoke one word. "Nonsense."

"What did you say!"

She turned, twinkling and unruffled, to find him on his feet and glaring at her across the table. "I said 'nonsense,' my lord," she replied equably, despite the storm warnings. "It is nonsense, you know—and don't contradict me again. You can't have thought. Your curricle? Surely, Teddy will have a trunk and other gear. You must take the carriage. And furthermore," she continued roughshod over his feeble attempts to interrupt, "furthermore, sir, even you would not condemn a freshly whipped child—for you do intend, do you not, that he shall be whipped, even though you've not heard his side of the matter—well, even so, you'd not condemn him to ride here from Eton in a bouncing, jolting curricle or in a well-sprung carriage, for that matter. You'll have to wait till you get him home, which will make it uncomfortable for both of you. You need Tiffany and me!" she finished triumphantly.

"I have no intention of making such a journey in a closed carriage with two witless females and a bothersome brat!" he declared, descending to nursery levels.

Catheryn fostered the illusion by agreeing kindly, "Of course not, my lord. You shall ride Chieftain. Much more pleasant for you, and Tiffany and I shall be quite comfortable in the carriage." At that, she whisked herself out the door, closing it upon a muttered epithet to the circumambient air—something to do with meddlesome females.

Fortunately, she had no trouble with Tiffany, who was delighted by the prospect of an impromptu outing; and, though she would not have been amazed to find that he had gone without them, the carriage was at the door when they stepped outside, and Chieftain stood quietly beside it. Without comment, the earl handed them up, mounted his horse, and they were off.

The journey was rapid, and by half past eleven they had arrived at the famous boys' school. Dambroke dismounted and strode to the carriage. "You may await us here," he said brusquely. "We shan't be long."

But, to Catheryn's relief, Tiffany took matters into her own hands. "Don't be silly, Richard." She pushed the door open, compelling him to take her hand and help her alight. Miss Westering followed. "Catheryn and I discussed it on the way," Tiffany added. "You cannot just explode all over poor Teddy and then take us to luncheon. We promise not to interfere, but you will keep your temper better if we come with you." Certain that Dambroke would be unwilling to engage in what amounted to a public argument, Catheryn applauded Tiffany's tactics. The earl had no choice. They entered the main building and were soon shown to the headmaster's study.

Dr. John Keate had been headmaster at Eton for not quite three years and was already known as a "famous flogger." It was said that, in a single afternoon, he had flogged all one hundred members of the lower fifth form for missing roll call on a holiday, so Catheryn understood why Teddy might have run away to escape a beating. She had imagined Keate as a sort of Goliath and was, therefore, a bit taken aback by the red-headed little man who rose to greet them from behind a massive desk. He was only five feet tall. Not that he was not powerful, for he was—like a bull—and he looked ferocious enough, with enormous shaggy red eyebrows standing out in angry tufts; but his eyes twinkled as he held a hamlike hand out to the earl. "Good morning, my lord."

"Dr. Keate." Dambroke nodded as he shook the outstretched hand. He indicated the ladies. "My sister, Lady Tiffany, and our cousin, Miss Westering."

Keate bowed from the waist with a surprisingly courtly air. "A pleasure, my lady, Miss Westering. Won't you be seated?" He pulled a bell rope, and Dambroke sat down in a wing chair near the desk. Tiffany and Catheryn took matching Kent armchairs nearer the door, as a boy of fourteen or fifteen entered. "Some refreshment, Pickens," ordered Keate, "and send someone to the Long Chamber to notify young Dambroke his brother is here." The boy jerked a bow and hastened from the room. Ignoring the earl's conspicuous impatience, Keate chatted desultorily about the unpredictable spring weather and other such harmless matters until Pickens returned with tea for the ladies and Madeira for the gentlemen. When the door closed behind him again, the headmaster settled back and peered at Dambroke. "I know you are anxious to get to the point, my lord."

"Indeed." Dambroke spoke quietly, but his expression was grim. Catheryn sighed. Clearly, the ride had blown away none of his ill humor. This would not be at all pleasant.

Dr. Keate hesitated, evidently expecting the earl to continue, then glanced at Catheryn. She was certain his eyes still twinkled. What an extraordinary man, she thought, smiling at him. Tiffany, made uneasy by the seeming levity, shot an apprehensive look at her brother; but if he was aware of anything other than his own desire to have the matter over and done with, Catheryn could see no sign of it. Keate set down his glass and pressed his fingers together.

"I cannot recall, my lord, that I have ever before been worsted by a ten-year-old." He frowned, shaking his shaggy red head, and Catheryn suddenly doubted that he had been worsted by anyone. He spread fat fingers in an impatient gesture. "In a nutshell, my lord, the boy is incorrigible. I lose track of the times he's been flogged." Catheryn closed her eyes, flinching. "He's been reprimanded, isolated, even sent to Coventry."

She opened her eyes again. "What! I mean . . . well, I beg your pardon. . . ." Encountering an ominous scowl from his lordship, she continued defiantly, "Well, why should they send him there, of all places?"

Dambroke's face relaxed almost to a smile, and Dr. Keate allowed himself a dry chuckle. "I have confused you, Miss Westering. The term derives from the punishment supposedly visited upon Peeping Tom by the citizens of Coventry after Lady Godiva's famous or, if you prefer, infamous ride there. They never spoke to him again after he alone defied the decision to allow her to ride unobserved. Here at Eton it means that the offender wears a yellow armband, and the other boys are not allowed to speak to him."

"I see. How horrid!"

"Don't hold with it myself. Prefer a good flogging!" Keate turned back to the earl. "The last time there was trouble—he picked a fist fight with a lad smaller than himself—I thrashed him myself and threatened to expel him if there were further such incidents. That was last week. Friday afternoon, he had another fight with the same lad. Left me no choice, my lord."

Dambroke frowned deeply. "Has he been beaten?"

The headmaster shook his head. "Thought you might wish that privilege reserved for yourself. He's been restricted to the Long Chamber on bread and water pending your arrival." The steady gaze had not moved from the earl, but now it flickered to the riding crop in his lap. Catheryn, who had been watching both men, believed Keate would like to have said more but that he was finding the earl unresponsive. There was nothing to be read in Dambroke's noble visage but irritation, anger, and perhaps embarrassment. She shifted her gaze back to the headmaster, willing him to look at her. In the silence that followed his last words, he began toying with his wine glass. Finally, lifting it to drink, he caught her puzzled look. When he set the glass down, he pulled the bell. The same boy answered. "Is young Dambroke here yet?"

"Yes, sir."

"Send him in, please."

The earl sat grimly regarding the carpet, his long legs stretched out before him, but Catheryn and Tiffany both turned to watch the culprit's entrance. The study door had been left ajar, and a moment later the Honorable Edward Dambroke entered, shutting it gently behind him.

He was a sturdy child with light brown, tousled hair and a roses-and-cream complexion. Bits of white shirttail pouched out on either side under his short blue jacket, and both stockings below his breeches were twisted—one, in fact, looked in imminent peril of collapse. Catheryn hid a smile. This small person who had disrupted the halls of Eton and the earl's day resembled nothing so much as a scruffy cherub.

Teddy looked quickly around the study. His vivid blue gaze flitted across Catheryn and Tiffany and came to rest upon his brother. Catheryn, watching closely, was amazed to see a spark of triumph in the boy's eyes. A grin actually flickered across his face before he recollected himself and let his gaze slide to the carpet. Triumph changed to contrition so rapidly that she realized neither

Tiffany nor Dambroke, who had swung his scowl toward the boy, had observed the former expression. She turned to find Keate's eyes peering at her from under those outrageous brows. When she quietly lowered her reticule to the floor by her chair, one eyebrow rose and fell almost as though it waved approval. Keate turned to Teddy.

"Well, Edward." His tone was grave, the twinkle gone. "Are you quite ready to leave us?"

"Yes, Dr. Keate." The boy spoke to the carpet.

"Look up when you speak, sir!" snapped Dambroke.

"Yes, sir." Teddy drew himself up, squaring his shoulders. His lower lip trembled, but he moistened it and looked steadily at Keate. "My gear is in the carriage, sir."

The headmaster stood, smiling faintly. "Fine, Edward. I'm sorry we didn't deal better together." He looked at the earl, who still sat at his ease. "I think perhaps your brother would like a private word with you before you leave." Teddy seemed to stiffen even more.

"No!" Belatedly, Catheryn remembered her promise not to interfere, but Dambroke stood up, raising his hand.

"Enough, Cousin." He turned to the headmaster with suave civility. "There is no need to take up more of your time, sir. Edward and I will discuss this further in London." He nodded. "Thank you for your trouble. I'm sorry he was such a bother. Come, Edward. Ladies."

Catheryn waited until they had nearly reached the carriage before making distracted noises about having left her reticule behind. Ignoring the earl's annoyed offer to send the footman and Tiffany's offer to accompany her, she hurried back to find Keate waiting for her. "Please be brief, sir. His lordship already thinks me meddlesome enough."

He smiled. "He won't appreciate advice from either of us at the moment, so I must leave matters to your judgment, Miss Westering. You seem perceptive. Saw it at once. In point of fact, I believe that young rattle contrived this whole affair. He outmaneuvered me, set me up. I threatened to expel him, thinking to end the nonsense. Instead, he cornered me into keeping my word."

"You may be right, sir," Catheryn agreed. "Dambroke will flay him for this, but Teddy actually looked almost smug."

"Precisely. He won't care for the beating. Boys don't as a rule. But you tell that lordship of yours that when he sends the boy back, I say he's to send him with his own tutor and to lodge him with one of the dames in town!"

"When he . . . but you said he isn't to come back at all!"

The twinkle was back. "In a rage, my dear. I'll come to my senses. When the boy apologizes for his sins, thereby notifying me that he's ready to return, I shall probably have a change of heart. Don't tell him right away. Just don't let Dambroke pack that boy off to any other school. I like him!"

"No indeed, sir! Thank you! Now, I must fly or he will be upon us." She left him, her opinion of him greatly changed, and rushed to the carriage, hoping the earl might not comment upon her long absence. She needn't have worried. He had gone ahead to bespeak their luncheon.

As the carriage lurched forward, Tiffany reported that Dambroke had first said that Teddy was to have no lunch but that she had prevailed upon him to change his mind by reminding him the boy had been two days on bread and water. The Honorable Edward looked up from his seat in the front corner with an impish grin. "She said she would send a maidservant out with a basket. That's when he relented!"

Catheryn laughed. "Well, I'm glad he changed his mind. You will need sustenance to carry you through this day."

Teddy grimaced and leaned over to straighten his stocking. His voice was gruff. "I expect he's pretty angry."

"Of course he is, stoopid." Tiffany smiled sympathetically. "But he will not eat you. Very likely, you are in for one of his scolds and will go supperless to bed. That's what Catheryn meant about needing sustenance."

Catheryn frowned at this interpretation of her words, but the boy's head came up, hope gleaming in his eyes.

"Really, Tiffy? Is that all?" When his sister seemed about to compound the error, Catheryn spoke more sharply than she had intended.

"No, Teddy, it is not all!" Squelching Tiffany with a look, she continued, "Dambroke is displeased and rightly so, though I'll say no more on that head, for Tiffany's no doubt right about the scold. However," she added with her customary frankness, "you must resign yourself to a thrashing as well. Dambroke has said so, and I doubt he makes idle threats." The boy wilted, and Tiffany's eyes reproached her, but Catheryn believed it would have been worse to allow him to think he would get off with only a scolding. "I'm sorry, Teddy, but you must not delude yourself." Breaking into a rueful chuckle, she added, "And we've not even been properly introduced. I am your sort of cousin, Catheryn Westering, you know."

The boy visibly pulled himself together and held out a slightly grubby fist. "Yes, ma'am. Tiffany told me about you while we waited. I am pleased to meet you."

Catheryn chuckled again, squeezing his hand. "Well, no one can call you rag-mannered. I believe we are going to be friends, Teddy." He smiled shyly at her.

Luncheon at the charming inn Dambroke had selected was no cheerful affair. Even Catheryn, fond as she was of food, was glad when it was done. The earl paid the shot, saw them back into the carriage, and rode off, leaving them to follow at his coachman's leisure. Somehow, the knowledge that he would be impatiently awaiting their arrival lowered their spirits even more, and they spoke little on the return journey.

When they entered the front hall, however, it was Lady Dambroke who greeted them, hurrying from the saloon with a rustle of skirts and arms outstretched. "Teddy, darling boy!" He started to run forward but stopped abruptly when the library doors snapped open. Hovering servants disappeared as if by magic.

"Edward!" The boy turned slowly toward Dambroke, who stood on the library threshold, holding the door with one hand, his riding whip with the other. "You will oblige me by stepping in here at once, young man. I have a deal to say to you." He flicked the short whip against his leg, and Catheryn trembled, rooted to the floor. Teddy hesitated, his eyes fixed upon the whip. "Now!" Startled by the sharp command, young Edward straightened his shoulders and strode determinedly across the hall and into the library. Dambroke shut the doors.

Catheryn still seemed unable to move. All her faculties were concentrated on those doors and what was happening behind them. Tiffany and Lady Dambroke also seemed frozen in place. The walls were thick and they could hear nothing at first, but Dambroke's voice soon rose. Catheryn could make out no more than an occasional word, but the tone was sufficient to inform her that Teddy was indeed receiving a thunderous scold. Silence fell again briefly before Teddy's voice, upraised in pain, told her what was taking place. She closed her eyes. Another silence, then the sound of the door. She opened her eyes.

Lady Dambroke started forward, but a look from the earl stopped her in her tracks. Dambroke still held the riding crop, and Teddy, shirttails hanging, was rubbing his eyes with the back of his sleeve, trying unsuccessfully to stifle his sobs. The earl looked down at him. "Seek your room, Edward. I do not look to see your face before morning, when we shall discuss what is to be done with you."

"Have you not done enough?" Tiffany asked bitterly.

"That will do, Tiffany. Go, Edward."

The boy started dejectedly up the stairs, dragging his jacket, and Catheryn drew a long breath and turned to Lady Dambroke. "I wonder if we might have tea, Aunt Elizabeth. It has been a very long day."

The countess looked at her gratefully, and the tension was broken. Tiffany gave a shaky laugh. "Trust Catheryn to think of food."

Even Dambroke permitted himself a slight smile, though Catheryn made a point of not responding to it. "It is a fine idea," he said. He motioned to the butler, who had taken advantage of his august position to remain on the scene. "See to it, Paulson. The yellow drawing room." When the butler had departed, he spoke further. "Edward is not to be coddled, Mama. I want him to understand the gravity of his offense. He is to be left to his own reflections until morning."

"It seems rather harsh, Richard. After all, he is my son. And what about his dinner?"

"He is not like to starve overnight, ma'am." His expression was grim, and his mother's protests subsided. Satisfied, the earl retired to his library.

IX

Once the ladies settled themselves and tea had been served, a silence fell. All three were thinking of Teddy, but none wished to discuss his misfortune. Finally, the countess roused herself to speech. "I had a visitor today, my dears. Your cousin, Mr. Caston, Catheryn. A nice young gentleman who thinks just as he ought, I'm sure."

"Dear me," Catheryn laughed. "Did he bore you to distraction, ma'am?"

"Don't be impertinent. I must admit, however, that he seems to have seen a great deal of London in the past few days. And he uses such long words. He seemed to think it necessary, oddly enough, to apologize—several times and at great length—for your presence in this house."

"Good heavens! I'm very sorry, Aunt Elizabeth!"

"Well, you should not be. I'm happy to have you here."

"Yes, indeed, Catheryn," Tiffany agreed. "You make it seem more cheerful than ever it was before. You won't let him take you away, will you?"

"No, not if you truly don't mind my imposing upon your generosity, Aunt Elizabeth." That lady shook her head, smiling. "Well, I didn't mean to apologize for being here, anyway," Catheryn went on. "Only for subjecting you to such a call from Edmund. I forgot all about him, or I should have realized he would call today. I'm still out of charity with him, however, so it's as well I didn't have to see him."

"As to that, my dear, you will. He dines with us."

"How could you invite him, Mama, when you must have known Catheryn would dislike it!" But Tiffany's eyes and Catheryn's, too, began to twinkle as the countess explained.

"I could do nothing else. The man seemed riveted to

the sofa! Fortunately, I chanced to recall that we are promised to Lady Heathcote tonight, so when he began to prose on about Lord Elgin's Greek marbles, I simply interrupted in the most unmannerly way and invited him to dine and lend us his escort. Naturally, he had to return to his hotel to change."

"Lady Heathcote's ball!" Tiffany leaped to her feet. "Catheryn, how could we forget! It's nearly four o'clock, and here we sit in all our dirt."

Catheryn grinned but rose obediently from her seat. "We have plenty of time, Tiff. But, Aunt Elizabeth, won't Lady Heathcote object if we bring an uninvited guest to her ball?"

"Dear Catheryn, don't be absurd," the countess replied calmly. "Her parties are always such crushes that she could not possibly remember the names of everyone on her invitation list. Don't bother your head about it."

Relieved, Catheryn went away with Tiffany to prepare for the evening ahead. As she luxuriated in a perfumed bath, it occurred to her that it would be better to meet Edmund in a social setting where they would be forced to be polite to one another. Then her thoughts turned to Teddy's predicament. She spent much of the late afternoon pondering ways of turning the rather uncomfortable situation to his favor, but the only thought in her mind when she went downstairs to join the family was the hope that the countess would not place Edmund next to her at dinner.

She need not have worried, for it became clear the instant she entered the drawing room that dinner was not to be a mere family affair. Upwards of twenty people were gathered there, including the entire Stanthorpe ménage, Lord Thomas Colby with the Ladies Prudence and Chastity, and Lady Easton with her husband. There were two strange gentlemen as well. One was a tall, fresh-faced young man with Tom Varling and clearly a friend of his. The other was just as clearly a man of the world. Dressed neatly in black evening dress and boasting none of the fashionable seals or fobs, he was precise to a pin with an air of simple elegance.

Tiffany approached, laughing. "Welcome, Catheryn. Was it not too bad of Mama not to warn us of her party? She says she never realized she had invited so many, just cast an invitation here and there, and here they all are. Luckily, she did remember to tell Paulson each time she added a name, so he and Jean-Pierre at least are prepared. I didn't even know the Beau was back in town. He has been down at Oatlands with the Duke of York, you know."

"The Beau?"

"Mr. Brummell. But you've not met him yet, have you?"

"No, I've not had that pleasure." She thought she should have realized the identity of the dandy in black sooner. Beau Brummell had certainly been described to her often enough. Someone had once told her his grandfather had been a valet; nevertheless, his background was perfectly respectable, for his father had been private secretary to Lord North, the Tory Prime Minister, and Brummell had attended both Eton and Oxford. She judged him to be a few years older than Dambroke and, despite the tales she had heard, thought he did not look odd at all. His nose had a disdainful tilt to it, but his smile was charming, and he had an aura of breeding that was not outmatched by anyone in the elegant company. Tiffany took her arm and drew her toward the group where everyone was laughing at some remark he had made. When the noise died away, she introduced him.

"Oh, Catheryn," laughed Maggie, "Mr. Brummell has just been telling us that he went to Berry Brothers this afternoon to be weighed!"

"To be weighed?" She regarded the Beau quizzically. "He must be joking you, Lady Margaret. Even I know Berry Brothers to be a grocers in St. James Street."

"Ah, but a prince of grocers, Miss Westering," responded Brummell instantly. "George Berry provides a novelty by weighing us on his great coffee scales!"

"Is this to be your latest fashion, George?" Dambroke inquired with his slow smile.

"Already is. Petersham is a constant customer. Purchases his tea there, you know. Prinny goes, too, but Berry says he actually blushed last time he was weighed and hasn't been back in a week." Laughter bubbled up again, and Catheryn saw that Mr. Caston had entered the room. She excused herself to greet him and had time to introduce him to one or two others before Paulson announced dinner.

At the table she found herself between Tom Varling's father and Lord Thomas, with Edmund across the table between Lady Trevaris and Lady Prudence. Catheryn observed with amusement that, though he was polite to the older woman, his attention was more drawn to the younger. Her own was claimed immediately by Colby.

"I declare, Miss Westering, you will break hearts tonight."

She had come to like him well enough to tease him and replied with a twinkle, "Not yours, certainly, my lord. My dowry keeps me quite beneath your notice, does it not?"

"Dear me, I seem to have developed quite a reputation."

"Undeserved, sir?"

"Unfortunately, no. I have cause now to wish it otherwise, however. It may well prove to be my undoing."

"Good heavens, my lord! Never tell me you have fallen in love!" She gazed at him expectantly, but his only response was a mournful smile. "You have! Who is she?"

But this question he would not answer. Lady Chastity, on his other side, spoke to him a moment later, and he turned away. Regretfully, Catheryn directed her attention to Mr. Varling. She spoke several times more to Lord Thomas, but he adroitly parried any reference to their original topic; so, when Lady Dambroke indicated the time had come to leave the gentlemen to their port, Catheryn was no wiser than before. Dambroke knew his duty. The men soon joined the ladies, and their carriages were called to take them to the ball.

Vehicles lined the street outside Lady Heathcote's great house, and linkboys scurried to and fro in a desperate effort to clear the way for new arrivals. At last, it was their turn to step down onto the red carpet, and soon they were greeting their hostess, who showed no dismay whatever at the sight of Mr. Caston. Moments later, they entered the great ballroom itself, a dazzling chamber lit by candles from no fewer than twenty-six crystal chandeliers. With nearly everyone who was anyone present, it was indeed a crush, a great compliment to any hostess. Catheryn recognized Lord and Lady Jersey, Lords Petersham and Alvanley, the Prince and Princess Esterhazy, and Lady Caroline Lamb with her long-suffering husband, William. His rival, Lord Bryon, leaned negligently against the wall in a position described by his admirers as a poetic trance and by his critics—mostly male—as a damned rude affectation. Catheryn thought Bryon a romantic figure and had enjoyed his new poem, *Childe Harold's Pilgrimage*, as much as anyone, but his airs and graces had begun to annoy her.

Her hand was claimed for a country dance, and she soon forgot the poet and his lady as she threw herself into the spirit of the party. Nearly an hour had passed when the orchestra struck up the first waltz of the evening. Catheryn felt a thrill of excitement and hoped the earl, standing nearby, would ask her to dance. Though she thought his treatment of Teddy unnecessarily harsh, it was not her business to interfere; and after all, she had not danced with him since the first subscription ball at Almack's. He was drawing an anecdote to its conclusion, however, and Mr. Caston was before him—if, indeed, Dambroke had even meant to claim her hand. She was surprised at Edmund but quickly perceived her error.

"I have waited all evening for an opportunity to speak with you, Catheryn, but did not care to interpose while you might be dancing. However, you will not take exception to our conversing just now, for I know you do not wish to make a figure of yourself by engaging in anything so improper as the waltz."

She stared at him, annoyed. "Well, you are quite out, Edmund. I adore to waltz. And if this means you have denied me an opportunity for which I have been waiting an hour and more, I shall be more vexed with you than ever."

This inauspicious beginning affected him not a whit. He smiled in his superior way and guided her inexorably into a small, conveniently empty withdrawing room. "Don't be infantile, Catheryn. I appreciate that you are taking this opportunity to make me aware of your displeasure, but it is superfluous, I assure you. To pretend to have so little elegance of mind that you would enjoy whirling about a ballroom clasped in the most saturnalian manner within a gentleman's embrace is to carry the matter too far. Even you could never be so wanting in delicacy as to disport yourself in a style that would scandalize your friends and family beyond bearing. No, no, do not interrupt me. It would only serve to convince me that your sojourn in London has done little toward improving your manners. Besides, I have no wish to quarrel, especially upon so spurious a topic. I have something to say to you."

Short of raising her voice to a level that would be overheard in the ballroom—for naturally, Edmund had not been so lacking the respect due her good name as to shut the door—there was nothing Catheryn could do to stop him. She resigned herself to listen.

"I cannot say that I relish the present situation, Cousin," he continued, "however, I desire you to know that I am not entirely insensible of your sentiments. It is not unusual for a young female to yearn for gaiety and frivolity. Nor is it remarkable for her to rebel against the restraints, however benevolent, of her family. I cannot help deprecating your methods, whatever the motivation may have been; however, to pursue that issue would be to belabor it. I desired this conversation in order that I might offer my apology to you in the matter of your inheritance. I do not admit that either Father or I was in error, but neither did we intend offense or deception. It simply didn't occur to us to explain. The fact that the inheritance has come to your notice now can make no difference, since my father will continue to administer the trust; however, if you persist in your decision to remain in town, I agree that funds must be placed at your disposal, and I shall speak to him. It is not right that you should continue to hang upon Lady Dambroke's sleeve."

Not seeing any good reason for informing him that it was Dambroke's sleeve rather than her ladyship's, Catheryn only murmured gratefully that Edmund was very generous. His more rhetorical periods always had the effect of leaving her dazed and making her lose track of things she wanted to say. It dawned upon her now, however, that for once he had said nothing of marriage. "Do you still wish to marry me, Edmund?"

"As to that, I believe I committed myself by stating my intent in Dambroke's presence," he said stiffly.

"Well, you need not bother your head about that, for

it doesn't signify! I stated quite firmly at the same time that I would have no part of it." She held out her hand. "Come, Edmund, surely you see that we should not suit."

He sighed, perhaps with relief. "Possibly you are right, my dear. I thought at one time . . . but I shall not press you further. Shall I partner you in the set now forming to make up for causing you to miss your waltz?" His eyes twinkled as though he were enjoying a good joke.

"No, thank you. I am promised to Lord Molyneux."

"Lord Molyneux! Do you look to be the next Lady Sefton, then?" Edmund teased.

She chuckled. "Not at all. His lordship only asked me out of politeness. Lady Tiffany's card was full and I was standing beside her. A good many of my partners come to me in that manner. The only reason I had the waltz free is that, being in her first season, she does not engage in it."

"Whereas you, being such an old hand, engage in it often? Doing it much too brown, miss."

"Well, it may be my first London season, but my age precludes my figuring as a debutante." She saw that he still did not believe her, but she could discuss the matter no further without offending Lord Molyneux; therefore, it was with great satisfaction a bit later that she accepted Mr. Brummell's invitation to join in the next waltz before going down to supper. Noting her cousin's shocked expression as she was swung onto the floor, she was guilty of a distinct smirk. Brummell raised a haughty brow and demanded to know what was so amusing.

She explained, adding, "I know Edmund would like nothing better than to scold me for indulging in such an impropriety. I only hope you don't find an opportunity for giving him one of your famous set-downs, sir. He wouldn't understand."

"Miss Westering, I protest! My set-downs are famous only because I never waste them on bumpkins who don't understand them."

She would have defended her cousin, but she had no wish to cross swords with the acknowledged master of repartee and allowed him, therefore, to change the subject. When the waltz ended, he guided her toward the supper room. Others had preceded them, and they could hear the rumble of conversation mixed with the light strains of a string quartet before they actually entered the room. Catheryn was shaking her head in amusement at something Brummell had said. "I must tell you that ... good God, sir! What on earth!"

A piercing shriek followed by screams of feminine horror brought the musicians to a discordant halt, while all around the room people craned their necks to see what had occurred. Miss Westering could see nothing but heads and shoulders. She turned in dismay to the Beau. "What is it, sir? Can you see?"

"No, but it—whatever it is—is up here. Come with me." He shouldered their way through the stunned gathering toward the buffet tables. Others began to fall back and suddenly Catheryn found herself at the front of the mob. "It's only one of Caro Lamb's distempered freaks," said Brummell in a bored tone, but Catheryn found the scene appalling. Lady Caroline, supported on either side by two gentlemen, seemed to be spattered with blood. The two men were likewise bedaubed with the stuff. "What happened here?" the Beau inquired of a wide-eyed damsel attempting to push her way through the onlookers.

"It's Lady Caroline! They were just having supper, sir, Lord Bryon and her ladyship. Suddenly, they were quarreling, and the next thing we knew, Lady Caroline stabbed herself with a knife from the table. I've got her blood on my dress!" She was nearly hysterical, so the Beau cleared a path for her, then turned back to Catheryn.

"Caro has no manners." Catheryn was as amazed by his attitude as by the incident itself. Chaos reigned around them, and Mr. Brummell was only bored. But then, her own shock began to give way to indignation when she realized Lady Caroline was not mortally wounded.

"What on earth possessed her?" she asked him.

"The key word is 'possessed,' I think," he answered casually. "The chief witness is over yonder."

Following his gaze, she perceived Bryon, his eyes wide with shock. Catheryn thought he looked disgusted and said so.

"Who isn't?" Brummell shrugged. "He might have been horrified if she'd tried it on in private. Can only be disgusted by a public display that makes him look ridiculous."

Catheryn observed that, while several persons displayed signs of shock or dismay, including one stout dowager who was indulging herself in a fit of vapors, most of those who crowded around seemed to agree with the Beau.

"Such a trial for the Melbournes," said one.

"How dare that stupid girl embarrass Lady Heathcote so!"

" 'Tis a pity she didn't succeed if she had to make such a cake of herself at all," commented another.

"The lad'll have a new poem out of this, mark my words!"

"Poor William Lamb! As if he weren't having trouble enough in the Commons."

"Why couldn't she have waited until after supper, for God's sake?" was the disgruntled reply of one gentleman to a wife who said that, if Caro was up to her tricks again, they might as well go home. Catheryn heard a chuckle behind her and then a familiar voice.

"So this is the *haut ton*, is it? Are you certain you won't come home to Somerset, Cousin?"

"Oh, Edmund!"

"Never mind. His lordship has called for the carriage. I am to escort you ladies home at once."

"Of course." She excused herself to Mr. Brummell and followed Edmund. Others with similar intentions were rapidly gathering in the antechamber, but they found the countess and Tiffany easily enough. Outside, they discovered that Dambroke's quick action had caused their carriage to be one of the first brought around. He was waiting beside it.

"Richard, isn't it dreadful!" cried the countess. "That wretched girl will be the death of them yet!"

"Quite so, Mama. I don't know if I can help here or not, but I mean to find out. I shall be home later." He packed them into the carriage and strode back toward the house.

Lady Dambroke whiled away their return journey with her opinion of the episode. It was difficult to ascertain which of her emotions was uppermost, sympathy for Lady Heathcote or relief that Lady Caroline had not chosen to enact her scene at the forthcoming Dambroke ball.

"For I sent invitations to all the Melbournes and they have accepted! But I daresay this scandal will at last force Melbourne to send her out of town for a while."

"I think the whole thing is absurd," stated Tiffany flatly. "I wonder why Richard sent us home. Surely, everyone won't leave. They hadn't even finished serving supper yet!"

Catheryn smiled at Edmund and saw that he, too, remembered the voice in the crowd expounding upon the same subject, but the countess was astonished. "Tiffany, how can you say such a thing! When you know how the least hint of Cheltenham drama oversets me. I could not have eaten a morsel. You cannot have wished to remain!"

"No, for I found the party had become a trifle insipid before Caro livened it up. I only wondered."

Lady Dambroke stared at her daughter. Miss Westering, on the other hand, having seen that Captain Varling did not choose to try his leg on the dance floor and had excused himself to his hostess at an early hour, had no difficulty interpreting her cousin's remark. Tiffany had danced with James Lawrence, of course, but only once, refusing a second invitation. He had persisted and showed his frustration openly. Catheryn was beginning to think him a bit of a nuisance.

They soon arrived in Grosvenor Square and Mr. Caston left them at the door, explaining that the coachman had orders to take him to his hotel before returning with the carriage for Dambroke. Both Lady Dambroke and Tiffany decided to retire at once, so Catheryn bade them good night and went to her own room. Mary soon answered her summons, curiosity plain on her face, but Catheryn gave no explanation for their early return.

Changing to an old stuff gown instead of her night dress, she announced that, since they had missed supper, she had a mind to raid the pantry. The maid offered to bring a tray, but Miss Westering explained glibly that she preferred to see for herself what delicacies might be available. She could think of no reason that would not sound odd, however, to keep Mary from going along to show where things were kept.

Downstairs in the great kitchen, the maid's eyes began to widen as two shiny apples followed thick slabs of buttered bread, juicy slices of roast beef, two chicken legs, and a generous wedge of Chantilly cake onto a tray. "Gracious me, miss, but you'll never manage to eat all that!"

"Oh, I've a prodigious appetite. Is there any milk?"

"Milk, miss?" Catheryn affirmed it and, shaking her head, Mary disappeared with her candle into the dark reaches of the kitchen, soon returning with a small earthenware jug and a blue mug painted with yellow roses. She placed these articles on the tray. "Will that be all, miss?"

Catheryn grinned at the incredulous tone. "I daresay you think me a sad glutton, Mary. Here, I'll take the tray."

"That you'll not! 'Twouldn't be proper, and I must go up to the maids' quarters anyway, Miss Catheryn," she continued firmly. "It won't take but a moment to take this tray up to your chamber on my way." Having forgotten that Mary would have to return to the upper part of the house, Catheryn gave in gracefully and thanked her for her trouble.

X

When the maid had gone, Catheryn counted slowly to fifty. Then she quietly opened her door and peeped up and down the long corridor. All was clear. Picking up the tray, she slipped out and pulled the door to with her foot, then tiptoed past Tiffany's room and on up to the nursery floor.

She hoped to discover the room she wanted without disturbing Mr. Ashley, who had the old nursery suite once occupied by Nanny Craig. Luckily, the door to the schoolroom was ajar. The next must be the room she sought. Balancing the tray carefully, she tapped on the door. A rather gruff but wide-awake voice bade her enter. She pushed the door wide.

"Hallo, Teddy. I thought you might be hungry."

The boy was sprawled on his stomach across the bed and, except for his jacket, still wore the clothes he had come home in. A stub of candle burned on the nightstand, its flickering light making no attempt to enter the deep corners of the room. When he realized who it was, Teddy turned over and sat up, grimacing slightly as he did so. "Miss Westering! I knew you were a great gun." He stood and moved to take the tray. "A feast! I tell you, my ribs have been gnawing at my backbone. But won't Richard be angry?"

"He isn't home so it doesn't signify. This place is like a tomb. Have you any more candles?"

"No, only the one."

"Then we'll make do. I'll put the jug here on the nightstand, and we'll share the mug. Mary wouldn't have understood my wanting two—or might have understood too well. I fear she already believes me an unnatural trencherwoman."

Teddy laughed. "Oh, Miss Westering, what a complete hand you are!"

"I think I must be," she grinned, "for I have contrived this very neatly, have I not? Set that tray on the bed," she added, pouring milk into the blue mug. "That way you may recline on your side in the manner of a Roman emperor while you eat. You will not want a chair."

"I shall very likely never want a chair again!" he exclaimed. Following her instructions, he moved gingerly, as much to avoid oversetting the tray as for his own comfort.

"It will pass," she said sympathetically. "I have vast experience of such matters. Do make yourself a sandwich of that bread and meat, Teddy."

He stared at her while she pulled up a chair. "Vast experience, Miss Westering?"

"Indeed, and I wish you will call me Catheryn." She paused. "Or perhaps you will prefer to call me Cathy. Grandpapa always did so, except when he was in a temper, and no one else does. I miss it."

"I'd like that. Was he often in a temper? Like Richard?"

Ignoring the rider, she smiled reminiscently. "Grandpapa was very strict in his notions of behavior for well-brought-up females. I believe it is often so with gentlemen, even those who are lax in their own affairs. I'm afraid I was not always well-behaved." She sighed. "Sometimes our man, Bert Ditchling, was able to bring me off before the tale reached Grandpapa's ears, but when he could not. . . ." She spread her hands expressively.

"But you must have hated your grandfather!"

"Do you hate Richard, Teddy?"

The question brought him up short, and he did not answer immediately, taking a large bite of his sandwich instead and munching slowly. Catheryn kept silent. She offered him the mug, but he shook his head and swallowed.

"He's not exactly first oars with me at the moment," he answered reflectively, "but I don't s'pose I hate him."

"Well, of course you don't. I think, if the truth be told, you have a great fondness for him."

"I don't know about that. I think I *could* like him a great deal, but I'm not very well acquainted with him yet, you know. Mostly, when I do see him, he's vexed with me. I wish we could be friends, but I daresay I'm too young."

"Oh, Teddy!" Her heart was wrung. Seventeen years was a wide gulf for friendship to bridge, but surely the brothers could deal together better than this. She let the silence lengthen while she considered how to gain his confidence, then reached for an apple. Though she had brought nothing with which to peel it, Catheryn had not been brought up so nicely as to blush for the omission; however, she discovered another oversight when she took a large bite and juice dribbled down her chin. "Good gracious, Teddy, I forgot the napkins!"

"Use your sleeve," he chuckled. She wrinkled her nose at him. "Oh, very well. There is a cloth on the washstand over there." He pointed and she went to fetch it, groping in the dark corner. By the time she returned, he had begun on a chicken leg. "This is a jolly good meal, Cathy."

"I'm glad you're enjoying it. I rather thought you might be hungry. I used to hate above all things to be sent to bed without supper."

"More than a whipping?"

"Oh, much! Whippings were always quickly over and done, but it seemed to take forever to get through a night without supper. I enjoy food too much, I expect."

"Well, I should much prefer going to bed without supper to one of Richard's thrashings, if I had a choice between the two." He paused, but Catheryn made no comment. "Has he said what he means to do now?" he asked in a small voice.

"No, but he's really had no chance. There were guests for dinner and then a ball, you know."

"A ball! But it's so early. Didn't you go?"

So Catheryn told him about the ball. Certain that the earl would disapprove if she repeated the whole sordid tale, she left out the choicest details and merely said Lady Caroline had been taken suddenly ill. She quickly found she had underestimated the astuteness of a young man lately home from Eton.

"Staging one of her freaks for Bryon, you mean." He nodded wisely. "I bet you've left out all the good bits, too."

"And just how do you know so much about Lady Caroline, Master Sly Boots?"

"Oh, Rags tells me all the best stories."

"Rags?"

"He's my best friend at Eton. A bang-up fellow! In fact, he's the one. . . ." His gaze slid momentarily from her face to the tray, but he picked up the wedge of cake and went on with studied nonchalance. "We call him Rags 'cause he thinks he's such a beau. Anyways, he's connected with the Melbournes one way or another and always has new bits to tell us about Crazy Caro. Like when she visited Bryon at his lodgings dressed like a page boy with red pantaloons and a plume in her cap. Bryon didn't know what to do!"

But Catheryn had not missed the pause or the heightened color, visible even in the dim candlelight, and refused to be diverted. "Tell me something, dear," she said gently, watching him closely. "Is Rags smaller than you are?" He shot her a quick look but seemed hesitant to meet her steady gaze and looked away again. "Is he the one you fought with, Teddy?" The boy went very still. "He is, isn't he?" she persisted. "You staged the whole performance between you, didn't you. Oh, Teddy!" The last was said with great sympathy and he looked at her again, but the color had drained from his face.

"You won't tell him, will you?" It was barely a whisper. She had no doubt to whom he referred.

"No. Not now, in any case. I hope one day you will be able to tell him yourself."

"I couldn't!" His eyes widened with dismay and he shook his head. "He would—oh gosh!—I don't know what he would do, but I can't tell him. Not ever! And you mustn't, Cathy."

"I can't promise that, Teddy, but I do promise never to mention it without discussing it with you first." The boy looked skeptical. "I can't be fairer than that. I don't make promises easily, dear, but I do keep the ones I make. Will you trust me?"

"I think so."

"Good enough. Will you tell me just why you cooked up such a scheme? I hope Rags wasn't really hurt."

"Course not," he retorted with boyish scorn. "Only,

we didn't think we'd have to do it but the one time though. I'd already been to Keate for fighting. A couple of times actually," he admitted with a lurking twinkle. "But I didn't start the others. They just sort of happened."

"I see."

"Well, you probably don't. I've discovered that females don't, as a rule, understand that sort of thing above half. Anyways, Keate said not to let it happen again or he'd send me off home. So we did, and he did, and here I am."

"Right where you want to be, restricted to your bedchamber with an aching backside," Catheryn mocked.

Teddy chuckled. "Well, I did want to come home and, sore or not, I'm here. The others all talk about their families, and I hardly know mine. I only wish Richard didn't hate me."

"Oh, Teddy, don't be nonsensical! Dambroke doesn't hate you. To be sure, he is angry with you, but that's a very different thing, believe me. It wouldn't be possible for him to achieve such wrath if he didn't care about you."

"Well," Teddy confided, rubbing his backside with a grimace, "if I am to know how much he cares by how angry he gets, he must care *prodigiously!*"

At that, Catheryn laughed out loud. Teddy watched her, grinning as she tried to control herself. But when she hiccoughed, he, too, began to laugh, sending her off again into fresh paroxysms.

"And *what*, may I ask, is the meaning of this?"

The laughter ceased abruptly as two guilty faces turned toward the grim figure in the doorway. Dambroke shut the door and moved into the circle of candlelight. "Mr. Ashley's rest is hard-earned," he said harshly. "There is no need to disturb him." Catheryn swallowed uncomfortably, waiting for him to continue. Teddy seemed to realize that his lounging position would not meet with approval and slid off the bed to stand beside her. "Have you lost your tongues?" the earl demanded angrily. They looked at one another, but neither spoke. "Very well. Perhaps I was not plain enough." He looked directly at Catheryn. "What are you doing here, Miss

Westering? I gave specific orders that Edward was not to be disturbed."

"You said Teddy must keep to his bedchamber until breakfast," she replied bravely. "He has not left it."

Dambroke's jaw was rigid, his eyes icy. "I do not wish to quibble, Miss Westering, but I said he was to be left alone and not mollycoddled."

"Until morning, my lord. It is past midnight, I promise you. I should not have dreamed of coming before," she added sweetly. His face relaxed slightly, and she sought to press her advantage. "Why did you come, sir?"

"To find you. Your door was clicking off the latch. When there was no answer to my knock, I looked in." He grimaced. "I knew you were not downstairs, since the lights have been extinguished, so it took no great mental effort to conclude that you had chosen to defy my orders. And don't try my patience by insisting that you have not done so."

"Perhaps I have not precisely followed your orders," she admitted. "I do think you were a little severe, but we needn't discuss that now. It is not my business to dispute your notions of discipline, after all."

"Certainly not!"

"No, sir. But perhaps, since you are here, you might relieve Teddy's mind a bit. Have you decided what you mean to do next?" The boy stiffened beside her.

"I have. I've arranged for a tutor, a very strict one," he added with a stern look at his brother.

But Teddy relaxed. "Then I may stay in London. Must I begin lessons at once?"

"Of course. You're not on holiday. I met Lord Elman from across the square tonight. I think you know his sons."

Teddy made a face. "Them!" Encountering a warning glint from Dambroke's eye, he went on more civilly, "I know them, sir. Philip is eight, and Clarence is a year or two older than I am." Catheryn noted with amusement that his expression still indicated a poor opinion of both.

"You will share their tutor, Mr. Appleby," the earl said. "It will be good for you. They say the older boy has the makings of quite a scholar."

"He's a bloody prig." The words, muttered low, did not, Catheryn realized gratefully, reach Dambroke's ears.

Hastily, she pointed out that Teddy would enjoy having friends nearby. He looked doubtful. "I s'pose so, Cathy. I just hope old Appleby ain't too strict."

"How did you call Miss Westering, Edward? Surely, I misheard you!"

"It's quite all right, my lord," Catheryn interposed calmly, though Teddy colored up to his ears. "I gave him leave to address me by my nickname."

Dambroke cocked his head with an ironic and reminiscent smile. "Did you now? It must be that, once again, my sense of propriety intrudes. I cannot approve this young rattle's addressing a lady of your years in such a style."

"A lady of my years! You make me sound a positive antidote, my lord!"

"Not precisely an antidote, my dear," he replied with a faint smile. Catheryn's brows rose comically.

"If we are to discuss the proper way to address a lady!"

"We shall discuss it no further tonight. Teddy may call you Cousin Cathy, if you like, but now I think we must all get some sleep." Dambroke did not speak again as he accompanied her downstairs to her bedchamber, but she was amazed and a little frightened when he followed her inside and shut the door. "You need not fear for your honor," he said. "It would take Gabriel's horn to wake Tiffany, but my mother is a tolerably light sleeper and will hear you if you scream. I've something to say to you."

"I do not fear you, sir," she muttered, but she braced herself so obviously that his smile mocked her.

"You deserve a scold, Catheryn," he said sternly. "Your interference has not improved a very trying day, and you needn't poker up like that. It won't help. What the boy did is inexcusable, and you said yourself that it is not your business to dispute my notions of discipline. Yet, by your actions, that is precisely what you have done!"

"Well, I do dispute them, then!" she retorted hotly. "I think you were much too severe. That boy needs love and understanding. He needs your guidance, my lord, but guidance with a light hand on the rein, not a heavy whiphand!" She was astonished to feel tears springing to her eyes and turned away abruptly that he might not see them. Blinking rapidly and striving for control, she waited for him to go on, certain that she had put him in a rage. But his voice was calm.

"Catheryn, I truly had not meant to scold. Perhaps I was too severe with the boy. I'll admit he puts me in a rage. And tonight, after the melodramatics at the Heathcote affair ... would you believe Caro slashed her wrists after you left?"

"Merciful heavens!" Her own emotions forgotten, she turned to face him again. "She must be demented!"

"You'll get no argument from me. Some poor fool gave her a glass of water. She smashed it and cut herself with the shards." He spread his hands. "Perhaps you understand why I was angry at finding you with Teddy after that."

"Oh, I understand, my lord." She thought she understood him better than he understood himself. It is sometimes difficult for a man to recognize his own pride, and Danbroke was a proud man. His mother accused him of arrogance. His sister said he took his own authority too seriously. But, however it was described, Catheryn knew he was proud of his name, his rank, and his position. Teddy had dared to embarrass him, and she had flouted his authority. No wonder he had been angry! She kept her opinions to herself for once, saying only, "I still think you should talk with Teddy instead of shouting at him. He knows he has misbehaved and is truly sorry, you know."

"If he's not, he's got a tougher hide than I ever had."

"Was your father very strict?" she asked, willing to change the subject.

"He had the Devil's own temper. And take that impertinent look off your face, miss. I know I've inherited it." He smiled at her, relaxing a bit. "Papa wasn't much interested in us. Too busy developing some of the finest succession houses in the country. I climbed one of his prize pear trees once and sampled several green pears before I got sick. I thought I was dying and shouted for the head gardener, who immediately sent for Papa. I had scarred the bark with my boots and broken off two of the lower branches. Dear Papa stood over me, ostentatiously cutting a switch from one of them until I finished being sick. There was also the time I took a shortcut through his rose garden on horseback. I remember both occasions vividly. I was sorry then, just as Teddy is sorry now."

"It's not precisely what I meant, my lord. Do you know, I think I am sorry for all three of you."

"Would you care to explain that? I don't expect pity for incidents that occurred fifteen or more years ago."

Catheryn had spoken without thinking and paused now to choose her words with care. "I'm not certain that I can explain, sir. I hardly knew my mother, and my father died when I was Teddy's age. Grandpapa raised me with the help of Bert Ditchling and various housekeepers. He was a thoughtless man in many ways, but there was never a moment when I doubted he loved me. Oh, we argued and shouted at one another often and often, but it never meant anything. Your family is different. Why, Teddy told me he is barely acquainted with the rest of you! That's a dreadful thing for a child to have to admit!"

"Did he truly say that?" The earl seemed shaken.

"Indeed he did! And I've watched you and your mother and sister. None of you speaks with fondness for his late lordship. In fact, I can't recall one of you saying much of anything kind about any one of the others. I believe your mother cares for you, but she said herself she doesn't like Tiffany much, and she hardly speaks of Teddy at all. I just wish you all could have some of what I shared with Grandpapa."

Dambroke's expression softened, and there was tenderness in his eyes when he spoke. "I think I begin to wish it, too," he said gently. "But you must realize that you had something very special. If you consider the families you have met, you must see that it simply isn't fashionable to be interested in one's offspring, particularly when they are small. One has nursemaids, nannies, governesses, and schools to raise one's children. A father is expected to introduce his son to his clubs and, if necessary, to explain the facts of life. A mother is expected to present her daughters to the Beau Monde as they emerge from the schoolroom and to help them find suitable husbands. Other than that. . . ." He shrugged. "I'll grant that there are exceptions. Lady Stanthorpe was thought to be dreadfully interfering. They went through several nannies before one was found who could tolerate her interference."

"Well, I think she was right. I couldn't bear to see my children only when a nanny thought it proper!"

"I believe you will be a tartar, ma'am." He smiled again with that nearly tender look. "But I don't mean to stand talking all night. I'm glad you've begun a friendship with Teddy. I've seen your influence with my sister and can only hope to see such beneficial results with him as well."

"My influence with Tiffany is small, my lord."

He grinned. "Don't think I didn't detect your fine hand in that very affecting apology the other morning."

"Apology?"

"Spreading it too thick, my dear. She came to the library the moment you returned from your ride. I never thought she'd apologize for that dress! I must congratulate you. I quite thought we should have to endure sulks for a fortnight."

"Oh, that. But I. . . ." Suddenly, she realized that the fine hand must have been Captain Varling's, and this was not the time to bring that little matter to his lordship's attention. He had enough on his plate. "I didn't know she had actually apologized," she ended vaguely.

"So it seems." She thought he looked at her a bit searchingly, but he let the matter drop. "I must not keep you longer, Catheryn. Do what you can with my repulsive brother and I shall be grateful." He was gone.

Catheryn stood where she was for a moment and was still thoughtful when finally she changed and got into bed. She had had the oddest notion while they were discussing children, when something in his expression had reminded her of that day in the library after Edmund's first visit. But perhaps it was only the late hour and the oddity of it all that made her think he had looked at her so. Whatever it was, she thrust the thought from her mind in much the same way as she had done on that previous occasion, as reluctant to analyze his behavior as she was to examine her own sentiments. Certainly, she reflected, it would never do to refine too much upon fleeting emotions that would no doubt disappear in light of day. It would be far more practical to thank the Fates that his lordship had managed to talk himself into a better humor. She snuggled up to her pillow with a small sigh and a tiny warm feeling in her breast that would not be denied. Her last conscious thought as she drifted into sleep was that it had been a very long day.

XI

The next few days the entire household was flung into a flurry of last-minute preparation for the countess's ball, giving Catheryn little opportunity for private reflection. Dambroke, declaring the confusion a damned nuisance, removed himself promptly after breakfast each morning, returning only to change clothes for the evening. Catheryn scarcely noticed his absence except to be grateful for it on Teddy's behalf. That young man, the picture of innocence at breakfast, would take himself off to the Elman schoolroom only to return later bursting with pent-up mischief. The telltale tray having been discovered the morning after the Heathcote ball, an approving staff quickly dubbed Catheryn Master Teddy's champion and brought their complaints directly to her. By turn amused and exasperated, she did her best to cope.

Called to the kitchen by a tearful maidservant, she spent an uncomfortable half-hour trying to placate an irate Jean-Pierre. That was followed by an equally unsuccessful attempt to convince a twinklingly unrepentant Teddy that the exchange of salt for sugar was not a matter to be taken lightly by one so puffed up in his own esteem as her ladyship's French chef. Next, she discovered, to her dismay, that the boy seemed to think that the proper way to dispose of dead rats was to put them in the beds of innocent maidservants. Mr. Ashley caught him red-handed at that revolting prank and promised to deal with the situation, but his methods must not have had much of an effect, for it was little more than an hour later that an agitated Paulson sent for Catheryn.

"I'm sure I didn't know what to do, miss," he said in an undertone as he guided her rapidly to the front saloon and pushed open the door. In front of the cold fireplace stood Captain Varling, his normally curly locks hanging straight and wet into his face and his blue superfine coat dripping water to the hearthstones. Catheryn stifled a grin and hurried forward.

"That wretched boy!" she exclaimed. "How did he manage this? For I'm sure that somehow he is responsible."

"He's responsible, all right," growled the captain. "As to the how of it, it's a simple child's trick. He made a pouch of brown waxed paper, filled it with water, and launched it from an appropriately placed window."

"Oh, just wait till I get my hands on him!"

"I'd enjoy a private moment or two with him myself."

"I believe it, sir." The clock on the mantlepiece caught her eye. "Good heavens! It's after five. Dambroke will be home at any moment!"

"I look forward to seeing him," Varling declared. "We were supposed to be dining together."

"Oh, no! You mustn't tell him. It will only widen the breach between them. Teddy is high-spirited and needs Dambroke's attention, but not this way. This prank would earn him a thrashing for sure. Please, sir, you can't really wish for that."

"I suppose not," he admitted with a rueful grin. "I've done it myself more than once and so perhaps have come by my just deserts. But I cannot dine with Dickon in this state."

"My dear sir, you cannot even meet him in that state! We must contrive." She rang for Morris, who suggested that the earl's valet might help. "Of course," she agreed. "Landon must bring him a change of clothes. He will know what is needed." Morris nodded and would have gone, but the captain stopped him with a laugh.

"Here now, Miss Westering! You don't seriously suggest that I dine with Dambroke wearing the man's own coat!"

"Whyever not? You are of a size with him, are you not?"

"Aye, close enough. But he'll know it's his and want to know why the devil I've pinched it."

"Begging your pardon, sir, but I don't think he will." Morris spoke in a properly deferential tone, but a gleam of pure devilment lurked in his eye. "Gentlemen dress much of a muchness to my way of thinking. Of course, my lord patronizes Weston, whilst you favor Scott, but

I've heard him with my own ears tease you to try his tailor instead. Perhaps, if he asks, you could say you had taken his advice in that matter."

Varling grinned. "We shall hope devoutly that he does not ask. We may be much the same size but I've not regained my full weight, so any coat of his will be a loose fit. He'd never believe it newly tailored, much less of Weston's cut."

Catheryn agreed but pointed out that it was their only chance, adding, "Teddy shall apologize for this, sir."

"That scamp! You'll be lucky if you find him. I hid for hours once after I made a direct hit."

He was right. The boy was nowhere to be found, so she soon gave up the search and went to look for the countess and Tiffany, finding them in the yellow drawing room.

"Catheryn!" exclaimed Lady Dambroke. "Where have you been, child? You've just missed Richard and Captain Varling." Hiding her relief, Catheryn inquired whether there was anything she could do for the countess before dinner. "No, thank you, dear. That is," she added anxiously, "did you remind Paulson to send someone to Gunter's tomorrow to check on the ices?"

"Yes, ma'am. Morris will go. But you need not fret. Gunter's reputation is excellent, and I'm certain the ices will be produced at exactly the right moment. Now, if you don't want me, I shall change for dinner."

"I'll come too," Tiffany said. As they went up the stairs together, she whispered, "Mama still has the fidgets because you badgered her into inviting James Lawrence. It wasn't necessary, Catheryn. Richard will be furious."

"Nonsense. Here, come into my room for a moment. I want to talk to you." She drew Tiffany inside and shut the door. "Now, I'm going to be blunt, Tiff. Are you still at all interested in Mr. Lawrence?"

The younger girl began to draw herself to her full height, but the effect was spoiled by reddening cheeks, and Catheryn's chuckle put an end to the attempted snub. "Oh, Catheryn, you know I don't care a snap for James anymore. I still don't know if you were right about him, but I'm not in love with him, so it doesn't signify."

"Have you told him?"

"Why, he's never asked me!"

"Well, he acts like a jealous lover. Which is why," she added hastily over Tiffany's rising indignation, "I got your mother to invite him. To let him see for himself."

"See what?"

"Why, that you love another man, you idiotish child!"

"But I don't! I mean . . . Catheryn, how dare you!"

The irrepressible chuckle rippled out once more. "How dare I, indeed? Anyone with something other than solid bone above the eyebrows could see what I see, if they but looked for it. You are head over ears in love with the hope of Stanthorpe, my girl. And don't try to cozen me. I've seen too much."

"That you have! Catheryn, you mustn't say a word! He hasn't . . . I mean, well, he treats me more like a sister than like one he intends to . . . oh, you know!"

"Indeed, but we needn't worry about it now. First things first, which means nudging Mr. Persistent Lawrence out of the picture. And even that can wait till after dinner. I'm hungry."

"You always are," Tiffany laughed with a quick hug. "I'm glad you ran away to us, Catheryn."

"So am I," Miss Westering agreed. A vision of a stern face with piercing blue eyes that could light with sudden laughter flashed through her mind, sending a flush to her cheeks. But there was no one to see, for Tiffany had gone. Scolding herself for foolishness beyond any yet displayed by her cousin, Catheryn turned her thoughts toward dinner.

Teddy did not appear at the table, but this circumstance seemed to cause neither his mother nor his sister the slightest qualm. The countess noted placidly that he had no doubt neglected, boylike, to inform them of his intention to dine across the way, but Catheryn knew he was not a guest at Lord Elman's table. After animadverting at length on the subject of being forced to spend his mornings with a prig, a sapskull, and a tyrant, he would not willingly dine with them.

She told herself that she would not worry unless the boy failed to show up for breakfast, but at midnight, when she checked his empty bedchamber for the third time, it occurred to her that he might have been locked out. Taking her candle, she made her way downstairs, going first to the garden door. She slipped the latch and opened it to look out. Immediately, there came the sound of a hesitant step on the gravel path.

"Morris?" A mere whisper, but she recognized the source all the same and felt a surge of relief.

"Teddy! Come here this minute, you wretched boy!" There was dead silence, and her voice took on a note of dangerous calm. "Edward, come here where I can see you. I am already displeased with you, and this foolishness is not like to mend matters. Show yourself at once, sir!"

Presently, a rather sheepish Teddy emerged from the darkness. His hands and face were grimy, and there was a rent in his coat. His blue eyes pleaded with her. "Are you really very angry, Cathy?"

"I am indeed. My palms are just itching to box your ears, young man. Come here to me."

Reluctantly, he moved closer, eyeing her warily. "Please don't. Is Richard angry, too?"

"He doesn't know about it. We got Captain Varling all rigged out in one of his coats before he returned. You owe the captain an apology, Teddy. It was a wicked thing to do."

An appreciative grin lit his face. "One of Richard's own coats, eh? But that means Landon knows."

"He won't say anything."

"Maybe." Teddy clearly wasn't convinced. "I'll apologize to Tony all right, and thank him, too. I never meant it to be him, you know. He was just the first one by."

"Never mind that," she scolded. "You are supposed to be a gentleman, and gentlemen do not behave in such a reprehensible manner. In only a few days you've made Jean-Pierre threaten to give notice, put the maids in an uproar, and doused Captain Varling. What will you do next!"

He traced a pattern with his shoe. "I dunno. I'm sorry, Cathy. It's just that there ain't much *to* do."

"Well, we must think of something. I simply won't have time tomorrow or Friday to rescue you from any more scrapes." He grinned at her but gave his fervent promise that he would try to behave. Shaking her head, Catheryn followed him upstairs. She didn't doubt his good intentions, but with two full afternoons ahead of him. . . . She decided, at last, to enlist Dambroke's aid.

Accordingly, she descended to the breakfast parlor at an early hour next morning, hoping to speak privately with him before Teddy came down to breakfast. She was not disappointed. The earl entered some moments later, attired in riding dress. He laid hat, whip, and gloves on a small table and sat opposite her. Since he looked to be in a pleasant frame of mind, she waited only until breakfast had been served and they were alone before plunging to the heart of the matter.

"I've a small favor to ask, sir, concerning Teddy."

"I thought things had been ominously quiet on that front," he smiled. "What's he done now?"

"It's not that," she said hastily. "It's only that his afternoons are free, and he is bored."

"I'll speak to Appleby. He can set the lad enough schoolwork to keep him occupied."

"That's not at all what I had in mind!" she exclaimed indignantly. "I thought it would be a good time for you to get to know him better. He's seen very little of London, you know."

"He is not meant to be on holiday."

"But it would be educational!" She peeped through her lashes at him. "It's a very historical city, my lord."

He sighed. "You are determined upon this course?"

"Yes, sir," she replied at her most demure.

"Baggage. Very well."

"Thank you, sir. Today?" Her eyes danced.

He shrugged. "If you insist. It will be educational for both of us, I daresay." He was as good as his word and, after a morning filled with errands for the countess, Catheryn was on hand to see Teddy climb proudly into the curricle. Her own afternoon was taken up by a steady stream of callers, including Ladies Prudence and Chastity, followed five minutes later by Mr. Caston.

Edmund smiled as he made his bow to the countess, but Catheryn thought the smile was more for Prudence, who stared with great concentration at the slim hands folded neatly in her lap. By the time the visitors rose to take their leave, Catheryn was certain Edmund was in love with Prudence and fairly certain the lady felt a tenderness for him. The discovery came as a bit of a shock, but the more she thought about it, the more she came to believe they might suit each other. Certainly, Aunt Agatha would be exhilarated by the idea of a duke's daughter joining the family.

Dambroke and Teddy returned a little after five o'clock, both grinning. Catheryn thought privately that his lordship looked a little worn around the edges, but it was evident that they had enjoyed their afternoon.

"We saw the Tower, Cathy! I mean Cousin Cathy," Teddy corrected with a flashing sidelong grin for Dambroke's benefit. "And we saw the riders at Astley's Amphitheater, and Richard took me to Manton's Shooting Gallery! He even let me shoot a pistol. And I hit the wafer twice!"

"Rather tolerable shooting, I thought," said the earl, responding to Catheryn's mocking grin with his guilty smile.

"Certainly, sir. And prodigiously educational."

The teasing note in her voice caused the boy to look doubtfully from one to the other. "But I learned a lot!"

Dambroke laughed and tweaked one of the brown curls. "To be sure you did, brat. Now, run along and get ready for your dinner. Not that he should be hungry," he added as they watched the boy run upstairs. "I believe he's been munching something or other since we left the house."

"Did you truly enjoy your afternoon, sir?"

His eyes twinkled. "I did. Teddy's a scamp, but he's not unintelligent. Knows more than I do about the history of the Tower."

"Ah, that explains Astley's Amphitheater and Manton's."

He grinned at her air of vast wisdom, acknowledging a hit. "You are impertinent, Miss Westering."

"Am I, sir?" But he would not be drawn again. He merely smiled and excused himself to change for dinner at Stanthorpe House, leaving her to a dreary meal with the others.

The day of the ball dawned bright and clear. Mary washed Catheryn's hair and helped to put the finishing touches to her dress, an exquisite confection of sea-green silk fashioned with a flared skirt, tiny puff sleeves, and a square-cut neck. It was trimmed with old lace, a band of which encircled the high waist and fell in a paneled demitrain down the back. For accessories, she would wear white gloves, sea-green slippers, and her grandmother's emerald necklace.

After a trying luncheon, during which the countess worried over one last-minute detail after another, Catheryn returned to her bedchamber to relax. Sunlight spilled across the carpet in much the same way it had done the day she arrived, but, as she leaned back against the door, she realized the room was no longer a guest chamber. It was hers. She had come to love it and to feel at home in it as she had never done in the bleak little room allotted to her at Caston Manor. For the first time since leaving Westering, she had a sense of belonging, for she loved the Dambroke family, from the countess to young Teddy.

Then, as she thought of another member, she tried to tell herself that love was certainly too strong a word, that perhaps fondness expressed it adequately, or affection. She straightened purposefully and, taking Mrs. Radcliffe's novel from the nightstand where Tiffany had left it, curled up in the chair near the window and soon lost herself in Gothic complexities. Sometime later, her stomach gently suggested that it might be time for tea; so, laying the book aside, she splashed cold water on her face, smoothed her hair, and set out in search of sustenance, only to meet Teddy on the stair.

Rapidly taking in the tear-stained face, barely stifled sobs, and the fact that he was rubbing his backside, Catheryn came to the only possible conclusion. "Teddy!" At the sound of her voice, the boy cast aside any thought of his advanced years and dignity and flung himself into her arms.

"He says I'm to leave for the Park in the morning!" he sobbed. "And it wasn't my fault, Cathy, it wasn't!"

"There, there, love," she soothed. "What happened?"

He sniffed, his sobs diminishing. "He gave me the lie!"

"Not Dambroke!"

"No, that prune-faced prig, Elman!" He sniffed again and, recalling his dignity, pulled a little away from her. "He said nobody could culp ten wafers in a row from twenty paces, so I planted him a facer. Drew his cork, too," he added, not without a touch of pride.

"But you said you only hit two wafers, Teddy."

"Not me. Richard."

"Oh." She digested the implications of this simple statement. "Did you explain it to his lordship?"

"Well, only the bit about being called liar." There was mute appeal in his eyes, and she realized he had taken the beating rather than confess that Dambroke's skill with a pistol had been doubted.

"You should have told him, Teddy, but I understand why you didn't. I'll speak with him if you like."

"You mustn't tell him, Cathy! It wouldn't make any difference anyway. He said I was not to fight, and I did. But, I don't want to leave London!"

"I'll do what I can, but I make no promises. Are you banished to your room without supper again?"

He nodded. "Will you bring me something?" The limpid gaze clearly expressed his confidence that, if she would sympathize with any part of his predicament, it would be with the fact that he might very likely starve before morning.

Catheryn grinned, shaking her head. "Not if he says I mustn't, scamp. But he may neglect to mention it." Teddy didn't look as though he had great hopes of such a lapse occurring, and she watched him go on upstairs, mentally damning the earl for his lack of patience. Just when things had begun to go well between them, he had to spoil everything by losing his temper. The more she thought about it, the angrier she became, and by the time she reached the library, her own temper had approached its zenith. Ignoring Walter, who stepped hastily forward to open the doors for her, she strode without ceremony into the room. Her precipitate entry brought Dambroke scrambling to his feet.

"Catheryn! What is it? Has something happened?"

"Indeed, my lord!" she snapped. She would have continued, but he cut in smoothly, signing to the wide-eyed footman still on the threshold to remove himself.

"Won't you sit down, Cousin, so that we may discuss whatever it is in a calm and rational manner?"

"I never sit when I am in a rage, Lord Dambroke, and

I do not wish to be calm. Whatever possessed you to order that poor child off to the country?"

He frowned but kept his own voice level. "So that's it. I should have known. It is not your concern, Cousin."

"Not my concern!" She clenched her fists into her skirt. "How can you say so, when you asked me to befriend him! What kind of friend would I be if I did not do my utmost to stop this ridiculous nonsense? I cannot allow Teddy to become a victim of your stupid temper, sir. He did nothing more than smack a boy who wanted smacking. Anyone with an ounce of pride would have done the same thing with similar provocation, but instead of supporting him as you should, you pack him off to the country because he has embarrassed you again."

"You know nothing about it!" Dambroke snapped. "The boy's nose may be broken, and I've received a very impertinent note from Elman regretting that Edward is no longer welcome in his house. I warned him what would happen if he indulged in any more fisticuffs. He leaves tomorrow, and that's the end of it!"

"So we reach the heart of the matter," Catheryn said scornfully, "and it's just as I thought. You are not nearly so angry about the fight between the two boys as you are about the embarrassment of so-called impertinence from a mere baron. A man dares to take umbrage at the fact that your brother flattened his son—a boy, I might remind you, who is both older and larger than Teddy and who should have known better than to taunt him. And do you exert yourself to explain the circumstances to Lord Elman? No, sir! You choose instead to punish a boy who was only defending his honor. And yours as well!"

"What the devil had my honor to do with anything?"

She paused, cursing her unruly tongue. But perhaps it would help him to see the situation more clearly. "The Elman boy said Teddy lied about your skill with a pistol," she said flatly. "That's why he hit him." She thought Dambroke looked a bit taken aback and hoped briefly that he might reconsider.

"That's very illuminating," he said finally, "however, the cause of the fight does not signify in the slightest. The only pertinent fact is that the boy disobeyed me."

"A scold would have been sufficient, my lord. The whipping was unnecessary, and sending him to the country is outrageous. You knew he despised the Elmans before you sent him there, so you are as much to blame as he is. But, for this one indiscretion, you exert the full force of your authority." Her voice trailed off on the last word, arrested by something in his expression. The silence that followed was uncomfortable, but she was sorry when he ended it, for his voice hardened with a bone-chilling note that she had never heard in it before.

"One indiscretion, Catheryn? Are you certain you mean to say that? Perhaps I have mistaken your integrity. I quite realize that I am not supposed to know of anything else, but do you mean to stand before me and insist, in all honesty, that Edward's behavior has been above reproach this week?"

She had the grace to blush. "Perhaps not, my lord."

"Indeed, and while we are on the subject, let me tell you, miss, that I do not approve the example you have set by practicing deceit, conspiracy, and other such underhand tactics. Oh, don't look so shocked. The terms may be severe, but you are guilty, my girl, and you know it!"

"I only tried to protect Teddy, my lord. I don't know what specific actions you condemn, so I am unable to defend myself." She spoke calmly enough, but her heart was pounding, and she felt curiously weak. How had he turned the tables so easily to put her in the wrong? His anger before had stimulated her; now it was frightening.

"In plainer language," he said grimly, "there have been so many incidents that you don't know what I have discovered. Isn't that it?" She could only be grateful that he didn't wait for an answer. "I won't take advantage of your ignorance. Landon was with me when I received Elman's note. He made a comment that seemed a bit suspicious, and I soon had a round tale of Tony's mishap out of him. It took little effort after that to learn about the salt and the dead rat."

"They were only boyish pranks, my lord!"

"I agree. Nonetheless, Edward must learn to conduct himself in a more proper style, and I won't have this house turned upside down in the meantime. He goes to the Park. I shall find a tutor for him there, and we'll join him in a few weeks. But for the present——"

"For the present," Catheryn interrupted, her anger with him overcoming any other emotion, "the great Earl of Dambroke must not be embarrassed! You could deal with Teddy right here, if you would exert yourself, for he loves you. But you cannot see what is under your nose, so you push him off to the Park to get him out of the way. By heaven, my lord, I believe you have greater patience with your horses!"

"Catheryn!" he exploded. "That will do! He's going because I promised to send him if he did not behave. That is the long and short of it. We shall discuss it no further!"

She realized he meant what he said and feared he would put her out bodily if she persisted, so, muttering wrathful things to herself, she turned on her heel and left the room. Halfway up the first flight of stairs, however, the echo of her words and his anger came back to her, and she looked over her shoulder almost expecting to find him at her heels. The hall was reassuringly empty. How had she dared to speak to him so, when he could send her away quite as easily as he was sending Teddy? Despite the fact that she had come to feel at home here, she was still no more than a guest in his house. Although, now that she came to think of it, he had not treated her as a guest. He had been amazingly angry himself. To a guest he would have been coldly polite, and he had not been polite at all. She smiled, her good humor oddly restored by the thought.

Catheryn was not one to tilt at windmills, nor to hold a grudge. Dambroke's final words had shown her that her cause was lost. Men could be so stubborn in matters of principle. If he had threatened Teddy earlier with exile to the country, he would believe himself committed now. Personally, she thought it a stupid way of doing things. One should always consider the ramifications of one's decisions. That she did not always do so herself was a mere bagatelle not worth considering. Dambroke should know better. Teddy would be better off in London under his eye than up to who knew what at Dambroke Park.

At least he had not forbidden her to visit the boy. Suiting thought to deed, she hurried down to the kitchen, piled a tray with various delicacies and, with a saucy smile to the scandalized chef, carried it upstairs to a grateful Teddy before returning to her own room to prepare for the evening ahead.

XII

The countess's ball was a success. After a magnificent dinner, the rest of the guests began to arrive, and Catheryn and Tiffany stood with the earl and the countess to receive them until the orchestra began to make tentative noises. Tiffany announced that she wanted to refresh herself before the dancing began, so Catheryn went ahead to the ballroom, escorted by Edmund. He soon left her to join Lady Prudence, and any lingering doubt Catheryn may have had about their developing relationship was put to rest by the ease of manner between Mr. Caston and Prudence's father. The light in Edmund's eye and the tenderness in his lady's meant a good deal, but these signs were as nothing compared to the duke's attitude, for the success of Edmund's suit depended entirely upon his grace's good will.

"Good evening, Miss Westering. A splendid dinner!"

"Indeed, Captain Varling." She smiled at him. "Jean-Pierre excelled himself."

"He is always to be relied upon. I only wish the same might be said of our Auguste. He is so puffed up in his own conceit that he exerts himself only for affairs like this one."

Catheryn laughed. "If you had tasted one or two meals here this past week, you would not commend Jean-Pierre so highly. It was not lack of hospitality that kept the countess from inviting you to dine, sir."

"Enough!" he exclaimed. "Spare me my illusions. Besides, I've been ungallant to mention food at all before informing you that you look prodigiously charming this evening. My sister has taught me better manners, I assure you. I like that dress." She thanked him with a demure twinkle. "I mean it," he insisted. "That color becomes you. Ah!"

Lady Tiffany had entered the ballroom. Her dress was

white, for the simple reason that the countess had insisted upon it. But the young beauty had rebelled at wearing the stark white of the debutante, insisting that it was not necessary so near the end of the season. A compromise had been contrived in a gown of beautiful white lace over an underskirt of sapphire-blue satin with matching sash and sapphires for her neck, wrists, and ears. The result was guaranteed to stun every gentleman at the ball; nevertheless, Catheryn was delighted to hear Varling's exclamation. She knew they were partnered for the first set, while she was to dance, ironically enough, with Mr. Lawrence. He had asked her ladyship first and Catheryn as a semipolite afterthought. Tiffany had allowed him to sign her card for the first and third country dances but refused his arch suggestion of a third dance on the grounds of impropriety and the likelihood of arousing Dambroke's displeasure. Lawrence had been visibly annoyed and Catheryn, seeing the younger girl's dance card a few days later, wondered rather wickedly how he would react to the fact that Captain Varling had been granted three dances, including the supper dance.

The captain excused himself. "I fear to see her ladyship snatched from beneath my very nose if I tarry."

Catheryn's chuckle was lost as he made a hasty bow and set off to claim his partner. Tiffany's eyes glowed at his approach, and Catheryn started at the sound of a harshly indrawn breath at her side. She turned to find Lawrence staring at the other couple, eyes narrowed, jaw clenched, and color draining from his face. Momentarily chilled by his expression, she gradually relaxed as he became aware of her attention and exerted himself to be pleasing. By the time her next partner arrived to claim her hand, the incident had slipped to the nether regions of her mind.

As the evening progressed and she bowed first to one friend and then another, Catheryn realized that she had acquired many since her arrival in London. Thanks to the Dambroke support, she had been easily accepted into their world and was amazed at how comfortable she found it. She loved the excitement and fast pace of the city, the parties, and the people. Her life had taken on a certain dreamlike quality for the moment, but she knew the novelty would wear off and wondered if she would long then for the peace and quiet of the country.

Mr. Brummell claimed her for a waltz and, as they swung onto the floor, Catheryn nearly missed her step. The Beau followed her gaze to where Edmund Caston danced with Lady Prudence. He smiled vaguely. "That's quite old news, Miss Westering. You must know they have been an *on dit* this week and longer."

"But Edmund is waltzing, sir! Just as though he never disapproved of it at all!"

"So he is," the Beau admitted, adding that Mr. Caston must have taken lessons, since he was doing the thing quite well. He spoke again a moment later, but Catheryn's reply was nearly absentminded as she watched the other couple.

"He seems so relaxed, so un-Edmundlike."

"The match will undoubtedly be the making of him." Brummell's tone was acid and Catheryn, quick to hear it, dimpled up at him.

"I beg your pardon, sir. I am boring you."

"Admitting a fault merely compounds the original error, Miss Westering," he replied sweetly.

She chuckled her appreciation. "My cousin's affairs must always interest me, sir, but I should not dwell upon them in your presence. I hope you will forgive me."

"Of course." He whirled her through an intricate pattern and into the closing steps of the dance, bringing her up breathless and laughing. Brummell smiled and then his attention was diverted to a point behind her. "I believe your next partner is impatient, ma'am. Your servant, my lord."

Catheryn turned to find Dambroke behind her. Some days before, he had scrawled his name for the set of country dances now forming as well as for the supper dance, but she had not spoken with him all evening. Seeing him now, she began to feel the same weakness she had felt earlier standing in front of his desk. The company smile with which he greeted her did not conceal an anxious look in his eye, and she scarcely noticed Mr. Brummell's departure.

"Do you mind very much if we do not dance, Catheryn?"

"Not at all, my lord," she answered with equal politeness. "Mr. Brummell has quite worn me out."

"Will you walk with me in the garden, or are you so tired that you would prefer to sit while I fetch some ratafia? Or, no, you prefer lemonade, if I remember correctly." He quirked an eyebrow and she chuckled. Dambroke relaxed. "I was afraid you were still vexed with me."

"Me too. That you were with me, I mean."

"I'm not. Shall it be the garden or the lemonade?"

"The garden. Some fresh air would be delightful." She glanced around. "I hope I've not offended Mr. Brummell again."

"Again?" She let him place her hand in the crook of his arm and, as they walked, began to tell him of her conversation with the Beau, thinking it would amuse him.

French windows at the end of the ballroom led onto a wide balcony with steps at either end leading down to the gardens. Torches had been placed in strategic areas, both to light the way for casual roamers and—in the countess's words—to deter the more outrageous young men from certain amorous strategies. When they reached the garden, Dambroke guided her to a marble bench and indicated that she should sit. He had not laughed at her tale. "I doubt he is offended," he said, "but since he has chosen to notice you, you must be careful, my dear. Should you truly offend him, he might cut the connection."

"I should survive it, my lord," she smiled.

"No doubt," he replied quietly. "But it could ruin you socially. Brummell still wields great influence. Not only do his tailor and bootmaker fear to dun him, lest he take his custom elsewhere, but no hostess who values his opinion would dare invite anyone he dislikes to a function honored by his presence."

"I see." She was thoughtful for a moment. "I shall have a care, my lord, while I remain in London."

"While you remain?" He sounded surprised.

Catheryn smiled. "I should like to stay, of course, and I should still like to set up housekeeping here. But although Edmund has said he will speak to my uncle, I doubt he will grant me an allowance large enough for the purpose, so I shall no doubt be returning to Somerset soon. I cannot remain indefinitely as your mother's guest, you know." He was silent. "Shall we walk again, my lord? It grows chilly."

Obligingly, he rose and took her hand again, but he remained silent and Catheryn lapsed into her own thoughts. She wondered briefly if anyone would comment on their absence. It was useless to hope no one had noticed. Dambroke was too great a matrimonial prize. She glanced up at his profile. He looked stern, almost forbidding, even under the softening rays of the golden moon shining above. It was not a full moon, more shame to it, but romantic enough at three-quarters. Nevertheless, it did nothing to make his profile look more loverlike. She thought him handsome but acknowledged that with the firm, sharp jawline, high cheekbones, and deepset eyes, his features were too harsh ever to allow him to look like one of the romantic heroes of literature. But then, most of those heroes were probably a bit on the soppy side, now she came to think of it.

"Must I raise the bid to a guinea?"

Jolted out of her reverie, Catheryn stammered, "Wh-what? I mean, I beg your pardon, my lord. Did you speak?"

"I merely offered the proverbial penny."

"Penny? Oh!" Flaming warmth swept across her face, and she had cause to be grateful to the gentle moonlight. Fighting her blushes, she took a deep breath, exerting herself to control her voice. "I'm sorry, sir. I was but daydreaming. My thoughts are scarcely worth your penny, let alone a guinea."

"Do you not trust me, little one, or is it that you are still angry with me in spite of your denial?"

Little one! "I believe the music has stopped, my lord," she said stupidly.

"So it has. You evade my question."

"I am not angry, my lord," she muttered.

"You were."

"Amazingly," she agreed. "Gentlemen are so idiotish."

"I beg your pardon!"

"Well, they are," she insisted, glad to pursue a subject she had hoped to avoid, since she wanted so much more to avoid the subject of her private thoughts. "Men always set such store by their own words. You are punishing Teddy because of something *you* said. It would make more sense to me if Teddy were being sent away because of a promise he made to you rather than one you made to him. Oh, I don't make any sense! Do you understand me?"

He laughed. "Of course I do. You mean it should have been Teddy who said, 'Now, look here, Dambroke. . . .'"

"Well, perhaps, 'Please, my lord. . . .'"

"Very well. I'm willing to accommodate. 'Please, my lord, I promise I shall never do it again, but if I do you must send me to the country.' Like that?"

"It does sound ridiculous put like that," she agreed, "but it was so harsh and unfeeling the other way. Females would never be so rigid."

He was still amused. "My dear Catheryn, does it occur to you that you have just reached the crux of the matter?" She looked up at him. "You have involved yourself in business between two males and are trying to understand it with a female mind. It can't be done any more than I could presume to understand business concocted between two females."

Her eyes widened into a gaze of such disarming innocence that the earl quite failed to note the spark of anger. "Tell me something, my lord." She spoke sweetly, and he smiled, clearly thinking he had made his point.

"What is it, my dear?"

"You have seemed until now to be a sensible man. Do you always talk such ridiculous fustian?"

"I beg your pardon!"

"Granted."

"Catheryn." The note of warning was there but overridden by amusement.

"Well, you should beg my pardon! Of all the conceited, despicable statements to make, to presume that a female's understanding is any less acute than a man's!"

"Don't take my head off, little one. I cry pardon." He sighed. "We weren't even going to discuss this issue."

"You began it."

"Must we descend to nursery recriminations?" he moaned.

She chuckled. "No, sir. That did sound childish."

They were silent, each thinking private thoughts while the moonlight danced on leaves made to quiver by a slight spring breeze. Music drifted from the ballroom punctuated occasionally by a note of laughter nearer to hand. Once or twice they passed another couple enjoying the fresh air, but neither noticed the appraising looks cast in their own direction. The music stopped.

"We must go back, sir. The last dance did not matter, but I am promised for this one."

"One moment." He turned her to face him, his hands lightly on her shoulders. They were completely alone for that moment. "I have wanted to do this since the day you first arrived." He bent down swiftly and kissed her.

It was the merest touch of his lips against her own, but it sent a tingling shock wave clear to Catheryn's toes. She was astounded, taken completely by surprise. Sense and nonsense collided with one another as her mind struggled to cope with a sudden flurry of thought and emotion. How dared he do such a thing! Could he possibly take her for a woman of easy virtue? Perhaps she was one at that, else why had she not evaded him? Of course, she reassured herself, it had happened so quickly that she had had no time to realize his intent before he had taken his liberty; but now, surely now, instead of staring up at him wide-eyed, she ought to react. Why was she standing like a stock, even granting him opportunity to repeat his action? A proper lady would never behave so stupidly. Indeed, a proper lady would smack his face for him. But she had no desire at all to do that. In fact, she realized with a shock nearly as great as that caused by the kiss itself that she rather wished he would do it again. When, instead, he gently took her arm and turned her back toward the balcony, she did not know whether to be glad or sorry.

"May I still take you down to supper?" He seemed anxious, and his voice was oddly gruff.

"Yes, sir." Her own wasn't any too steady. She took a deep breath and glanced at him through her lashes. He certainly didn't look as though he were taking her lightly. On the contrary, his relief when she consented to his supper invitation was patently obvious. Reassured by this attitude, her sensibilities began returning to normal. "It is kind of you to ask me this time," she said demurely, even smiling when, momentarily puzzled, he raised an eyebrow. "Well, you didn't ask before, you know. You just took my card and scribbled 'Dambroke' across the two dances."

"I do not scribble." His voice was steady now.

"No, my lord. My error. You have an elegant hand."

"Baggage."

"Just so, my lord." She had recovered her poise. Her partner stepped up to claim her, and she was quickly swept into the next dance. For the following hour she enjoyed herself hugely, though she wondered what it was about the tall and dashing redhead or the buxom brunette that had attracted his lordship's attention to the point of his having asked first the one and then the other to dance. The plump girl with the dreadful complexion and overfrilled dress was clearly a duty dance, but those others! Especially the redhead—so tall, so elegant—just the way one would wish to look oneself. Miss Westering sighed.

The time passed quickly enough before the supper dance. It was a quadrille, so they had to attend to the figures and could spare little time for conversation. Before they realized it, they were beyond *la pastorale* and into *la finale*. The whole was danced with spirit and energy, the final figure ending with laughter and heaving sides.

Captain Varling and Tiffany were also in their set, so it was natural to go down to supper together. They met Mr. Caston and Lady Prudence, and soon Varling was pushing tables together to accommodate a growing party. It was not until everyone was seated with high-piled plates and the footmen were pouring out the wine that Catheryn saw that Lady Chastity's partner was none other than the ubiquitous Mr. Lawrence. Dambroke's sudden frown gave her to realize that he had also noticed the pair. She could only be grateful that they sat at the opposite end of the tables.

"I have been meaning to ask you," the earl said, his voice low, "what that puppy is doing here in this house."

"Have you, my lord?"

"He has twice danced with my sister."

"As have several other young men."

"To be sure. But again you evade my primary question."

"He is here because your mother invited him, of course."

"I shall speak to my mother."

"Oh, pray do not, sir! You would only upset her. She was not in favor of the notion, I promise you. I had to exert all my powers of persuasion to convince her."

"You!" He looked at her suspiciously. "Are you certain you are not now trying to protect my sister just as you would have protected Teddy?"

Catheryn stared at him in amazement. "You think Tiffany wanted Mr. Lawrence here?"

"Of course she did. Really, Catheryn, I am more than seven, you know."

"Dambroke, you are blind!"

He would have responded, but her agitated whispers had caught the ear of the gentleman on her right. "What's toward here? You two ain't branglin' at my supper party!"

Dambroke answered across Catheryn. "Don't be daft, Tony. As a matter of fact, I was telling Miss Westering that I appreciate the way you've been keeping Tiffany occupied and out of the clutches of that damned Lawrence fellow."

"Have you now, Dickon?" The captain's eyes twinkled merrily. "My pleasure, I assure you."

Just then, they were interrupted by Tiffany, sitting between Varling and Lord Thomas. "Catheryn, you'll never imagine! Lord Thomas's mama is going to give a masquerade ball! The invitations went out today and we will each receive one!"

Dambroke frowned. "A masquerade?"

"Yes, Richard, a masqued ball!" Tiffany tried to keep her voice low, but it was difficult when she had to speak across two other people. The constant buzz of polite conversation made it difficult to speak to anyone except one's immediate neighbor, which of course was all one was expected to do. But Tiffany seemed determined not to allow her brother to spoil the fun. She continued, "Surely, you will not object to a masquerade at Clairdon Court! It's perfectly respectable. Why, the duke is a paragon of virtue, and the duchess is very strict!"

"I'm surprised they would allow such a party under their roof," Dambroke observed.

"Overborne by sheer numbers, my dear boy. Sheer numbers. Six daughters, you know. Imagine having six daughters!" Varling threw up his hands in mock dismay.

"Put a sock in it, Tony," Dambroke recommended.

"Yes, do," Tiffany agreed. "Besides, it was Lord Thomas. You know it was, Tony. The girls can never persuade the duke to do anything exciting. It was Lord Thomas, and he got the idea from me," she added with pride.

"From you!" Dambroke's brows rose alarmingly. It was clear that he would have liked to continue but was deterred by the public nature of the moment. The set of his jaw and the way his lips thinned to a straight line indicated that he would have more to say to his sister in the not distant future. Tiffany wisely lapsed into silence, but the captain, with a glance at each of them, put the matter into its proper perspective.

"Relax, Dickon," he said quietly. "It was my sister, not yours, who put the notion in Colby's head." Tiffany moved as though to speak, but he kept her silent simply by laying a light hand on her wrist. Catheryn watched in awe. "It was indirectly Tiffany's doing," Varling added, "but only in that she mentioned to Maggie how unfair she thought it that they are not allowed to attend the public masques. Maggie spoke of it to Colby, who mentioned it to the duchess, and bingo! A proper masquerade with proper chaperones."

Dambroke's expression relaxed, but when Tiffany encountered his direct gaze she dropped her eyes. "I shall have to consider the matter," he said at last. "I cannot approve of masqued balls."

Catheryn spoke up innocently. "I think a masque where we knew everyone would be great fun. I should adore to dress as a shepherdess or a moonbeam or some such odd thing."

"Tonight, you are a sea nymph," laughed Varling.

"Well, I have never been to a masque before," she confided, "but I think the best fun would be guessing who everyone is before the unmasking."

"I suppose there can be no great harm in a private masquerade, if Clairdon approves it," mused the earl.

XIII

After so much bustle, the peace and quiet of the weekend was almost unnerving. Teddy's departure Saturday morning went without a hitch. The boy was a trifle subdued and even allowed Catheryn to give him a hug. Interrupting to give final instructions, Dambroke spoke in such stern tones that she turned away to spare Teddy further embarrassment. To her astonishment, she saw Peter Ashley coming out the front door with a leather satchel under his arm.

"Good morning, Mr. Ashley. You are leaving us?"

He allowed the youngest footman to relieve him of his satchel. "Thank you, Michael," he nodded. "Only for a short time, Miss Westering." He nodded toward Dambroke and the solemn Teddy. "His lordship has kindly given me leave until Tuesday. I shall visit my father and see if I can prevail upon my cousin Mark to bearlead that cub for the summer."

Catheryn knew Ashley was the younger son of a clergyman whose living was within the earl's jurisdiction. "What a good idea!" she exclaimed. "I'm certain a cousin of yours will be unexceptionable. Teddy will be so pleased!"

"Well, he will, because he will like Mark. He's a second-year man at Oxford, but he became ill shortly after Easter term began and had to go home. He is well now but won't go back till Michaelmas. If he accepts the post, he will probably stay with Father, since his family lives near Baldock."

"Could he not stay at the Park?"

Ashley laughed, his blue eyes dancing. "Too independent by half is Mark. I think he will agree to tutor the boy, but I'm not such a gudgeon as to think he will want to be responsible for him twenty-four hours a day!"

"Then, who will look after Teddy?"

"Her ladyship's cousin, Miss Lucy Felmersham, and two dozen or so servants, I expect." He smiled. "I know what you mean, Miss Westering, but it will be better for him there. It's his home, after all, much more so than London, and he has friends in the neighborhood; though, I admit, they are not all approved by the family. Truly," he added seriously, "you needn't worry. Straley, the chief groundsman, and Mrs. Trent, the housekeeper, are particularly fond of him." He saw Teddy climb into the carriage and hastily bade her farewell. A few moments later, the carriage lumbered off, and Dambroke offered her his arm.

"You are unnaturally quiet, Cousin," he said when they reached the front hall.

She opened her mouth to answer him but thought better of it. She was tired and knew he must be as well. She had no wish to quarrel with him.

"Still angry, Catheryn? Last night you seemed to be in charity with me again." His voice was gentle, but she remembered how stern he had been with Teddy. She thought, also, that it was no time to think about last night in the garden. The silence lengthened, deepened, became nearly tactile. Finally, Dambroke laid a firm hand upon her shoulder and directed her into the library. The expression in his eyes was tender, but his jaw was set as though he intended to see the matter through once and for all. He shut the door with a snap and leaned against it. "Now, you may say whatever you like without fear of interruption."

Catheryn pushed an errant curl into place and took a deep breath. This was getting out of hand. She glanced into his eyes and away again. "My lord, you make too much of this."

"Do I?" It was his lazy drawl, the tone he used when he meant to exert the firmest control over himself. It was odd to hear it now. She hadn't thought him angry. Not yet.

She eyed him doubtfully. "I believe so," she said slowly. "I have no right to take you to task, sir. Certainly not the right to say what I like to you."

"Rubbish." It was merely a comment, but his eyes began to twinkle, and Catheryn relaxed.

"Did you say 'rubbish,' sir?"

"Yes, certainly. You did not hesitate to speak your mind yesterday, little one."

She felt the telltale color creeping into her cheeks at the endearment and looked down. "I was angry yesterday. Today I am not. Today I am only sad to see Teddy leave." She looked up and saw one mobile brow arch quizzically. "It's true, Dambroke. Do not look at me so!"

He shook his head in amusement. "Oh, Catheryn, I am a fool to bait you. I know you still disapprove of my sending Teddy away, but I hope it won't cause further constraint between us. It is done now."

"I hold no grudge, sir. I just wish you had not found it necessary to be so stern with him this morning."

"Did I seem harsh? I assure you it was not my intention to be." She stole another look at him from under her lashes. He seemed sincere. She sighed.

"I believe you mean that, my lord. It's a pity you were unable to see or hear yourself. I don't understand why that boy idolizes you so."

"He should not." The words were crisp. "I am a poor subject for hero worship."

Catheryn chuckled. "I know that, but it's good to hear that you do, too. You must excuse me now, my lord." She moved straight toward him, wondering if he would allow her to leave. "I've a hundred things to do," she added firmly. His gaze rested upon her long enough that she had to pause, but when she cocked her head inquiringly, he stepped aside and opened the door.

The rest of the weekend was quite dull. Dambroke, Colby, and the captain went to a town twenty miles away to watch a boxing match, a fine pastime, Catheryn thought, for a man who disapproved of boyish fisticuffs! Instead of the hundred things she had told him she had to do, she was hard-pressed to think of one, and she missed the activity that preceded the ball. More than that, she missed Teddy. Not knowing from one minute to the next what mischief he would create had, she realized, added a certain piquance to life.

The invitations to the duchess's masque arrived by first post Monday morning, and Tiffany was promptly thrown into a frenzy. How would she contrive? The ball was to be held Friday, May twenty-second, only a fortnight hence. Only a few short days to work a miracle! She was determined not to be recognized and scorned Catheryn's intention of wearing a domino and not, as she had previously indicated, some ingenious costume.

"Catheryn, this may be my only opportunity to attend a masque before I am married! We must do the thing properly."

"Are you marrying so soon, then?"

"Of course not!" But her ladyship was surely blushing. She recovered herself. "Perhaps, I shall be a shepherdess."

"If you are, you will probably melt right into the crowd," responded Catheryn, tiring of the subject. "I daresay the place will abound with shepherdesses. Marie Antoinette made the pose quite respectable, you know."

"A polite way of informing you that you are in a fair way to losing your head over this affair, my dear," commented a familiar voice from the doorway. Catheryn nearly choked on her toast, and Dambroke stepped forward to offer her a glass of water. Tiffany laughed but kept a wary eye on her brother, believing him unpredictable on the subject of masqued balls.

"You are very late this morning, Richard."

"The devil I am!" He grinned. "Tony and I ate hours ago and have been twice round the park. I only stopped in to tell you that I shall be out most of the day."

"White's, most likely," Tiffany laughed. "Where is Captain Varling?"

"Gone home. And I shall not be at any of my clubs. Tony tells me he is thinking of selling out."

"Is he, indeed?" asked his sister at her most nonchalant.

"Yes. Tired of military life already, I expect. Some of our business pertains to that, and later I've other appointments of my own. I miss Peter."

"Poor Mr. Ashley," mocked Catheryn. "I wonder he has not contrived by now to be in two places at once. Surely, he understands that the Earl of Dambroke requires his secretary to possess such talents."

Dambroke grinned but refused the gambit and soon departed, leaving Catheryn to be drawn into further discussion of Tiffany's costume. The countess joined them later in the morning room and finished off any lingering desire her daughter may have had to become a shepherdess.

"Too, too common, my dear. I don't know why you are so crazy for a masque anyway. So wearing not to know one's partners." But Tiffany was undeterred. Her tentative suggestion that she might go as an houri being squashed flat, veils notwithstanding, she proposed the idea of dressing as Cleopatra. "Nearly as ordinary as the shepherdess," scorned the countess, taking up a piece of her exquisite embroidery. She quickly became absorbed in her work. Catheryn put forth a few suggestions, feeling the exertion was expected of her, but Tiffany rejected them all. She did hesitate over the possibility of posing as Leda and carrying a stuffed swan, until the countess wondered aloud how she would dance with a reticule in one hand and the swan in the other. The conversation deteriorated after that until Tiffany declared in frustration that she would ask Maggie Varling.

"I daresay I shall eat luncheon there, so don't look for me till teatime. Won't you come, too, Catheryn?"

But Catheryn was steadfast in her refusal and saw her cousin off with relief. The countess was right! Masqued balls were very wearing! On the other hand, she was left with nothing to do. After a light luncheon with the countess, she was debating whether to venture out with Bert Ditchling to Hyde Park, which at this hour would be alive with Cits and other rabble, when Lady Prudence arrived.

"I've come to carry you off to my sister's for tea," she announced. "At least, when it's time for it, I'm sure Patience will give us tea. But do say you will come, Catheryn, for I've ever so much to tell you."

Catheryn accepted with alacrity and was not surprised, when they were settled in the Easton's comfortable drawing room, to learn that the duke had accepted Edmund's suit. That Prudence had actually fallen in love with Edmund still amazed her. She said as much.

"But he is so solid, so dependable, Catheryn," was the reasonable and unruffled reply. "Compared to London beaux, who are forever prosing on about fashion or curricle racing or cockfights, Edmund is such a sensible man!"

Catheryn stared at her. "He is?"

"Well, you are close to him," said Prudence quietly. "Perhaps that is why you do not recognize his virtues. I'm sure I shall stare just so, if Maggie accepts Tom's suit."

"Maggie! Tom! You mean Lord Thomas?" Catheryn's eyes danced when Prudence nodded. "Never say so, Prue!"

"There!" declared Lady Easton. "I knew it. Even you, Prue, cannot keep your tongue between your teeth. Nothing has been said, Catheryn. It's Prue's imagination."

"Well, it isn't," twinkled Catheryn. "It's as plain as plain. That sly devil! I see it all now. No wonder he's worried. If anyone knows his views on the necessity of marrying an heiress, it's the Earl and Countess of Stanthorpe!"

"Not to mention Captain Varling," added Prudence dryly. "Nevertheless, if his own suit prospers, perhaps he will stand Tom's friend." They looked at each other in that conspiratorial way females have when they know they have rumbled something that is not yet public knowledge.

"How is Lady Tiffany?" asked Patience sweetly.

Catheryn chuckled appreciatively. "Up to her laces in ideas for fancy dress!" She put her hands up in mock dismay. "If I hear one more idea for a costume, I shall scream!"

They laughed and spent the rest of the afternoon discussing Prudence's plans for a ceremony in late June. Her ladyship had opted for a country wedding at the ducal seat, but the duke insisted on St. George's, Hanover Square. "London will be thin of company by then, of course, but I daresay our guests will come," Prudence said in her quiet way.

"Of course they will, and I know of several who will be grateful you're being married here and not in Wiltshire," replied Catheryn. She also learned that, when Edmund had written to inform his parents of his good fortune, the duchess had included an invitation to Sir Horace and Lady Caston to visit as soon as it would be convenient.

"Suppose they should arrive in time for the masque?"

Prudence's voice was tinged with worry. "Your aunt may disapprove of such a function."

Despite having often heard Lady Caston's disparaging remarks on the folly of such uncivilized activities, Catheryn was easily able to soothe Prudence's fears. No party given by a duchess—especially by the duchess soon to become her son's mother-in-law—would be condemned by Lady Caston.

Not long after a generous tea, Prudence and Catheryn took their leave, and Catheryn was soon set down at Dambroke House. There being no one in the front hall, she proceeded to the yellow drawing room, where she could be certain, at this time of day, to find the countess at least. When she pushed open the door, she had the odd feeling that she had left civilized reality down in the street and had stepped instead onto a stage. Morris, standing just inside the door with a small tambour frame in his hand, moved obligingly aside to give her the full effect.

The countess had fainted and lay back on the settee, her feet still on the floor. A lachrymose Tiffany hovered over her, and Paulson's usually placid wife jabbed smelling salts ineffectively at her mistress's nose while waving her free hand angrily at a strange lad who carried with him a marked aura of the stables and who listened with downcast face and shifting feet while she shouted at him.

"Wicked boy! Wicked, wicked boy! What have you done!"

"Warn't my fault," he mumbled wretchedly.

"No business here at all! There, there, my lamb," she added soothingly to the now stirring countess.

"I tell yer, it warn't my fault. I was sent."

"Sent, schment! You don't belong in my lady's drawing room," grated Mrs. Paulson. "Your sort stay in the stables. I shall have a word with Mr. Hobbs about this, I will."

"I brung a message from the Park, I did," insisted the poor lad. "Can't 'elp it if the man says bring it up, can I? Just does like 'e says, is all. 'E says 'is lordship ain't 'ere, go tell 'er la'yship, so I does."

Catheryn looked at Morris. He shrugged and spoke in an undertone. "That Michael, like as not, miss. Not much in his cockloft saving open space. Mr. Paulson'll have a strip off him for this, I'm thinking. His lordship, too, an he gets wind of it. I was upstairs." He gestured with the tambour frame. "Walked in just before you did."

"Well, if Michael did indeed send a groom to her ladyship instead of bringing the message himself, he deserves a trimming," Catheryn agreed. "What was the message?"

Morris had no idea, but their voices had penetrated to the others. "Catheryn! Oh, Catheryn!" cried Tiffany. "Teddy's been hurt, maybe even killed!"

A cold chill trickled down Catheryn's spine, but her first thought was for Dambroke. Dear God, she prayed, don't let his action result in Teddy's death! Don't let there be any way he can blame himself.

"My baby!" moaned the countess, coming to her senses in time to hear Tiffany's cry. "My poor darling boy. He must not be dead!"

"He ain't."

The words were lost as Mrs. Paulson rounded on Tiffany, commanding her to hush now and mind her poor mama's nerves. "Here now, my lady," she added, bending over the countess, "just you have a whiff of these good salts. And you there!" she snapped at Morris. "Don't stand like a stock, man. Fetch Miss Fowler. And Miss Catheryn, will you be a dear and fetch some hartshorn and water? If you will be so kind."

But Catheryn had recovered sufficiently to take command of the situation. A glance at Morris assured her that he would see to the hartshorn, so she turned her attention first to her cousin, who had burst into fresh tears. "Tiffany, compose yourself at once or leave the room! You are behaving like an underbred kitchenmaid. If you wish to remain, you may help your mother. Mrs. Paulson, do you give the salts to Lady Tiffany and be so good as to explain this charade to me."

Bowing, however reluctantly, to the note of authority in Catheryn's voice, the housekeeper passed the salts to a startled Tiffany. The younger girl had never heard Catheryn speak so sharply before and made an effort to stifle her tears, but her sniffs and an occasional weak moan from the countess punctuated the housekeeper's next words.

"I don't know as I can give much of a round tale, Miss Catheryn. That Michael came to me all of a dither saying her ladyship had got word Master Teddy was throwed from that great black beast of his lordship's and was sure the lad was killed."

"He warn't."

Diverted, Catheryn turned to the groom. "Who are you?"

"Ben Fincham, an it please ye, miss. From down to the Park. Young Master b'ain't dead. Leastwise not yet."

Wise in the ways of countryfolk, she knew better than to take Ben's pessimism too seriously. Nevertheless, the knowledge that Blaze had thrown Teddy sent another chill slithering down her spine. No wonder the countess and Tiffany were in such a state! "Can you tell us about the accident, Ben?"

"Didn't see it. Miss Lucy, she just says take the letter quick to 'is lordship. But 'e warn't 'ere, so——"

"Yes, Ben, we know that bit. Did you say letter? Did Miss Felmersham send a letter?" The lad nodded.

"Well, I never!" exclaimed Mrs. Paulson. "You never said about any letter!"

"No one arst me."

"Never mind," Catheryn interposed hastily before the housekeeper could vent her indignation. "Where is the letter, Ben? Let me have it, please."

Obligingly, he pulled a crumpled note from his jacket and handed it to her. Ignoring the fact that it was directed in firm copperplate to the earl, Catheryn tore it opened and scanned the contents rapidly before giving a sigh of relief. "It's all right, Aunt Elizabeth. He's merely taken a tumble. Miss Felmersham writes that he's badly bruised, but she thinks no bones are broken. He hit his head and was unconscious for a moment or two, so there's a possibility of concussion, which is why she sent for Dambroke. She also sent for Dr. Quigley, she says, but only to be on the safe side."

"Oh, for heaven's sake!" exclaimed Tiffany, sinking into a chair. "That dreadful boy!"

Ben Fincham shifted his feet uneasily, and Catheryn smiled. "She means Master Teddy, Ben. I'm sorry there was such a dust-up, but we are grateful to you for bringing the news so quickly. Go on to the kitchen now and someone will feed you. You must be hungry."

"Aye, miss. Thank you, miss." His ears and neck reddening, he cast her a look of shy gratitude.

"I'll show him, Miss Catheryn," offered the housekeeper, seeming glad of an excuse to leave. Catheryn nodded. As they left, Fowler entered briskly and proceeded to the countess, plumping cushions behind her and dragging up a footstool for her feet. Then she measured out a dose of hartshorn and water and saw to it that her mistress swallowed it, while she bathed her forehead with lavender water.

Tiffany waited only to hand Fowler the salts before she said, "I did mean Teddy, Catheryn, but I might just as easily have meant that nodcock. To let Mama think. . . ."

"I know," Catheryn replied, "but it wasn't his fault. He's only an ignorant country lad. You know he didn't mean to distress you, don't you, Aunt Elizabeth?"

Lady Dambroke pushed herself upright, her spirits revived by Fowler's tender care. "Well, he did upset me," she said. "Coming in here smelling of the stables and saying that great, horrid stallion of Richard's had thrown poor Teddy. Well, naturally, I thought. . . ." She settled herself firmly. "Concussion, Catheryn? That can be quite serious, can it not? Ought I to go to him, do you think?"

XIV

A brief silence fell. Catheryn tried to imagine the countess in a purely maternal role and found the task beyond her mental skill. Even Fowler paused. Tiffany recovered first. "Mama! You can't! The duchess's masquerade!" She jumped up only to fling herself down beseechingly at the countess's feet. "Richard will never let me go if you are at the Park. In fact, he will most likely pack me off, too. It isn't fair! Only because Teddy has got himself into another scrape."

"Very true, my dear," agreed her mother. "But he may need nursing, and Cousin Lucy is a featherhead. Besides," she went on, resigned, "I *am* his mother."

Catheryn intervened before Tiffany, rapidly rising from her affecting pose on the floor, could initiate another scene. "It apears to me, ma'am, that the sensible thing to do is to wait for his lordship. He will decide what is to be done."

"But nobody knows where he is!" protested the countess. "If Mr. Ashley were here, he would know, but we can't ask him if he is at the Park. And why didn't he send a message, I should like to know!" Since no one attempted a reply, she went on. "Richard could be anywhere, and he wouldn't know what to do if he did go to Teddy. He would just send for me, and by then it might be too late. I *must* go! Not," she added vaguely, "that I have the least confidence in my ability as a nurse. I have never had to nurse any of my children. Nanny Craig always did it. But she is dead these two years and more, so she cannot help. I expect I shall manage well enough. Maternal instinct and all, you know."

"But you mustn't, Mama! It would ruin my whole life if I have to leave London now!" cried Tiffany, once more on the verge of tears.

"So help me, Tiffany," grated Catheryn in exasperation, "if you shed one more tear, I shall personally box your ears. Both of them!" The others stared at her in shock, but she lapsed into thought and did not notice. "Do you know what effort, if any, has been made to find his lordship?"

It was Fowler who answered, collecting the hartshorn and lavender water but wisely leaving the smelling salts within reach. "I must apologize, Miss Catheryn. Morris asked me to relay that information to you, but my lady's condition upon my arrival swept it from my mind." There was no trace of regret in her voice. Fowler knew her first duty.

"Perhaps you might recall that message now, Fowler."

"To be sure, miss. It's only that Mr. Paulson has sent runners to his lordship's clubs and to Stanthorpe House. In Mr. Ashley's absence, he can think of nothing further to answer the purpose."

"I suppose not. Thank you, Fowler." She lapsed into a brown study, staring at the mantlepiece, and hardly noticed Fowler's departure. The other two remained silent. Her gaze rested unseeing upon the comical Godin of Paris clock, but for once, the little men failed to make her smile. Her gray eyes focused at last upon the dial. It was nearly six o'clock. Her reverie was interrupted when the drawing room door suddenly opened and Paulson entered, shaken out of his usual calm. "My lady," he announced abruptly, "we have located my lord, but he is unable to return!"

"Nonsense, Paulson!" Tiffany cried before the countess could reply. "Your messenger must have got things mixed or failed to explain the matter properly. There is nothing so important that it would keep him away at a time like this!"

"My lady, Mr. Perceval has been assassinated!"

"Merciful heavens!" The countess reached for her salts.

"The Prime Minister! But how? When?" Catheryn passed a hand across her brow, trying to digest Paulson's news.

"I haven't had details yet, Miss Catheryn," he apologized. "The tragedy occurred less than half an hour ago at the Commons. In the lobby, I believe. The assassin has been caught and his lordship, my lord Stanthorpe, and Captain Varling are at the scene. A messenger had been sent to Stanthorpe House, and they were about to send to us when young Michael arrived."

"Michael!" Tiffany spoke caustically, and the butler replied with as near a grimace as he ever allowed himself.

"Just so, my lady. I have spoken with him. He will not make the error again. But I knew you would wish to know that his lordship is detained."

"Thank you, Paulson," the countess said, dismissing him. She turned to Catheryn, her salts still gripped in her hand but forgotten. "He has a wife and twelve children!"

"I'm sure they will be provided for," Catheryn reassured her. "But have you thought what this means?"

"Well, I hope it does not mean we shall be expected to put on black gloves," Tiffany declared with asperity. "We don't . . . didn't even know the man, after all, and if this means the masquerade will be canceled. . . ."

"Tiffany!" Catheryn exclaimed, truly shocked, but the countess looked thoughtful and then spoke to the point.

"You know, my dear, I don't think it will come to that, for the Regent didn't like Mr. Perceval. And where he does not mourn, no one else will either, except poor Mr. Perceval's family, of course. Twelve children! But it is not as though he were a member of the royal family," she added comfortably.

"Excuse me, Aunt Elizabeth," Catheryn interrupted with a glance at the clock. "I was not thinking of the masquerade but of Teddy. Someone ought to go down at once, and since Dambroke may be detained some hours——"

"Hours! It may be days, Catheryn! If he was actually on the scene, as Paulson seems to think, then he will be called to give evidence. There's no telling how long he will be detained. I shall just have to go myself."

"Mama!"

"Hush, Tiffany!" Catheryn ordered sharply. "Aunt Elizabeth, it will cause much less upheaval if I go. I am a tolerably good nurse and Teddy likes me."

"Oh, Catheryn, the very thing!"

"Absolutely not!" the countess exclaimed flatly at the

same time. "No, hush, Tiffany. I cannot allow it. You have done far too much for us already, my dear. Besides, what would Sir Horace and Lady Caston say to such an odd arrangement? Not to mention Dambroke!"

Catheryn had expected initial resistance and was not at all cast down. "I am of age, ma'am, so my aunt and uncle have nothing at all to do with the matter," she answered calmly, thinking it best not to mention that Sir Horace and his lady had been invited to Clairdon Court and would, no doubt, arrive within the week. "Nor does his lordship, for that matter," she added, "since I would be doing this as a favor to you and to spare you unnecessary exertion. It would be much more awkward for you to leave London. Not only would Tiffany have to go with you, but I could not remain here either. It is much more sensible for me to go." The countess began to look thoughtful, and Catheryn went on firmly, "Bert Ditchling will drive me with Ben Fincham to show the way and Mary for propriety's sake. If I think it necessary, I can always send for you or his lordship. Now, what do you think, Aunt Elizabeth?"

Tiffany held her breath and the countess smiled ruefully. "I don't know what we have done to deserve you, Catheryn. You leave me nothing to say. I doubt that Richard will approve, but you may go to Teddy with my blessing and my gratitude. You must travel post, however," she added more briskly, "else you will be all night on the road. You may take Bert and Mary, of course, but you must not be dependent upon that dreadful Ben."

"Then that's settled. Will you be comfortable now, if Tiffany comes to help me pack? That is," she added with a twinkle, "if she doesn't mind."

"Mind! I guess I don't!" exclaimed that young lady. The countess assured them that she would do nicely, thank you, now that she knew Teddy would be in capable hands. "More capable than if she went herself, I promise you," Tiffany confided with a giggle as they were climbing the stairs a moment later. "Mama always retires to her sofa with hartshorn and salts when one of us is ill." Catheryn smiled vaguely, her mind occupied with a mental list of things to be done. She had no desire to be caught by darkness on the road, and Dambroke

Park was nearly thirty miles away. To be leaving at half past six would be cutting it very fine. Tiffany paused on the step, biting her lip, and Catheryn turned impatiently to see what kept her. "I ought not to have said that about Mama," Tiffany said in a small voice. "It was unkind, just as my behavior in the drawing room was childish. Richard is right. I shall never learn."

"Nonsense," was the crisp reply. "You simply want to learn to think before you act instead of afterward. I was angry before because you were making a bad situation worse. As to what you said just now about your mother, I am afraid I wasn't attending. No, no, I beg you won't repeat it. It is enough that you think I shall disapprove. If you think it, you are very likely right. Now, come along, do!"

As soon as they reached Catheryn's room she rang for Mary and a footman. The latter, an abashed and profoundly apologetic Michael, was sent to give the order for the chaise and to alert the postillions and Ditchling. Tiffany informed Catheryn that Dambroke kept his own teams stabled along the Great North Road. "He usually only changes twice," she said, "at Barnet and Welwyn, but he keeps horses in two or three other places as well, so he can travel more rapidly if need be. I'm not certain where, but the boys will know. Just tell them you wish to make all speed. It usually takes two and a half to three hours. You'll never make it before dark, Catheryn."

She feared Tiffany was right. Although she moved as quickly as possible and spurred the others to similar activity, it was twenty minutes to seven before Catheryn and Mary were tucked into the chaise under fur rugs. Nestled at their feet was a woven basket sent by Jean-Pierre, for even in the flurry of packing, Catheryn had not forgotten to send word requesting something with which to ward off starvation.

Ditchling and young Ben were waiting, and Catheryn's eyes widened when she realized Bert was riding her own Psyche. He caught the look and grinned, begging her pardon for the presumption but pointing out that she might like to have the nag along in case she had time to indulge in her favorite form of exercise. Laughing, she agreed it was an excellent notion, and moments later, the team of matched grays leaped forward.

They rolled along over the cobbled streets to the Holloway Road, then through Islington Spa and across Finchley Common to the Great North Road. Two miles later, they drew into Barnet and pulled up at the small inn where the earl kept his team. Although the kitchen basket had been opened before they reached the Great North Road, there was plenty left, and Catheryn passed bread, meat, and fruit out to Ditchling and the young groom, while they waited for the change. The postillions had supped before leaving. So had Ben, but he confessed to hunger pangs, and Catheryn, recognizing a kindred spirit, was generous.

By the time they completed the second stage, splashes of crimson, apricot, and lavender had spread across the western sky; and by the time they reached Welwyn, it was dusk. Catheryn leaned out long enough to order the post boys to relax the pace a bit as it grew darker. It wouldn't do to lose a wheel or have a horse step in a chuckhole. But no such mishap occurred, and before she realized how much time had passed, Ditchling was leaning down to shout that they were nearly there.

Dambroke Park was located southwest of Stevenage and some two or three miles off the Great North Road. The chaise turned into a private road just after passing a wayside inn, proclaimed by a torchlit sign to be the Running Bull. From the noise issuing from the taproom when they passed, Catheryn deduced it to be a popular gathering place for the local country folk. She could still hear faint echoes of revelry when the chaise slowed for the turn. A short time later, by the light of a rising full moon, she saw the large gates of the Park swing open. One of the postillions called out a cheerful greeting to the lodgekeeper, and she soon caught a glimpse of that worthy himself, plump and smiling, his lantern casting a warm glow across his ruddy cheeks.

It was still some distance to the house. The drive was lined on both sides with trees and thick shrubs; and, had it not been for the moonlight trickling and dancing on the branches and leaves, it would have seemed almost as though they traveled through a tunnel. The drive widened, and the trees broke away in a line that would eventually encircle the house and gardens. The house itself was now visible, and it was evident that they were expected. Light blazed from nearly every window of the massive central block and spilled out the front door. Catheryn just had time to take in the immense size of the place before the chaise swung between two stone lions on pedestals and onto a circular drive. Moments later, it rolled to a stop. She heard Mary let out a long breath.

"My, miss, but the place is huge!"

"Have you not been here before, Mary?" They had spoken occasionally on the journey, but the dust from the road and the constant noise of the horses and chaise made lengthy conversation difficult, and the subject had not arisen.

"No, miss," Mary replied, peering out with wonder in her eyes. "I'm a Londoner, I am." The door to the chaise was jerked open, and Catheryn found herself looking into the surprised face of a strange footman. She allowed him to help her alight and, with Mary right behind her, proceeded up the broad steps and into the great hall.

Twin fireplaces blazed merrily at either end, and chandeliers glowed with hundreds of little flames. Catheryn paid little heed to the splendor of the huge room, however, as she introduced herself to Carlson, the underbutler, and asked to see Miss Felmersham or, if she had retired, Mr. Ashley. She rather hoped it would be Mr. Ashley, since both the footman and Carlson had looked at her rather oddly. There was the unquestionable crest on the chaise door, however, as well as the familiar post boys, and now she seemed to have mentioned magic names. Carlson smiled, seeming at once more approachable.

"Miss Lucy was expecting his lordship, Miss Westering. She keeps early hours but left orders to be called when my lord arrived. I sent to advise her when we heard the chaise."

Catheryn could restrain herself no longer. "How is Master Teddy, Carlson?"

"He's fair knocked up, miss, but not in danger. Miss Lucy will tell you. Mr. Ashley is with him now. He won't have heard the chaise, but I can send for him if you like."

A moment before she would have accepted the offer with gratitude, but Carlson's friendliness restored her courage. "No, thank you," she replied. "I shall want to go up to him myself after I've spoken to Miss Felmersham. But perhaps someone could show Mary where I am to sleep, so that she can get settled." Carlson immediately began to give instructions to the young footman but broke off when a door to the left of the entry was flung open. An elderly woman emerged, fastening a gray wool dressing gown that had seen better days.

"Richard!" she exclaimed without looking up. "So you are here at last, my lord. I expect I ought to beg your pardon for barging through your study, but it *is* the quickest way, you know. Dear me!" She stopped short and adjusted her spectacles with a rather bewildered look on her face. "Who are you and where is Dambroke?"

Miss Felmersham wore her serviceable dressing gown over a high-necked nightdress and quite obviously had been roused from her sleep. Her nightcap was not exactly askew, but strands of gray hair had escaped its confines, and her pale blue eyes were bleary behind the wire-rimmed spectacles. She was not much taller than Catheryn and weighed a great deal less, so it was more than a little disconcerting when she thrust her head forward to peer at her, rather, thought Catheryn, like some strange bird ready to peck out the eyes of an intruder to her nest. Hastily introducing herself, Catheryn extracted a note written by the countess from her reticule and handed it to her.

"Indeed," said Miss Felmersham testily, unfolding the note, "but where is Dambroke?" Catheryn explained and, while the old lady grunted and began to scan the note, reviewed what she had heard about her. Miss Lucy Felmersham had more than sixty years in her dish and had supposedly decided long since that she had no need to please anyone but herself. Criticized by an elder brother for not making a push to nab a husband who would support her in his place, she had applied to her cousin, Elizabeth, recently married to the sixth Earl of Dambroke. Elizabeth had welcomed her as companion and friend. In the course of years and differing interests, the two drifted apart but, by that time, Miss Felmersham was so much a fixture at the Park that it occurred to no one to wonder why she did not leave. She pursued her own interests and made herself useful by managing things when the family was in town. She folded the note and pushed her spectacles higher on her nose.

"So, you've come to tend the boy. Well, you're welcome, of course, though I can't imagine why Dambroke should waste his time over a man known only for wars and riots when his own kin have need of him. However, that's neither here nor there. May as well go on up, I expect." Without waiting for a response, she turned away, clearly expecting Catheryn to follow. "Young Ashley will be glad to see you, no doubt. Insisted on sitting with Edward himself, though there's no need for it, I'm thinking. Still, Peter always was a stubborn lad, from the cradle."

They had passed into an octagonal staircase hall, and half of Catheryn's attention digressed to the magnificent stone staircase and intricately carved oak paneling. Dambroke family portraits followed the graceful curve of the stair as it swooped up and around six sides of the hall to a landing from which three doors opened. Miss Felmersham, silent now, charged through the nearest and turned left with near military precision, then turned again and proceeded up a carpeted service stair. Catheryn puffed after her. "Then Teddy is not seriously injured?"

"Early days yet, Dr. Quigley tells us." Her words were crisp, and she had a habit of clipping them as though to be done with each one as quickly as possible. "Boy's like a blasted cat though. Always lands on his feet. Figuratively, of course, but I do not think he landed on his head. Quigley fears concussion. More of an old woman than I am! Naught ails that lad but a cracked rib or two and a passel of bruises. Deserves them, too, to my way of thinking," she added bluntly, pushing open the schoolroom door without ceremony.

XV.

Peter Ashley scrambled to his feet, letting the book he had been reading slip to the floor. "How you startled me!" he exclaimed. "This room is nearly soundproof. Welcome, Miss Westering. You can't know how grateful I am to see you."

Catheryn smiled as he bent to retrieve his book, but she spoke anxiously. "How is Teddy, Mr. Ashley? Miss Felmersham insists it is not so bad as we'd feared."

"As to that, ma'am, and not knowing what you feared——"

"That he was dead, like as not," interjected Miss Felmersham tartly.

Catheryn blushed. "There was a slight misunderstanding at first," she admitted, "but we truly didn't know what to think."

"I see. Well, just let me shut this door a bit. Quigley dosed him with laudanum. Didn't like to with possible concussion, but he said the pain would keep the boy awake otherwise, and he wanted him to sleep." He glanced into the darkened night nursery before pulling the door to and motioning them to seats in front of the fire. Miss Felmersham sighed.

"Might as well ring for tea," she said. "Brevity is not one of your virtues." She gave the bell a tug. Ashley was just explaining how he had returned with his cousin from Baldock only that afternoon and had received word at his father's house via the servants' grapevine of Teddy's accident, when the young footman entered with the tea tray. It occurred to Catheryn that Carlson must have given the order even before Miss Felmersham rang, in order for the tea to have arrived so quickly.

She examined the contents of the tray with approval. A chubby teapot nestled between a large plate of buttered toast and a basket of apple muffins. Thick mugs and small crocks of creamy butter and jam rattled against cutlery as the tray was deposited. Catheryn helped herself to a muffin and passed the plate to Ashley while Miss Felmersham poured out the tea.

"Thank you, John," Ashley said to the departing footman. Then he grinned at Catheryn. "I daresay I've not had tea by a schoolroom fire since I left my old school."

"Well, I never have," stated Miss Westering between bites of buttered muffin, "never having had a schoolroom."

"Get on with your tale, Peter," ordered Miss Felmersham, "else we'll be here all night. Did they find young Nat?"

"No, Miss Lucy. At least, if they did, I've heard nothing about it. Nat Tripler is Teddy's friend," he explained to Catheryn, adding with a grin, "one of the sort I mentioned before. Seems he was here when Teddy was thrown. I heard about it from young Hobbs. You met his father in London." Catheryn nodded. "Well, he saw the accident but couldn't tell from where he stood whether Teddy landed on his head or not. He thought young Nat might know. Nat's father, Ben Tripler, owns the Running Bull, that inn you passed on the road, and John is sweet on Nat's sister, Hilda, so he knows the family fairly well. I sent him to see if Nat could tell us anything, but they hadn't seen hide nor hair of the boy. Seems he's supposed to be off helping his Uncle Harry, one of Dambroke's tenants, with some job or other." Catheryn's head was beginning to spin with all the unfamiliar names, but she didn't want to interrupt. Ashley went on. "Ben said he'd send Nat over if he could add to what we know. I think Miss Lucy's right, though, and Teddy landed on his shoulder. It's very badly bruised." He grinned at the old lady. "Miss Lucy is not happy with the situation."

"Certainly not," she asserted. "Dambroke ought to have known what would happen when he sent that dratted boy down here to cut up all my peace!"

Catheryn restrained a chuckle and tried to sound sympathetic, for she found Miss Felmersham rather formidable and had no wish to offend her. "But his lordship could not possibly have anticipated that Teddy would try to ride Blaze," she protested mildly. "I know he gave strict orders when he sent the horse down here that no one was to ride him." Miss Felmersham responded with a sound very like a snort, and Ashley carefully avoided meeting Catheryn's eye.

"Don't I know it, ma'am?" He shrugged expressively, his voice tinged with amusement. "You should have heard poor young Hobbs! I don't know whether he's more afraid of facing his father or the earl! He thinks Nat dared Teddy, but isn't sure the whole idea wasn't Teddy's from the outset. Hobbs told one of the undergrooms to put a lead on Blaze so they could turn him out to graze. The boy said later that Teddy offered to do it for him. The upshot is that Teddy bridled him, mounted him, and before Hobbs or anyone knew what he was about, bolted out of the stable toward the paddock. He's a bruising rider and might have been all right but for Straley's big yellow mongrel. The mutt ripped after them, barking like mad, and spooked Blaze. With a saddle he might have stayed put, but when the horse wheeled on the dog, horse and boy parted company." Ashley grimaced. "I'm glad I'm telling you and not his lordship. When I anticipated this conversation I pictured it being a shade more uncomfortable than it is. I expect I've still got that bit to look forward to in London, however."

Catheryn appreciated the fact that he had not questioned her arrival in place of either Dambroke or the countess but had just accepted her and been grateful. She explained the earl's absence, and Ashley expressed great shock over Perceval's assassination, much more than Miss Felmersham had shown. Catheryn knew he wanted to pursue politics as an eventual career, though she thought personally that, if Dambroke could spare him, Peter would be a greater success as a diplomat. He had that rare knack for making each person within his sphere of influence feel special, and she knew the countess's ball would never have been such a success had he not constantly served as a buffer between her ladyship's capricious whims and the servants' outraged sensibilities. He was frowning now.

"I must return as quickly as possible. His lordship no doubt has much for me to do. I had hoped to be here to introduce Mark to you tomorrow, but now...."

"You cannot leave before morning, Peter," Miss Felmersham declared, "but you will want to be away at first light, I daresay, so I suggest we go to bed at once." She stood up, brushed crumbs from her dressing gown, and pushed a loose strand of hair under her cap. Catheryn volunteered to sit with Teddy, but the old lady scoffed at the idea and Ashley insisted it was unnecessary. A bed had been made up for him in the old nanny's room and, with the doors open, he would be certain to hear the boy if he called out in the night.

Catheryn let herself be persuaded but tiptoed into the nursery before allowing Miss Felmersham to show her to her own chamber. Holding a candle to light her way and with Ashley close behind her, she looked down at the sleeping boy. He was very still and pale, his breathing harsh. Ashley whispered that, according to Quigley, these symptoms were but normal effects of the laudanum, and with that explanation she had to be satisfied.

She awoke early the following morning. Not bothering to ring for Mary, she dressed quickly in a simple round gown and found her way to the schoolroom. It gave view to the east, where the glow of sunrise outlined dark trees. She was not surprised to hear voices in the nursery and entered to find Ashley sitting on the edge of Teddy's cot. The boy seemed restless.

"Relax, Teddy. You are quite safe. It is only the medicine making you feel queer." His voice was gentle, soothing. Something made him turn and he saw Catheryn. "I'm glad you came. Look, Teddy. Look who's here."

The boy's feverish eyes rested upon her and she thought he relaxed a little, but his voice was weak. "You came." He closed his eyes. Ashley's brows knit.

"He's been drifting in and out this past hour and more. I don't like it. Seems feverish, too, and complains of the headache. What do you think?"

Catheryn hoped her smile was reassuring, though she felt anything but confident. "It's most likely the drug, as you said yourself, sir. My grandfather commonly took laudanum in the last years to help him sleep and was a constant victim of morning headaches. Perhaps you might ring for some strong tea with plenty of milk and sugar. If it is only the drug, it will help, and if he has concussion it won't harm him."

He did not question her judgment but went immediately to pull the bell in the schoolroom. Catheryn took his place on the cot. Laying a cool hand on Teddy's forehead, she did not think him warm enough to have a fever. But then, she reminded herself, she had no idea whether fever accompanied concussion or not.

Teddy opened his eyes. "Where is Richard, Cathy?"

"In London, dear. He has been detained."

"He will be very angry." He sighed deeply.

"You deserve that he should be, do you not?" But she smiled gently. "Whatever possessed you to do such a foolish thing?"

"Nat. He's the best of good fellows. Full of ginger. Said I'd fall off, that I was pigeon-hearted. Had to try then." He moved uncomfortably. "Didn't know it would hurt so much."

"Teddy, did you land on your head when you fell?"

He frowned. "I dunno. Remember riding. Don't remember falling, only waking on the ground. Told 'em yesterday." He sounded impatient.

"They didn't tell me." She smoothed the tousled hair.

"Did they tell you Blaze is all right? Wasn't hurt a bit. Mr. Ashley said he bolted but Hobbs caught him easily enough. Did they tell you?"

"I didn't think to ask, Teddy, but I'm sure Dambroke will be glad the stupid animal is unharmed."

Her comment drew a weak grin, which had been its purpose. "He won't 'preciate you calling Blaze stupid, you know. But you didn't say when he's coming," he added anxiously.

"I don't know, Teddy." She started to explain about the Prime Minister but soon realized he wasn't listening, that he had drifted off again. She sat quietly for a moment, watching him, noting that his breathing was steady and lacked the harshness of the previous night. Relieved, she went to find Mr. Ashley. He was standing by the schoolroom window.

"The tea will be here soon," he said, "and I've sent for Quigley as well. I cannot like this. Even if it is only the drug, I'll feel better if I hear it from him, since I must report to his lordship."

"Of course. I shall also be interested in his opinion, though Teddy spoke to me just now and seemed quite lucid. He's anxious about what Dambroke will say about all this."

"Then he is in good company, is he not?" Ashley's expression seemed almost grim, but a near twinkle lurked in his eye. She looked at him suspiciously, but there was no opportunity to question his meaning, since Teddy's tea arrived at that moment.

The boy awoke when they carried it in to him, and it revived him a bit. He still seemed drowsy but managed to stay awake until the doctor arrived. After introducing her to the grizzled old gentleman, Ashley suggested she might go along to the breakfast parlor, since Teddy would not appreciate her presence during the examination. She agreed to go only when he promised to report the doctor's findings as soon as possible.

Catheryn went downstairs to the first floor and a chambermaid directed her to a room filled with sunshine. The fact that the walls of the breakfast parlor were bright yellow with crisp white woodwork and a white marble mantle over the fireplace only added to the effect. It was a corner room facing south and east, and it was empty. She stepped to the window and found herself overlooking a courtyard flanked on two sides by double-story wings, which she later discovered to be the chapel wing on the north and a residential wing on the south. Mr. Ashley's apartments were there, and Miss Felmersham's were above his and connected to the breakfast parlor by means of a passageway. Beyond the courtyard was the low roofline of the stables and carriage house, then the succession houses, sloping well-scythed lawns, and the deer park.

Catheryn loved watching the day wake up in the country, for the morning had an exhilarating freshness about it. Much of this flavor was lost in the bustle and noise of the city, particularly in London, which woke up so long before dawn, with the calls of street vendors and the rattle of milk wagons and other vehicles. She let out a long breath, drinking in the landscape. The warm courtyard evidently produced an early spring, and a circular flower bed in the center boasted red roses surrounded by circles of daisies, cornflowers, yellow pansies, and alyssum.

"Have you rung for breakfast, Miss Westering?"

Catheryn nearly jumped out of her skin. She whirled around to discover Miss Felmersham standing only a few feet to her right at the passage door, her head cocked a little to one side. If Catheryn had thought her odd the previous evening, there was certainly nothing in her matutinal appearance to alter that opinion though, admittedly, her hair was tidier. It had been brushed severely back from her face and forced at the nape of her neck into a tight little gray bun from which not one wisp had as yet dared to escape. But her costume was little short of sartorial disaster.

From the down-at-heels boots to her tiny little waist, she was dressed for riding. Both boots and dun-colored skirt had seen better days, but they were as nothing compared to the disreputable thing that served as her upper garment. It was actually one of Dambroke's shooting jackets, long since outgrown, which she had appropriated to her own use. One of the many bulging pockets was ripped, and several others showed distinct signs of having been mended, hastily and haphazardly, with varicolored threads. But the most outrageous detail, in Catheryn's opinion, was the old leather belt fastened tightly around her middle over jacket and all. Extra holes had been punched in order to make the belt fit, but no one had bothered to adjust the length, and the excess leather simply dangled where it would. The whole incredible outfit was topped off by a dashing and expertly knitted red-and-white-patterned scarf knotted around her neck with its ends stuffed any which way into the front of the jacket.

Catheryn realized she was staring rudely while Miss Felmersham waited for an answer to her question. She blushed. "I beg your pardon! I don't know where my wits have wandered, ma'am. I was diverted by the view." The warmth in her cheeks increased when she realized exactly what she had said.

But Miss Felmersham did not seem the least disturbed. She strode purposefully toward the bell. "In effect, my dear Miss Westering, you have not rung."

"No, ma'am." Catheryn had never had a governess,

but she suddenly had the strangest feeling that if she had had one, that lady might have been very like Miss Felmersham, except for her manner of dress, of course.

"No matter. Save a trip for someone. What about Ashley?"

"He will be along momentarily, I believe," Catheryn replied, dragging her eyes away from her hostess with difficulty. "He is with Teddy and Dr. Quigley."

"Good." Miss Felmersham stepped briskly to the table and whisked out a chair. "Sit down, child, sit down! Doesn't matter where. But do, for God's sake, have a good hard look at me and be done with it! I dress for my own convenience and no one else's. You'll get used to it."

Flushing to the roots of her hair, Catheryn begged her pardon but was ruthlessly told to sit down and put a sock in it, unless she had something of worth to impart. Meekly, she obeyed and sat staring at the polished surface of the table wishing she could think of something to say and thinking that even Dambroke at his fiercest would be more easily dealt with than this difficult old lady. Silence reigned for several seconds. Finally, she looked up to find Miss Felmersham, elbows on the table, staring at her with amusement. Her natural courage bolstered by that look, Catheryn asserted with only a hint of defensiveness that it was rather an odd costume.

"I daresay." Miss Felmersham let the propping hand fall to the table and directed a more piercing stare at her guest. "I expect I was rude to you last night. Never at my best when I'm wakened. Often rude anyway," she added with wry candor and a slight shrug. "However, I think I might like you, Miss Westering. Believe you've got spunk. I shall call you Catheryn, and you'd best call me Miss Lucy like the rest of them. What's going to be done about that dratted boy?"

Completely disconcerted, Catheryn was grateful for the interruption of John the footman and two maids with their breakfast, or the first part of it at any rate. She discovered that Miss Lucy took only hot chocolate, toast, and fruit as a morning repast. She disdained early chocolate served in her bedchamber, saying she disliked crumbs in her bed and had a nagging fear that Belinda, her cat, would overset the tray one day. As for having it served upon a table in her room rather than in bed, why, if she were to arise from the bed at all, she was certainly capable of tottering so far as the breakfast parlor—quite the closest room in the main house to her own—to be served in a proper Christian style. As a result of her well-known tastes, the servants had not arrived empty-handed but produced a basket of fresh fruits from the succession houses, a large silver pot of chocolate, and a covered basket of fresh buttered toast. John ascertained that Miss Westering preferred an expanded menu, and she agreed enthusiastically to his smiling suggestion of a cheese omelet prepared in the French style, to be accompanied by thin slices of Yorkshire ham. In the meantime, she helped herself to toast, jam, and chocolate.

Mr. Ashley arrived as the servants were leaving, paused long enough to confer briefly with the footman, and then took his place at the table. He smiled. "Good morning, Miss Lucy." She bent her head in response and he continued, "You will both be pleased to know that Quigley thinks Teddy is going to be fine. He looked him over carefully and believes he is only shaking off the effects of the drug, just as you thought, Miss Westering."

"Oh, I am glad!" Her relief checked when he frowned. "There's more, Mr. Ashley?"

"Well, he thinks the boy does have a mild concussion and doesn't want to dose him any more if it can be avoided, since the stuff seems to affect him so severely. Said he ought to have shaken off the small amount he gave him last night well before dawn. At any rate, Teddy's going to be in a good deal of pain and will likely have trouble sleeping. I'm afraid it will mean a lot of nursing, if only to make certain that he stays put and doesn't die of boredom. Your Mary is with him now. She came looking for you and offered to stay. And Mark will be here later this morning. I know he will help keep the boy entertained, though Teddy won't be wanting lessons for a while yet. Mark's a great one for reading aloud and for making up hair-raising tales as well."

"I'm certain he will be very helpful, and I know I can depend upon Mary. We'll do nicely, sir."

"Well, there's servants aplenty," declared Miss Lucy, "which is a blessing, since the Lord knows I'm no nurse-maid." She pushed back her chair. "I've things to do, so if you'll excuse me. . . ." She nodded in her curt way and left the room.

Catheryn stared after the old lady, her temper aroused by the suggestion that Teddy should be tended by servants. Ashley, watching closely, seemed to read her mind. "Miss Lucy is a bit disconcerting at first," he said quietly, "but she is only being honest when she says she is no nursemaid. She hasn't the patience for it. She'll leave Teddy to you, Miss Westering, and I know you will not be distressed by her blunt manner. She dotes on his lordship, but no one would know it from the way she speaks to him."

Since he seemed to expect it, she returned a smile, but her heart wasn't in it. Embarrassed that he had read her thoughts so accurately, she still didn't quite know what to think about Miss Lucy, and she didn't particularly want to think about Dambroke at all. The servants arrived with breakfast, and their conversation turned to Ashley's forthcoming journey. The chaise had been ordered for half past nine.

XVI

After breakfast, Catheryn wished Ashley a safe and speedy journey and returned to the schoolroom feeling a little forlorn. At least while Ashley remained she knew she had an ally. Once he had gone she couldn't be sure. She dismissed Mary and turned her attention to the boy. He was wan and pettish, his eyes still seemed too bright, and he complained of headache, but he seemed to have his senses about him. Mary had ordered toast and an egg for him, but both were untouched. There was also the teapot, still warm under its thick cozy. Catheryn poured out a second cup, adding plenty of cream and sugar, then fluffed up his pillows and helped him to a more comfortable position. He grumbled.

"Don't fret, Teddy." She spoke briskly. "You're bound to be uncomfortable for a while, but it's no use moaning and groaning about it. Drink your tea like a good boy."

He hitched himself up obediently but muttered in fractious tones, "Just like a flogging."

"I beg your pardon?"

"What they say. 'Six of the best,' he droned, imitating a master, " 'to be taken as delivered. No moaning and groaning, young Dambroke. You know the drill.' " He grimaced. "Same thing."

"Oh." She thought for a moment, watching him scowl over his tea. "Perhaps it *is* a kind of punishment, Teddy, for disobeying Dambroke." Grimacing again, he shrugged, but he had forgotten his bruises. His face clouded over with pain.

"What did he say before you left? About me, I mean." She explained again about the assassination and her own decision to come to him. Clearly, the boy's only interest in Perceval was a certain gratitude that the tragedy had delayed Dambroke, but his eyes widened when she told him about convincing the countess to let her come. "Do you mean to say that Richard didn't even know you were leaving London?"

"No, dear, how could he when he was still at the Commons? He will understand that it was the sensible thing to do. For your mama to come would have meant disrupting the entire household."

"That's true enough," he agreed, "and I'll wager Tiffany kicked up a dust, too. But Richard won't care about 'sensible,' Cathy." He gazed at her shrewdly over his teacup. "I believe you've already thought of that. He don't care to have his authority set aside."

"Nonsense, Teddy." She took the cup and motioned for him to eat his egg. "What could he possibly find to say?" Her protest sounded weak even to her own ears, and the boy actually grinned, looking normal for the moment.

"I think he will find plenty to say to us both, and I doubt much of it will be very comfortable to hear."

"Well, I think he will be too worried at first to say much," Catheryn said, "and, hopefully, by the time he realizes there is nothing further to worry about, he will have forgotten to be angry. He may still have something to say to you about your little ride, but only because he cares about your safety and not till you are recovered from your injuries."

The boy looked doubtful but left her to her own reflections while he finished his egg and toast. She remembered Ashley's comment about Teddy being in good company. She had hoped he referred to himself but knew now that he had not. He, too, understood the earl's nature and knew Dambroke would oppose any decision he had had no part in making. She sighed. It would do no good to worry about it now. When Teddy finished, she took the tray and the teapot into the schoolroom and rang for someone to take them away. While waiting, she glanced over the books on the shelf. They were not precisely dusty but looked as though they ought to be. Cheek by jowl with an outdated geography was an ancient book of rules for proper conduct. After rejecting its fusty neighbors, she plucked the latter from the shelf, thinking it might prove amusing, and carried it in to Teddy. They were chuckling over the author's advice to children when Miss Lucy entered, accompanied by a sturdy young gentleman.

"Miss Westering, this is Mr. MacClaren, the new tutor."

"MacClaren!" She realized immediately what must have happened and laughed, letting him shake her hand. "How silly of me! Mr. Ashley has spoken of you only as Mark, and I just assumed you would be Mark Ashley. How do you do!"

MacClaren grinned. "Cousins on the distaff side, Miss Westering. Is this my charge?" Teddy had been eyeing him warily and Catheryn quickly made the introductions. Mark MacClaren was fair with crisp curls and broad shoulders. He was not as tall as his slim cousin and, despite his recent illness, had more the look of sportsman than scholar. Even his well-made coat fit loosely, as though his muscular body needed room to breathe. His eyes twinkled merrily when he realized Teddy was sizing him up. He hefted the load of books under his arm and grinned when the boy blinked. "I am supposed to be a tutor," he mocked. "Did you expect me to arrive with a trained monkey on a string?"

"Wouldn't half mind it if you did, sir." He showed relief to discover that, though MacClaren had brought along Magnall's *Questions*, Lindley Murray's *English Grammar*, and the first volume of Oliver Goldsmith's *History of England*—all unhappily familiar to the boy—he also had a copy of Defoe's *Robinson Crusoe*. Teddy's eyes lit up, and Catheryn and Miss Lucy left him confiding to MacClaren that he had never read the famous tale.

"That relationship looks promising."

"Yes, indeed," Catheryn agreed. "Mr. Ashley's cousin seems to be perfect for Teddy."

"I don't know about perfect," declared Miss Lucy. "Seems a bit easy-going. That lad's a handful and no mistake. Ought to have a birch rod along with all those books, if you ask me."

Catheryn held her peace and was delighted when Miss Lucy offered to show her over the house. They had reached the ground floor and stood in the octagonal stair hall. Miss Lucy pushed open one of a set of double doors set under the curve of the great stone stair and preceded Catheryn into a magnificent drawing room. The north wall was fully glazed with French doors leading onto a lovely, symmetrical terrace. Broad, curved steps swept down to the gardens, and Catheryn had a clear view beyond to the lake and the Home Wood. The view was incredible.

From the drawing room Miss Lucy turned west and guided her through a saloon to the long gallery, pausing to view a charming inner courtyard with a fountain in the center. Catheryn soon came to realize that the house was symmetrical, a huge four-story central block with wings attached by stairway passages at each corner. East and west courtyards balanced each other, as did the pedimented portico and colonnade of the south entrance balance the magnificent terrace to the north. She wondered aloud that the lovely inner court had no mate on the east side.

Miss Lucy nodded. "I'll show you." They passed through the great hall and into the room from which the old lady had made her entrance the night before. "Dambroke's study," she noted briefly, turning briskly to the left into a narrow alcove. At the end was a door somewhat smaller than the others in the house, so Catheryn was totally unprepared for what lay on the other side. Dambroke's library was large enough to be a ballroom; but, unlike the other rooms she had seen, it was cavernous and gloomy, for the only light came from clerestory windows above the bookshelves lining its walls. Surrounded as it was by other rooms—the study, East Hall, dining room, and another saloon—the library had no direct egress to the outside. One could enter through the alcove door from the study or through the larger double doors from the East Hall. Miss Lucy pointed out that, though it was a bit dim by day, it was lovely in the evenings with a cheerful fire, and added that it was Dambroke's favorite room.

When they parted company after the tour, Catheryn still didn't know what to make of the old lady, for she seemed to maintain a polite distance between them. As the days settled into a pattern, Catheryn saw her only at meals, for Miss Lucy spent the mornings busy with her own affairs, avoided the schoolroom, and retired early in the evenings. Thanks to MacClaren, Catheryn spent her own mornings riding Psyche or walking in the gardens;

but, once he had gone for the day, she found herself racking her brain for ways to keep Teddy amused. She sent word to the countess of the boy's improvement and, Friday morning, she received a letter from Tiffany.

It was mostly town gossip. She mentioned the assassination briefly, with no indication that it had cast a cloud over her activities, except that Dambroke, she added, was going about like a bear with a sore head. Catheryn read more carefully. Evidently, the earl had said very little after a conversation with his mother, from which that lady seemed, if Catheryn read the crossed and recrossed lines correctly, to have emerged in tears. There was room for doubt, however, since he had also given his sister permission to have a new gown made for the forthcoming masque. Tiffany neglected to mention when or even if he intended to visit the Park. Catheryn set the letter aside with a sigh of frustration. Teddy was beginning to rebel against staying in bed, and she knew that he was also anxious to know when Dambroke was coming.

She was engaged in a dispute with her young charge that very afternoon and had just agreed to send for Dr. Quigley so Teddy could ask for himself when he might be let out of bed, when John brought the message. "Miss Catheryn, his lordship would like to speak with you in the study, if you please."

For a moment, Catheryn and Teddy looked at each other in dismay; then Teddy spoke with studied nonchalance. "I don't s'pose you need get Quigley here today, Cathy. I'd just as lief stay in bed till tomorrow."

She smiled her understanding. "You may tell his lordship that I shall be down as soon as I have changed my gown, John."

The young footman hesitated. "Begging your pardon, miss, but he said 'at once.' He's in a bit of a temper, Miss Catheryn."

She glanced at Teddy, but the boy was relaxed, clearly trusting her to deal with Dambroke, for the moment at least. Very well, she thought, then she would need her wits about her, and she could not face him in a plain round gown with her hair very likely mussed. She spoke firmly. "You tell him I shall be down directly,

John." Reluctantly, he departed as Teddy shot her an impudent wink and wished her luck.

Catheryn hurried to her room and rang for Mary, repressing an excitement that had nothing to do with the earl's probable temper. Without waiting, she stripped off her dress, splashed cold water on her face, and was halfway into a lovely gown of pale blue mull muslin trimmed with ribbons of shaded silk by the time her maid arrived. Mary quickly brushed her hair into a simple tumble of curls and, in a very short time indeed, Miss Westering descended to the study. John waited unhappily by the door. She smiled at him, took a deep breath, and nodded for him to admit her.

Dambroke stood behind the desk, his expression uncompromising. Catheryn eyed him warily as she approached. By the look of things, his lordship meant to be difficult. "Good afternoon, my lord," she said calmly, holding out a friendly hand. Dambroke ignored it and gestured to a nearby chair.

"Sit down, Miss Westering. I sent for you twenty minutes ago."

Miss Westering! Reduced to the ranks indeed, Catheryn thought to herself. He certainly looked implacable, but not frighteningly so this time. "I prefer to stand, sir."

"No doubt, but I should prefer to sit and cannot do so if you do not. Be seated, if you please."

"Very well, my lord." She settled herself with a graceful swirl of skirts and watched as he sat back in his chair on the other side of the desk.

"And now, my girl, perhaps you would care to explain your outrageous journey to me."

Much better. "Outrageous, my lord?"

"Quite outrageous," he growled. "There was no need for you to go haring off in such a way."

"Perhaps you would have preferred that your mother make the journey, my lord."

"There was no need for anyone to do so, and I——"

"I disagree, my lord, and you were unavailable."

"Don't interrupt, and stop peppering every sentence with my damned title!"

"Yes, my lord." He glared at her.

"I am waiting for an explanation, Catheryn."

"If you truly require one, my lord, I came as a favor to your mother. And I cannot help calling you so," she added when he bristled, "if you will continue to look so stuffy."

"Stuffy! Look here, my girl, I have had a difficult week and am in no mood for impertinence. You had no business to dash down here as you did without so much as a by your leave. It is not your affair to nurse that young hellion, assuming that he needs nursing at all."

"He does, my lord," she replied, keeping her own temper now with difficulty. "And whose affair is it, if not mine?"

"That is obvious. I am his guardian."

"Well, you were not there." She dared a small chuckle. "And when did you last nurse a sick child, my lord?"

"Lucy Felmersham can nurse him."

"Your mother said Miss Lucy is a featherhead, and Mr. Ashley said she lacks the patience for nursing."

"Well, you should not say such things," he reproved, "and as for Ashley, I've already told him what I think of his part in this. Were you aware that he was up nearly the whole of Monday night with the boy?"

"No, I wasn't, but if you scolded him, you should not have done so. He was only worried about Teddy."

"Would you protect everyone from my wrath, Catheryn?" he asked softly. "You may put your mind at rest. I didn't scold him. I merely pointed out that he is no use to me in a state of exhaustion, told him he was an addlebrained idiot to put himself to so much trouble, and packed him off to bed."

"And that was not scolding!"

"Certainly not. Ashley knows the difference, believe me. He is my secretary, you know, and is useless in that capacity if he wears himself out staying up all night, whatever the reason. Particularly when he knows very well that he has never been able to sleep while traveling! If he was worried about Edward, it was his duty to call one of the servants to sit up with him. But I do not wish to discuss Ashley," he went on when she moved to protest. "I am still dissatisfied. I should certainly have been consulted before you took it into your head to dash down here. And what makes you such an expert, for that matter? I daresay you've never nursed a sick child before either."

"No, I haven't, my lord. I did nurse a cantankerous old man, however, for quite some time before he d-died, and I am perfectly capable of nursing a small b-boy, whom no one else seems to c-care a whit for. He is better now and at least he knows that someone l-loves him. And . . . and, even had you been there, you could not have stopped me!" It was not until she was forced to choke back a sob that Catheryn realized she was crying and, to her astonishment, well on the way to hysteria. She could hear the echo of her words in her mind and was overwhelmed. It had been a trying week, but she had not realized the depth of her feelings until his taunt unleashed them.

He was on his feet, but his words came like a bucket of cold water. "That will do, miss! I find this sort of emotional drivel revolting. Spare me your tears, if you please."

Catheryn's head came up and she stared at him in shock. "Emotional drivel!" Her tears ceased, stanched by fury. "How dare you, sir! You descend upon us with your petty anger—yes, petty, my lord!—and expect us to bow before it. Well, I shall not!" She stood, her breasts heaving, and turned away from him. Her tone was scathing. "You are angry, my lord Dambroke, because we dared to make a decision without your precious advice and consent, because you think your damned authority had been flouted again. You don't care for your mother's anxiety. You don't care about any of us at all—just yourself! You are far and away the most self-centered, arrogant, contemptible——"

"Enough, Catheryn!" he snapped. His face was drained of color. "I made that stupid statement about 'emotional drivel' simply to check your hysterics. This conversation will never be finished if you go to pieces. As for the rest, you are right about only one thing. I was angry that you failed to consult me before you left. You knew where I was and could easily have sent a messenger, and I would certainly have advised restraint. Cousin Lucy's letter was hardly so agitating as to demand instant action. By God, do you realize that your aunt and uncle are in town and that they think I *sent* you down here!"

"Sent me!"

"Yes, sent you. Your aunt actually insinuated that it was meant to be a payment for my generosity or some such garbage, and your uncle went to great pains to inform me that he has arranged for you to draw upon your own funds."

"Excellent," she said flatly. "I'm sorry if Aunt Agatha injured your sensibilities, sir, but I am grateful for my uncle's news. As soon as I get back to town I shall begin arrangements for setting up my own household as I had originally intended. I shall then be a trouble to you no longer!" She moved purposefully toward the door.

"No! Catheryn, wait!" He stepped toward her.

"This conversation is finished, my lord." She left the room and fled to her own, half expecting him to follow but not really surprised when he didn't. Her thoughts and emotions were in a dizzying whirl. She had expected him to be displeased, but his anger seemed out of proportion to the situation. And her own temper amazed her. She had been prepared, she thought, to face his displeasure, so why had she flared up so easily? And why was her heart pounding? And why did the idea of setting up her own household seem so utterly depressing? She flung herself down on the bed, emotionally exhausted, and cried herself to sleep.

When she awoke she visited briefly with Teddy before dinner and discovered that Dambroke had been to see him and had also spoken with the doctor. Teddy expressed the thought that his brother had seemed a bit subdued. They had talked about Teddy's ride and Dambroke had promised dire consequences should he ever attempt so crackbrained a trick again, but he had not been nearly so angry as the boy had expected.

At dinner, Catheryn said very little and avoided the earl's eye, but to her astonishment Miss Lucy became nearly affable. She inquired into the details of the assassination and discovered that Dambroke, Varling, and Lord Stanthorpe had walked into the lobby of the Commons just after the fatal shot had been fired. The assassin, a man named Bellingham, had given himself up at the scene, and it had been necessary for the three gentlemen to remain in town to give evidence at his trial. Dambroke didn't know what the outcome had been, since he had left the courtroom directly after speaking his piece.

After dinner, the earl requested that his port be served in the library. He had brought Miss Lucy a new book, *Sense and Sensibility*, by a young gentlewoman who preferred to remain anonymous, and he readily agreed to the old lady's suggestion that he read aloud to them while they tended to their needlework. He said nothing to Catheryn, but a momentary truce seemed to be declared. Miss Lucy's early bedtime was forgotten, and even Catheryn soon found herself chuckling over the absurd conversations between John Dashwood and his parsimonious spouse. This comfortable diversion became their evening routine.

Teddy emerged from his bedchamber Saturday morning, still wobbly but determined, and escaped thankfully to the great outdoors. Catheryn knew his freedom was not as complete as he would have wished, because Dr. Quigley insisted that he must proceed cautiously. Added to this was his lordship's assertion that, if he was well enough to traipse around outside, he was well enough to attend to proper lessons. Therefore, at his first meeting with the earl, Mr. MacClaren was instructed to set up a regular study schedule and see that Teddy adhered to it. What with the doctor on one side and Dambroke on the other, Catheryn thought it spoke volumes for MacClaren's skill that he seemed to satisfy them both. Teddy had lessons every morning and was left a light schedule of tasks to perform each afternoon. Indeed, these tasks were so light at first that Monday young Master Dambroke neglected to do them at all. He quickly discovered that merry Mr. MacClaren had a rough edge to his tongue if roused sufficiently to use it, and virtuously informed Catheryn that he would not repeat the error.

The earl had not mentioned returning to town, and Catheryn was oddly reluctant to bring up the subject. It was nearly anticlimactic, and she wasn't certain why she continued to avoid conversation with him, unless it was out of fear that she would need to make good her own threat. Miss Lucy's attitude seemed to have changed considerably since Dambroke's arrival and Catheryn found her much more approachable. They had several interesting conversations, and when Catheryn suggested that she would like to make Teddy a shirt, Miss Lucy provided both pattern and material.

While she spent her mornings with Miss Lucy or with Teddy and MacClaren in the schoolroom, she discovered from Bert that he and Dambroke were working with Blaze, schooling him to more civil conduct. The earl had been ready to sell the horse but had evidently changed his mind after seeing the progress Ditchling had made working on his own. She knew he spent his afternoons taking long rides, visiting tenants, or discussing business with his bailiff. Once or twice he even took Teddy with him in the gig, since Quigley had vetoed riding for the time being. Dambroke also took the boy fishing. Catheryn was delighted with their warming relationship and began, as each day passed, to feel more in charity with the earl. He seemed content enough, though she caught his pensive gaze upon her more than once.

XVII

The days passed quickly, and soon another week was gone. Friday morning Dambroke received a letter from his sister, which he read with amusement to Catheryn and Miss Lucy. Aside from a passing mention of the fact that he would be pleased to hear that the assassin Bellingham had been found guilty and publicly hanged at Newgate the previous Monday and a confirmation of Mr. Caston's betrothal, Tiffany's letter dealt mostly with her own raptures and hints about her costume for the duchess's ball, to be held that very evening.

"She's full of gossip," added the earl, scanning ahead to decipher the next paragraph. "Here's a bit about Tony's latest prank. He made off with one from each pair of Maggie's shoes. Tiff says, 'he devised a clever treasure hunt, sending her hither and yon.' I'll wager poor Maggie didn't think it so clever. 'Hither' seems to have been our house and 'yon' was Hyde Park!"

"Captain Varling has always had a rather highly developed sense of humor," observed Miss Lucy dryly.

"It can be a damned nuisance," said Dambroke.

"But it makes him understanding of others," Catheryn mused, remembering his reaction to Teddy's prank.

Either her words or Miss Lucy's glare at his use of the epithet drew a grin from his lordship. "Tiff ends with a postscript inquiring about Teddy. Glad she thought of it, though he does seem to be on the mend at last." Catheryn held her breath, expecting him to say something about returning to town, but he merely turned the conversation to another topic.

Teddy was late to dinner and had to be sent away again to make himself presentable. When he returned at last with face and hands polished to a rosy glow and wearing a clean shirt, Catheryn smiled, thinking how right the earl was and how much better he looked. She knew his shoulder and ribs were still painful but, boylike, he seemed to ignore his aches and to do much as he pleased despite the doctor's orders. He grinned at her now with a look that made her wonder what mischief he had been up to.

She knew that, after Monday's episode and with Dambroke having made it clear that the association with Nat Tripler was to be discouraged as much as possible, MacClaren had begun to increase his study load. But she also knew that Teddy had not been at his books all afternoon and suspected that he had been with Nat instead. The earl was also aware of his disappearance, because he had looked for him to take him fishing. He didn't ask for any explanations, however, and Miss Westering applauded his restraint. But when they rose to adjourn, Dambroke laid a restraining hand on the boy's good shoulder.

"Where are you off to, my lad?"

"Oh, nowhere in particular. Just out, I expect." Teddy's voice was airy and casual, though not enough to be impertinent.

"I hesitate to contradict you or to bring up unpleasant subjects, but did not Mr. MacClaren leave lessons to be done?"

"Yes, sir." Some of the air had gone.

"Have you done them?"

There was a slight hesitation while Teddy clearly weighed the possibility of asserting that of course he had done them. He sighed. "No, sir. But I can do them later," he added hopefully.

"You ought to have done them this afternoon," Dambroke said gently but with a glint of amusement. He ruffled the boy's curls. "I do understand, you know, that other things seemed more important at the time. I have often been in that position myself. But the lessons must be done and not, I'm afraid, at your convenience. Go now, and when you have done I think you had best go straight to bed. No," he added when Teddy looked up in protest, "I am not punishing you, but I am going to insist. You still need a good deal of rest, my lad. Whether you like it or not, you are not yet entirely mended, you know."

All the air had gone and Catheryn couldn't bear it. The evenings had somehow become precious and she knew this one would be spoiled if the boy were banished to the lonely schoolroom. "Perhaps Teddy might bring his work down to the library," she suggested almost shyly. "He can do his lessons just as well there, and it will be warmer than the schoolroom."

Dambroke consented immediately, but Catheryn was surprised to note that Teddy seemed to weigh the suggestion for a moment before going up to get his books and papers. By the time he returned the earl was seated in his favorite chair with his feet stretched out to the roaring fire, a small glass of port resting companionably on the table at his elbow. Catheryn had sent for extra working candles and was in the process of arranging a branch in such a way that they would cast their light most beneficially upon Miss Lucy's knitting.

"Thank you, my dear. Quite admirable. I shall now have no excuse for dropping my stitches."

"I don't believe you've dropped a stitch in all your life, Miss Lucy," Catheryn retorted, laughing. "Come in, Teddy. I've cleared a space on the long table. Will these candles do? I thought two branches would be better than one."

He put his paraphernalia down and grinned. "Thanks, Cathy." He pulled out the heavy chair and, with a sigh nearly as heavy, slid into it and opened his book. Hiding a smile, Catheryn turned to find the earl's amused gaze upon her. Warming to him, she chuckled and moved to pick up her workbasket. She had nearly finished Teddy's shirt, but she still had to attach the narrow lace at the cuffs. It required tiny blindstitches, and she hoped she would have enough light. The room was still except for the noise of the crackling fire and Miss Lucy's clicking needles. Dambroke shifted his feet. Teddy turned a page. She missed *Sense and Sensibility* and the earl's deep, steady voice as he read. Somehow sewing in silence was not as much fun, but it would be worth it for Teddy's sake. She had reckoned without the earl.

"Must you fuss with that thing now, Catheryn?" he demanded after a quarter hour of silence. "I'm persuaded there is not sufficient light in here."

"Have you another suggestion, my lord? I assure you it would be more than welcome."

"Good. Let's have a game of backgammon. Or perhaps," he added with more grace than sincerity, "Cousin Lucy would care to take a hand of whist?"

Miss Lucy declined politely, assuring him with a laugh that she preferred to finish her shawl, thank you, and Dambroke unfolded from his chair to procure the backgammon set from the high cabinet near the fireplace. They pushed their two chairs closer together, facing each other across the low table, and he laid out the leather board and ivory stones.

Catheryn was experienced and conservative, but she rapidly discovered the earl to be a daring and innovative player, much like her grandfather had been. Playing carefully, and with the aid of some lucky throws for herself and several disastrous ones for her opponent, she won the first game. Without looking up from the board to comment, Dambroke began to set out his stones once more.

"Another game, my lord?" she asked demurely.

"Silence, Impertinence." But he grinned at her.

Thinking her luck was holding, Catheryn cheerfully covered her five-point when she won the opening roll. His lordship, however, promptly retaliated with double sixes and covered both bar points. Her next roll proved singularly unhelpful. Dambroke, with a smile that was nearly smug, managed to complete a four-point block, and Catheryn rolled double sixes. She had only one option and made the move with a grimace.

"At least it has the advantage of leaving you with no major decision to make," Dambroke teased.

"If," she replied with dangerous calm, "you have nothing to say to the purpose, my lord, I beg you will hold your tongue. You disturb Teddy." She glanced at the boy and found him grinning from ear to ear. Dambroke winked and Teddy stifled a laugh. The earl rolled double twos. "Oh, for heaven's sake!" Catheryn exclaimed.

"Sh-h. You'll disturb Teddy." The earl chose to leave a blot, quite impudently, she thought, on her twelve-point.

"You will be well served if I roll double ones, my lord," she whispered.

"Never mind, my girl," he answered with a grin and in his normal voice. "Your luck is out, and I shall soon have my prime." He was right. She rolled a double but useless six, and he promptly rolled four-two, giving himself prime and effectively trapping two of her stones on his one-point. From then on it seemed hopeless. Catheryn moved her pieces methodically into her inner board, except for the two that had, so to speak, been caught behind enemy lines. The earl gloatingly maintained prime until the last possible moment. When he began to bear off, she was still stuck. By the time he had removed four stones, she had only succeeded in closing her board.

"Sir?" Dambroke, about to throw the dice, looked up to find Teddy at his elbow.

"Yes, what is it?"

"I've finished."

"Well, then, off with you."

"May I watch the end of this game?"

"No need for you to gloat over Catheryn's ignominious defeat, my boy," his brother laughed. "Just bid the ladies good night and be off."

Catheryn wrinkled her nose at the earl and turned to Teddy. "Do you want Mary, Teddy? I know it's still difficult for you to manage shirts and so forth."

But he declined, grinning. "I hope you trounce him!"

"Begone, rascal!" Dambroke raised a hand in mock threat, but Catheryn only sighed.

"Do go, Teddy. He has it all his own way, and you are only delaying the inevitable. I need a miracle to save me."

Teddy obediently began gathering his books while Dambroke flourished for the throw. The dice rattled out of the leather cup and across the board. "Damn!"

"Richard, mind your tongue!"

"Sorry, Cousin Lucy. But of all the luck! It would try a saint, I promise you. I've rolled double sixes."

"Is that so bad?"

"Not usually, but this time... disaster?"

Miss Lucy only commented that it seemed insufficient reason for blasphemy and went back to her knitting. Catheryn twinkled at the earl. "I don't know why you make such a piece of work about a single blot, sir. My luck being what it is, I doubt I'll hit it." She rolled double fours and sat staring at them. Dambroke swore again, but under his breath this time.

"She did it! She did it!" Teddy crowed. "Now you'll

sing a different tune." Ignoring the earl's glare, he moved closer; and, while Dambroke sat helplessly, unable even to throw the dice because of her closed board, Catheryn alternately threw and moved her stones to the inner board. When, finally, she opened the six-point, he was allowed to throw but, with perverse consistency, threw none but low numbers. He fumed while Catheryn continued to bear off. Not until the three-point was open was he able to escape. He did not, however, avoid sound defeat.

"Good show, Cathy!" Teddy applauded. "Oh, well done!"

Dambroke pushed his chair back and stood up. "I'll take you upstairs myself, you scallawag!" He shook his fist at Catheryn. "And don't you dare move, miss. We're having another game!" She only chuckled, watching them go. Teddy's protests that he could so put on his own nightshirt and didn't need a nursemaid of any sort, let alone one who still needed a valet to put himself to bed, were effectively squelched by the calm rejoinder that his lordship would just see about that. The door closed behind them.

"That goes rather well now, does it not?"

Catheryn turned to smile at Miss Lucy. "Very well, I think. I'm glad his lordship decided to stay on."

"Humph!" snorted Miss Lucy, as though she had her own ideas about that. "Told him about Eton yet?" It had not been long once the ice was broken before Catheryn had confided most of what she knew about Teddy and his family to the old lady.

She sighed deeply. "Not yet. I haven't really spoken privately with him since just after he arrived, you know." She could feel color creeping into her cheeks and, though Miss Lucy seemed not to notice, went on quickly, "I don't want to tell him if it means he will exert pressure on Teddy about his lessons. Mr. MacClaren handles him well, but Dambroke might replace him if he thought a stricter man would get Teddy back in school sooner. He sets great store by Eton."

" 'Course he does," replied Miss Lucy crisply. "His old school. Though, considering he was there under George Heath, I don't know why he would retain a fondness for the place. Used to flog the boys for the fun of it, I think.

Hear that Keate fellow is cut from the same cloth, too." She paused.

"Dr. Keate said boys don't care about the flogging," Catheryn observed uncertainly.

"Much he knows." Miss Lucy paused again to begin a new ball of yarn. When she spoke, her attention was divided between the task and her words. "I suppose you know best, my dear," she said doubtfully, "but I believe you ought to tell him. Dambroke don't look kindly on female meddling."

Catheryn sighed again. "I know. He isn't likely to approve of my private conversation with Dr. Keate no matter when I tell him about it. He warned me, too, but I couldn't help meddling. I think he will be pleased that Teddy can return. I'd just prefer to wait till I know Teddy will also be pleased."

"Up to you, of course, my dear," Miss Lucy replied equably. She turned the subject, and Dambroke soon returned. Catheryn had rearranged the board.

"So, you are ready for me," he laughed.

"As you see, sir. Did Teddy get to bed all right?"

"Of course. He made a few faces while putting on his nightshirt and protested the whole time that he didn't need any help from the likes of me."

"Being yourself, as he said, the sort who needs a valet to tuck you up at night," Catheryn mocked.

"I am not!" he retorted indignantly. "I've survived more than once without Landon, I assure you. It was a good line, though. I'll give him that." He hitched his chair up to the board. "Now, miss, are you ready to pay the piper?"

Catheryn chuckled at the reference but agreed that she was ready. She concentrated upon her careful play, but the earl's superior skill and daring tactics began to have their effect. It seemed that he left blots indiscriminately, keeping an eye only for the main chance. He did not play that way with impunity, of course, but her strategy could not prevail against him. At the end of the first game she found herself humiliatingly gammoned, but the play was more even in the next and she held her own. When Dambroke bore off his last stone, she had only one remaining.

"A win, but scarcely worthy of being called so," he

observed. "If you had thrown a double any of the last few times, you would have won. So, now we must have a tie-breaker." He raised his brows hopefully, much as a child does who wonders if he has pushed his luck too far.

"No, sir! Not until I have had my tea, my lord. And I will not be bullied." She began putting the stones away, but his expression did not change. She laughed. "If Miss Lucy can bear to stay up, I shall allow you one game after tea." He grinned, but she ignored him. "I daresay your sense of propriety is interfering with your usual early hours, ma'am, but you must not let us take advantage of your good nature."

"I enjoy the company," Miss Lucy admitted with a placid smile. The door opened to admit John and a maidservant with the tea tray, and the old lady briskly bestowed her knitting.

"Are those apple tarts?" Dambroke inquired with interest.

"They are. Help yourself." Liberally taking her advice, he passed the plate to Catheryn and the three of them tucked into their tea with energy, while conversation ambled from one topic to another as cozily as though they had known one another forever. It occurred to Catheryn once again that it was the night of the Clairdon masquerade, and she noted that the ball must be well underway by now.

Miss Lucy's only comment was a snort, but Dambroke smiled contritely. "I'm sorry you're missing the fun."

She felt very comfortable with him tonight. "Rubbish, sir. I've no great yen to disport myself as a shepherdess."

He cocked his head quizzically. "I only approved the plan because you said you'd always wanted to go to a masque."

"Did you?" She grinned.

"I did. I expect you said so in the hope that I would do just that. You are incorrigible, little one." Mentally hugging herself, she suggested he have another tart. "Baggage. I hope my sister is enjoying herself. I don't suppose you know what costume she finally decided upon." Catheryn shook her head. "Well, she never confided in me. Probably a shepherdess." As John and the maid began to clear away the tea things, Dambroke brushed crumbs off his cream-colored breeches. "Ready, miss?"

She cast a doubtful glance at the old lady. "Are you so set upon this game, sir? Miss Lucy must be longing for her bed."

"Nonsense. We'll play rapidly and she won't mind a bit. Will you, ma'am?" The appeal, accompanied as it was by his most charming smile, achieved its purpose. Miss Lucy drew out her knitting again, observing as she did so that they might as well get on with their silly game, since she wanted to knot her fringe and could do so as well tonight as tomorrow.

Accordingly, the stones were once again set out in the starting pattern, but the new game soon promised, despite the earl's assurances, to be a long one. By midnight, they were well into the middle game when John came in and began replacing burnt candles with new ones. Diverted by his entrance, Dambroke glanced up and told him he might take himself off to bed when he finished. Both players forgot Miss Lucy who, though her fringe was but half done, had dozed off in her chair. John headed for the door, his tray full of candle bits. Dambroke threw the dice.

"The devil!" he exclaimed. "Now, how in blazes do I make use of that!" His attention was fully engaged, so he did not notice John's sudden start when he opened the door into the East Hall. Catheryn did, however, and likewise heard the gruff voice speaking from beyond.

"His lordship there, is 'e?"

"Aye," John answered in surprise. He looked back over his shoulder. "It's Mr. Straley, my lord."

"Straley!" Dambroke muttered, counting his move. "What's he want at this hour? Poachers?" He looked up to see his footman still poised at the door and looking very uncomfortable. "Why does instinct warn me that it's nothing so simple as mere poachers? Send him in, John."

John motioned to the keeper with a nod and stood aside. The reason for his discomfort as well as his subsequent hasty exit became perfectly clear when Straley entered, a shotgun under one arm and a wriggling, red-faced Teddy under the other. The elderly man set the boy on his feet, retaining a grip on his arm, and made his bow. Miss Lucy came wide awake.

"Beggin' yer pardon, my lord, but I had no choice," Straley growled. "I've sent my Jack to the Running Bull with t'other, but this'un I'm delivering myself." He seemed to realize the boy wasn't going anywhere and released him. Teddy looked as though he'd sell his soul to be elsewhere, but he stood his ground. He even braved a glance at his brother but blanched at the expression he encountered and lowered his eyes quickly to the floor.

Since they had long since thought him asleep, it took a moment to recover, but Dambroke was not long in demanding an explanation. Straley answered, his anger still patently obvious. He and his elder son, making their usual rounds, had discovered Teddy and Nat Tripler playing at smugglers in the Home Wood. In order to add a touch of realism, they had appropriated one of Dambroke's shotguns and were pretending to find revenue men behind every bush. Straley and Jack had spent the best part of the afternoon and early evening laying rabbit snares, hoping to decimate the inordinate number of rabbits presently abiding in the Park. The boys had sprung nearly every trap.

At this point, Dambroke interrupted, his steely gaze upon the culprit, his tone withering. "I trust there was an excellent reason for destroying the snares." A terrible silence followed his statement. Miserably, Teddy shifted his feet. "Well, Edward?"

The boy swallowed audibly. "I . . . I'm sorry," he muttered. Dambroke looked ready to explode, but Catheryn gathering her courage, laid her hand upon his arm and spoke calmly.

"Teddy, dear, please explain why you released poor Mr. Straley's traps after he and Jack worked so hard to lay them." She caught his gaze and held it, giving him time to compose himself, knowing he was on the verge of tears. He swallowed again and, by avoiding Dambroke's eye, contrived to answer her.

"We . . . we didn't think. W-we only made up the game. The snares was . . . were revenuers, and if we stepped in one we were caught. But if we could slip it first, then the revenuer was disarmed and captured. We just didn't think about the work of it, or we wouldn't have. I promise, Cathy!"

"And the gun?" Dambroke's drawl was deceptively calm, making his words all the more ominous. Another, heavier silence fell. Miss Lucy began working her fringe again with fierce concentration. Catheryn, remembering what Tiffany had said about Dambroke and his guns, felt perfectly helpless. Even Straley began to regard the boy with something akin to sympathy.

XVIII

Straley was dismissed and when he had gone, taking the shotgun with him, Teddy looked smaller, more defenseless. He shifted his feet again. Dambroke spoke, his voice holding that chilling note that Catheryn had heard only once before. "You know the rule about the guns, do you not, Edward?"

"Yes, sir," Teddy muttered.

"Well, then?"

"It wasn't loaded."

"Are you quite certain of that?"

"Course I am. I'd remember loading it, wouldn't I?"

Dambroke stood up. "Don't be impertinent, young man. Did you examine the gun before you took it out?"

Teddy saw the chasm yawning before him and caught his breath. "No, sir." The reply was barely audible.

"So you don't know that it wasn't left loaded in the gun room, do you?" The boy shook his head, wisely refraining from pointing out that there were strict rules about that, too. Dambroke went on in the same icy tone, "I think we will resume this discussion in the schoolroom. Will you excuse us, ladies?"

Miss Lucy nodded without comment, but no one noticed, because Catheryn jumped to her feet and grasped the earl's forearm. "Please, sir! It's so late. Won't you deal better with this in the morning after you've both had a night's sleep?"

He turned toward her, anger plain on his face, but when his gaze met hers his expression softened. He glanced at the wretched boy and Catheryn held her breath. "You may be right, Cousin," he agreed. "After breakfast then, young man. In my study. I suggest you think carefully about what you have done."

Hope gleamed in Teddy's eyes as he turned away and Catheryn knew he expected another miracle. The great door was just swinging shut when the earl said, "It's only a reprieve, Catheryn. It may even do some good to let him stew, but the boy must be beaten, and he knows it." Having noted a hesitation in the movement of the door, she watched now as it closed softly. If Teddy had not known before, she mused, he knew now. She was not surprised a moment later to see the alcove door behind the earl open a hair's breadth. Clearly, Teddy expected her to speak for him, to convince Dambroke to be lenient.

She gave it her best effort, pleading his youth, his injuries, and his lack of criminal intent. The earl listened with more patience than she might have expected, but her last point proved one too many. He scorned it outright, adjuring in stentorian accents that the taking of the gun had nothing whatever to do with Teddy's youth or his injuries but damned well spoke volumes for criminal intent, it having been understood since he was in short coats that he was not to touch Dambroke's guns without both permission and adult supervision. When he capped his argument by stating that he had postponed matters till morning only that they might finish their game, Catheryn sighed and the alcove door shut quietly.

She did not give up as the game dragged on, but Dambroke firmly resisted every plea and finally, quite unfairly, prohibited further discussion of the subject. Unwilling to risk their own fragile relationship for a lost cause, she held her peace until he defeated her at last on the board as well. Then, bidding Miss Lucy a warm and grateful good night and his lordship a rather cooler one, she made her way upstairs to her own bedchamber, intending to retire immediately. But thoughts of a lonely, possibly frightened boy intruded. It would take only a moment to run up and see that he was asleep and not fretting about the upcoming confrontation with Dambroke.

Dismissing a sleepy Mary to her bed, she hurried up to the schoolroom. Everything was dark, and the very darkness nearly convinced her that he must be asleep. Even while she hesitated, the heavy silence made itself felt, and she stepped quickly to the night nursery, pushed wide the door, and caught her breath in dismay at the sight of the empty bed. Too late, she recalled the reason Teddy had once run away from school.

A myriad of thoughts chased through her head as she ran back to her own room to change to her riding habit. Meddling again, my girl, and just when things were beginning to look up! But if she could bring Teddy back before he was found to be missing, perhaps the earl would not discover the meddling this time. She hoped she could find Nat Tripler, for surely he would know where to look for Teddy. Fifteen minutes later, she was throwing a saddle over Psyche's back and praying she would not wake Bert or any of the grooms. Within twenty, she was on her way to the Running Bull.

Nat was not difficult to find, for he was standing smack in the middle of the innyard, and his eyes rounded in disbelief when she rode up and swung from the saddle. A year or two older than Teddy and half a head taller, he was well-muscled with untidy orange curls and freckles so thick they seemed to blend together. She quickly confirmed his identity, introduced herself, and demanded to know Teddy's whereabouts. Nat seemed oddly relieved once he knew who she was and began to tell an amazing tale.

Teddy had come to him some time before with the suggestion that he might like to go smuggling for real, insisting that they wouldn't be running from punishment but merely seeking their fortunes in the way of knights and crusaders and such. It was clear that Nat hadn't much needed to rationalize his enthusiasm. His father was away for the night but, like Teddy, he anticipated a painful morning interview. Evidently, they had been discussing and arguing details of the plan when they were interrupted by the sound of a carriage approaching rapidly from the south. Nat explained that, though the Running Bull was not a posting house, his father occasionally provided a change of horses to persons hoping to get a lower rate by changing before Stevenage. Sure enough, despite the late hour, the carriage had pulled into the yard and someone shouted for the change. Then another voice had sounded, calling the first a fool for stopping. It had sounded like blowing into a full-scale argument, and Teddy had suddenly pricked up his ears, thinking he recognized one of the voices.

"Who was it?" Catheryn asked sharply.

"Fella name o' Lawrence, I reckon," replied Nat. "Ted said as 'ow 'e warn't sure, so 'e went round an' listened whilst I unhitched the team. Met me back inside an' said as 'ow yon gennemun was abductin' some 'un—a lady bundled on the floor. They was in an awful 'urry—I give 'im that—but when 'e says it be 'is sister . . . well, I arsk ye, mum, daft, ain't 'e?"

Catheryn felt faint. "Good God!" she exclaimed. "Of course, it's Tiffany. The way he looked at the ball, his persistence—and I practically flaunted the captain at him! What a ninny I've been!" Nat's amazement sobered her. "What happened next?"

"Ted clumb in the boot, mum."

"He what!"

Repeating the information, he added that there had been no one nearby to help them and they had been afraid to confront the two men for fear they would have pistols. Teddy thought that if he could rescue Tiffany it might mitigate the earl's wrath, and he had made Nat swear not to tell Dambroke. Catheryn gathered that Nat had been torn between loyalty to his friend and fear of repercussions to himself should anything go wrong.

"Look here, Nat," she said when he had finished, "you won't thank me for this, but you must run for his lordship. We are going to need him." Nat's expression clearly indicated his aversion to the errand, and Catheryn sympathized but insisted. "Tell him the whole, just as you've told me. I daresay you can leave out the bit about going smuggling, but tell him the rest. Be as quick as you can, because I'm going after them. If they turn off, I'll leave a signal, so tell his lordship to look out for it." Quickly she led Psyche to the mounting block and was soon turning her onto the high road.

Passing through Stevenage some time later, she felt suddenly alone and vulnerable, even grateful for the late hour and cover of darkness. Just the other side of town, however, she spied the carriage rumbling ahead. A cloud drifted across the new moon, and she had to strain to see her quarry, but she hesitated to shorten the distance, lest she be seen. Patting Psyche's neck, she shivered in the chilly night air. Lord, what a dust-up there would be over this! It would be a miracle, she thought, if Dambroke didn't have an apoplectic fit before the night was done. He would be furious with Tiffany for being abducted, furious with Teddy for running away, and furious with herself for meddling instead of informing him of Teddy's departure. Heaven help them all!

The cloud passed and the carriage seemed suddenly closer. It was slowing. Suddenly it swung off to the right and disappeared, but she found the turning easily, a narrowish though not untraveled road. Quickly pulling off her yellow neckscarf, she tied it to the lower branch of a nearby tree, where moonlight turned it white as it fluttered in the breeze. Dambroke couldn't miss it. A little chill went up her spine as the thought crossed her mind that Nat might have been too frightened to go for him, and she wondered what she would do if the earl did not come. Then she gave herself a shake. How stupid. Surely Lawrence would not persist when he realized his plot had failed. Her own presence would provide all the propriety the occasion warranted, if such an occasion could ever meet standards of propriety. And Teddy would be there as well. The whole affair would take on more the flavor of a family outing than an abduction. She chuckled, imagining how Lawrence would look when she and Teddy appeared on the scene.

She heard Lawrence shouting up ahead. The trees, which had been growing up close to the road, suddenly fell away to her left, forming a large clearing. The carriage had stopped in a yard before a ramshackle house, and Lawrence shouted again. They were too far ahead to see her, but to be on the safe side, she rode back the way she had come for about twenty yards, dismounted, and tethered the mare. Since she could not leave Dambroke a written message, Psyche would have to do. When she returned to the clearing, there were lights in the windows of the house, which she saw now was a sort of hedge tavern. Suddenly, as she approached, she heard a muffled oath from the far side of the carriage and then a scuffle. Next came Teddy's voice, first in pain and then shouting to be put down and left alone. When she could see them, Catheryn stood very still, hoping that if Teddy's burly captor turned she would be invisible against the trees. She watched him carry the struggling boy into the house and then circled quickly to approach from the side and thus lessen the chances of being seen. A few minutes later she crept slowly up to a front window and peeped inside.

The window was filthy, but there was no curtain and she could see well enough. She looked in upon a taproom lit by candles in wall sconces. Directly opposite, Tiffany slumped against the chimney corner of a large oak settle. Catheryn could see her face dimly, but the rest of her was just a blob through the dirty window. She heard Lawrence and the fellow who held Teddy talking, but Lawrence was out of sight and their words were muffled. Tiffany said something, sounding frightened, but Catheryn couldn't make out her words either. This would never do. She ducked down below the window, crept to the front stoop, and pushed the door open, hoping it would not squeak. It was as silent as though freshly soaped, but she did not pause to wonder why. She found herself in a dark hallway, and when she neared the taproom door, Teddy's voice came clearly.

"You just wait till my brother gets hold of you, Mr. Lawrence! He'll fix your wagon!"

"'Ere now, Jimmy, you ain't got no more of these coves acomin', I 'ope!" It was an elderly voice. Certainly not the coachman, she thought. "This b'ain't no posh postin' 'ouse. 'Sides, I don't want no part of it!" Catheryn was wondering if the voice might belong to the coachman after all, when a second unfamiliar voice recommended that the speaker stop jawing and think what to do. There were three men in the room!

"Never mind, Uncle." That was Lawrence. "We can't stay here. That's clear enough. Someone's likely to come looking for the boy. We'll move along. Duff, mind that brat. Uncle Jig can let him go once we've got away."

"'Ere now!" the elderly voice protested. "Ye can't leave 'im 'ere! Ye'll 'ave t' busies all over me ken!"

"Put a sock in it, Uncle Jig. The boy will be my message bearer. Nobody will bother you. All he has to do is tell Dambroke Tiffany and I are married." Catheryn gasped. "By the time the lad gets to the Park, we will be." She relaxed again.

"I'll never marry you!"

"Don't be childish, Tiffany. You will." His tone was

lazy, even amused. "Hurry it up, Duff. We've got to move."

Catheryn squared her shoulders and pushed the door wide, making as grand an entrance, she thought, as the duchess must have made at her ball. "Good evening, Mr. Lawrence," she said calmly, silently congratulating herself on her poise. "Don't you think this charade has gone far enough?"

"Good God! Miss Westering!"

"As you see, sir. Now be so kind as to release Lady Tiffany and the boy. You must see your plan has failed."

"I'm damned if I will," Lawrence retorted angrily.

Tiffany let out a squeal of surprise and Teddy laughed excitedly. "Good for you, Cathy! That's one in the eye!"

Catheryn ignored them, keeping her steady gaze upon Lawrence. "I'm very much afraid you are damned if you don't, sir," she replied equably. "Dambroke will be here shortly, probably with a number of men. It will go ill with you if he finds his sister trussed up like a Christmas goose." She glanced at Tiffany, who was wrapped in a dirty blanket.

Lawrence shrugged his shoulders angrily, defiantly. "Thank you for the warning," he growled. "We'll see he don't find us here. You perhaps. The boy. But not us."

" 'Ere Jimmy!" The old man's voice was shrill. "T' mort says a ruddy flash cove's bearin' down wi' a ruddy posse, and ye say I'm t' stay 'ere! Not ruddy likely!"

"As you wish, Uncle Jig. Leave the place for a few days. No one among your thieving customers will miss you." Catheryn thought of the well-soaped hinges of the front door and wondered if Lawrence had not given an accurate description of the clientele. Since no one seemed disposed to release Tiffany, she moved to do so herself. But Lawrence's tone changed sharply from derision to command when he noted her purpose. "Here you! Get away from her!"

"Nonsense, Mr. Lawrence," she said without turning. "You must see that you cannot succeed in this villainy."

"It is not nonsense, Miss Westering," he grated. Something in his tone or, perhaps, a look in Tiffany's eyes caused Catheryn to glance back at him and then to go very still. Mr. Lawrence did have a pistol. It was firmly gripped in his right hand and leveled at a point somewhere between Miss Westering's neck and her high waistline. She shivered. "Just so, my dear. I am held to be a better than average marksman, you know. Though no one," he added unnecessarily, "could miss at this range. Tie her up, Duff."

"Begging yer pardon, sir," that rascal replied, "but we ain't got no more rope. Used the last bit on the lad there."

"Then get more, dolthead! We must get out of here!"

Uncle Jig diffidently suggested there might be a bit of string or the like in the kitchen. Duff dumped Teddy onto the settle beside Tiffany and went with the old man to look, while Lawrence kept the pistol steadily aimed at Catheryn.

"Don't think for a moment that I should hesitate, Miss Westering," he advised smoothly. "I shouldn't have to kill you, you know. A simple wound would keep you out of my way and delay his lordship as well."

"What on earth do you hope to accomplish, sir?"

"Wealth, my dear. You must know her ladyship's quite an heiress. After I've compromised her reputation by that most effective of means, even Dambroke will insist upon our marriage." Catheryn nodded. Certainly marriage would be the only acceptable course if Lawrence succeeded. However, she still had a card or two up her elegant sleeve, possibly even an ace. "Once she marries me—and you will marry me," Lawrence went on in a grim aside to Tiffany, "all that lovely money. . . ." He gestured expressively and sighed with complacency.

". . . will still be controlled by Lord Dambroke," Catheryn finished for him. "He does control her fortune, you know, sir."

"Don't take me for a fool, girl! His guardianship ends with her marriage. Anyone knows that! Once she marries me, I shall have complete control of her fortune."

"It's no use, Catheryn," Tiffany interposed dismally. "I explained the situation to this idiotish man myself. He knows Richard must relinquish when I marry."

"But you were wrong, Tiffany dear." Catheryn kept her tone pacific, not knowing how the younger girl would react. "Dambroke told me himself. You accused him of something or other during one of your quarrels. I don't remember the details of it, what he said they were anyway, but when you flung it in his teeth that you knew he would lose control when you marry, he left it at that. He does control though—I believe the expression is 'at his discretion'—until you are twenty-five, whether you marry or not. So you see, sir...."

He did not see. He regarded her, in fact, with a good deal of suspicion and roared at his henchmen to get a move on with the damned rope. "It isn't true," he insisted. "You're making that up, and even if you're not, Dambroke will fork over the dibs. He won't want his pampered little sister living in squalor for eight years. Or perhaps I ought to consider ransom as a better choice," he added with a black scowl. "He'd pay handsomely, I daresay. Maybe more for the three of you." Catheryn felt a chill and clenched her teeth. Surely he wouldn't hold them all captive! He grinned suddenly. "That pierced your armor, didn't it, Miss High-and-Mighty. It might be interesting to watch you squirm, but not interesting enough to give up the grand prize. I'm willing to wait." Catheryn looked up sharply. "Ah, you get my meaning. Unless I marry her, you see, I have naught to look forward to but poverty. I've no wealthy relatives that matter. But when I marry Tiffany it will come—in the long run perhaps—but it will come. Oh, yes, ma'am, I can wait!"

Catheryn sighed. "I do not think you can know Lord Dambroke very well." She grimaced as the man called Duff, coming unheralded from behind, yanked her arms together tightly behind her back. Evidently he had found a piece of rope. The old man seemed to have disappeared. Catheryn sighed elaborately and, with effort, kept her voice conversational. "You will, if you are silly enough to force the Lady Tiffany to marry you, only find that you have given Dambroke reason to make her an instant widow. And, likewise, I believe he would arrange for your disposal rather than part with a penny's ransom, sir. He's a bit of a pinch-purse, as I'm certain her ladyship must have mentioned once or twice." Pausing, she noted with satisfaction that the shot had gone home. Tiffany had surely complained to him of Dambroke's miserliness more than once.

"Your best recourse, Mr. Lawrence, would be to leave now without her. Dambroke may still want to kill you, of course." She shook her head sadly at such waste. "But at least you would travel unencumbered and, therefore, have better odds of escaping him." Lawrence's face reddened, and he looked about to sputter again. Duff, on the other hand, having finished binding her wrists, had moved closer to his leader and seemed to be listening intently. Catheryn went on with a little smile, trying to keep her mind off the unwavering pistol in the meantime. "There is also, of course, Captain Varling. A gentleman," she mused, "a very easygoing gentleman, for the most part. But I do think he will not take kindly to your designs upon the Lady Tiffany or her fortune. If I am not mistaken, he sets great store by her happiness and has designs of his own. Her fortune matches his, you see, so much better than it matches yours, Mr. Lawrence. You interfere, sir, and I'm afraid the captain will be displeased."

Tiffany's eyes were expressive and Catheryn, catching a glimpse of them, was relieved that her ladyship was sensible enough for once to keep still.

"I can take care of Varling!" Lawrence sputtered. "I can take care of his bloody lordship, too, girl! You think you are so clever! I know what you're up to. Don't think for a moment that I don't! You'll try whatever you can to convince me to hare off and leave the lot of you right here. Which makes me wonder very much about his bloody lordship. Now I come to think of it. . . ." He paused, studying her bland countenance with deep mistrust. "Yes, sir, now I think of it, where is he? If he's coming, which I doubt, what are you doing here, Miss Clever Westering? It's all havey-cavey, if you ask me. Dambroke would never have allowed a female to follow us if he'd known about it. Even I know him well enough to know that much. You've been bluffing, Miss Clever Westering. Not even a very good bluff, either. I'll wager Dambroke don't know a damned thing about all this yet."

"You lose, Lawrence." The words, uttered softly but with an edge of steel, were followed immediately by the explosion of a pistol. Lawrence's weapon spun away out of his hand and across the floor, coming to rest with a grating smack against the hearthstone. Lawrence grabbed his bleeding hand in an attempt to stanch both pain and flow, and turned furiously to face Lord Dambroke.

XIX

The earl stood in the doorway, legs spread, a smoking pistol already shifted to his left hand, its primed and cocked mate securely in his right. He looked, Catheryn thought, for all the world like an Elizabethan buccaneer must have looked; though Edmund Caston, appearing behind him, rather spoiled the effect with his air of solid, prosaic competence.

"I must say, my friend," Dambroke went on in that same hard tone to Lawrence, "you do ask appropriate questions. I should like very much to hear the answers to several of them before we're any of us much older." He let his uncompromising gaze drift toward Catheryn.

"You come in good time, my lord," she said, feeling somewhat like a character in a play—hopefully one by Shakespeare rather than Sheridan. One did hope for a shred of dignity. And why must her heart choose this of all times to thud against her ribs? She inhaled slowly, willing herself to be calm, telling herself that it was only a reaction to the dreadful experience she had just gone through and not to the fury in his lordship's steely blue eyes.

Dambroke did not answer her but moved aside to allow Edmund, likewise and to Catheryn's astonishment brandishing a pistol, to pass into the room. "Release them, Caston." His voice was crisp as he gestured toward the captives. "You there!" he snapped at the coachman, once more hovering near Miss Westering. "Move away from her at once!" Cringing, the man did as he was told, and Catheryn soon felt Edmund's strong fingers dealing with the knots. She watched Dambroke.

"Are you all right, Miss Westering?" he asked when she began to rub feeling back into her hands. His glance was brief, but his expression caused her to moisten her lips. She was saved the necessity of answering by the clatter of booted and spurred feet across the kitchen floor heralding the rather boisterous entrance of Captain Varling and Lord Thomas, dragging the hapless and vociferously reluctant Uncle Jig between them.

"Ho there, Dickon! What's the ruckus?" Varling exclaimed after a swift visual search assured him of Lady Tiffany's safety. "Look what we've got! Led us a chase through yon woods, but we brought him to earth all right and tight. What now?" He saw Caston about to release Tiffany and abruptly relinquished his hold on the old man. "Here, Caston! I'll do that. Tend to the boy." He knelt in front of Tiffany. "Are you all right, my lady?" Catheryn watched, thinking that, though his concern was much like Dambroke's, his attitude was completely different, so gentle, so thoughtful. She looked again at the earl, mentally shaking her head at herself. Definitely getting in over your head, my girl, she mused contentedly.

With a gesture from Dambroke, Mr. Lawrence and Duff sat down on a bench under the window, and the earl lowered his pistols, at the same time ordering Lord Thomas to keep an eye on the scoundrels. Thomas gave the old man a push, and he joined the others. Neither Tiffany nor Teddy had made a sound except for a slight squeal from her ladyship when the pistol discharged. Both had simply stared wide-eyed at their brother. Now, as Varling freed her, Tiffany began to respond to his anxious questions in a low murmur.

"If that's an explanation for this imbroglio, Tony, we'd all like to hear it, if you don't mind," Dambroke barked.

Varling, his expression sober now, got up from his half-kneeling position beside Tiffany and turned to face the earl. "It's as we speculated back at the Park, my lord," he said quietly but with an odd touch of formality and a withering glance of contempt at the three men on the bench. "She had a note and thought it from me—one of my stupid jests. Idiotic child." He glanced at her fondly. Dambroke's mouth began to develop recognizably mulish lines at the corners, but the captain persevered. "Her ladyship got out to the carriage and those two ruffians," indicating Lawrence and Duff, "just bundled her in. Made a neat job of it, too, since they must have pulled it off under the very noses of Clairdon's link boys."

"I confess a certain curiosity about that bit myself," asserted Lord Thomas sternly.

"Don't blame the boys, my lord." Tiffany spoke quickly, pleadingly, but with a weather eye on Dambroke. "There was nothing for them to notice. The carriage pulled up and, as I ran down the steps from the garden gate, the door was flung open and the steps let down from within. I just hopped in before either of the boys could move to help me. Like a lamb to the slaughter," she added bitterly. "James—Mr. Lawrence, that is—grabbed me and bundled me onto the floor in a blanket before I could even scream. Then he complained that he had no place to put his feet!"

"By God!" Varling turned angrily toward Lawrence, hands clenched into ominous fists. The men on the bench shrank away involuntarily.

"Tony!" Dambroke called sharply. "None of that, if you please. I want him well enough to travel. He's got a journey ahead of him." Reluctantly, the captain subsided.

Now that Dambroke had laid his pistols aside and stopped the irate captain midstride, Mr. Lawrence began to recover himself. He straightened up on the bench, though he seemed to lack the temerity to rise. "Journey, my lord?" There was just a touch of insolence in the tone.

"Yes, journey, Lawrence," returned his lordship harshly. "You may consider yourself lucky that I choose to avoid scandal. My primary, albeit selfish, inclination was to school you to better conduct with a horsewhip before giving you over to the nearest magistrate. Instead, I choose to be lenient, provided you show some sense in the matter. I realize my sister led you to believe that she held a tenderness for you."

"I *never* did!" interrupted Tiffany in accents of mingled indignation and loathing.

"You did, my love," Varling reproved gently.

"Did I, Tony?" He nodded, and Tiffany desisted at once, her whole attitude sobering as she turned to Lawrence. "I must apologize then, sir. I never meant to do so."

Lawrence was taken aback by her frank gesture but no more so, Catheryn noted, than the earl. Casting a startled look at his sister and one a bit more speculative at his friend, Dambroke continued, "I don't care where you take yourself, Lawrence, so long as you put distance—great distance—between us. I'd heartily recommend volunteering for duty in America, if I thought the military would want you."

"Seems to me, you're asking a great deal, my lord," sneered Lawrence. "Seems to me, you ought to be willing to pay a bit to keep me away from London. I could tell a tale there, right enough."

"You won't attempt such a foolhardy course if you value your life, Lawrence." Varling's voice was icier than Catheryn would have believed possible, and Dambroke looked about to add a comment of his own, when Edmund spoke up in his grave and measured way.

"If you'll pardon the obtrusion, Mr. Lawrence, there would be, if I may so speculate, little benefaction to yourself through such a course as you propose. It would not avail, sir. There is insufficient evidence to substantiate your ... uh ... tale. In short, sir, no one would believe you."

Duff, the erstwhile coachman, listened with awe. "Gawd damn," he breathed. "Do he yammer like that alla time? I never 'eard the like afore."

Lord Thomas recognized a kindred spirit of sorts. "He does indeed," he answered, not without a little pride. "Good as a play, ain't he? My sister's going to marry him, you know," he confided in low tones. "Bound to improve her vocabulary out of all reason, don't you think?" Duff only looked at him, and the byplay was forgotten when Catheryn picked up the thread of Edmund's argument.

"He's right, you know, Mr. Lawrence. Against the word of their lordships and Captain Varling, not to mention myself and Lady Tiffany——"

"And Maggie," added Varling, now grinning.

"Maggie!"

"Aye," answered Dambroke, watching her through narrowed eyes. "She's at the Park. The disobedient chit followed them from London, Tony said. Like a damned puppy!"

"Oh, good for Maggie!" applauded Miss Westering. "But you must see now, Mr. Lawrence. Lady Margaret can say that she was with the Lady Tiffany from the outset if necessary. And I daresay Lady Dambroke will arrive in the morning as well, with the duchess perhaps, and my aunt and uncle Caston," she added, getting carried away.

Dambroke waved her to silence and spoke pointedly to the rapidly deflating Lawrence. "All these arguments are impressive, my friends, but since the question will not arise, they are unnecessary. When I mentioned the military earlier, sir, I spoke facetiously. But I promise that if I so much as lay eyes upon you at any time in the future—and I shall make it my business to lay eyes upon you, if you cause distress to me or mine—I shall volunteer your services to his majesty's Navy by making a gift of your person to the nearest interested press gang!"

Lawrence blanched and Catheryn knew it was with good reason. Only about one-third of the crews aboard British naval vessels were regular sailors, due for the most part to the appalling conditions below decks. Many came from workhouses and debtors' prisons. Some were even hardened criminals, allowed to volunteer simply because there were so few volunteers from the regular civilian population. In order to make up crews of a proper number, brutal press gangs worked the coastal villages and towns, waylaying the unwary and "pressing" them to shipboard duty. Wages were low, if paid at all, discipline was maintained with the bo'sun's cat, and food consisted of jerked beef and hardtack. Duff and Uncle Jig looked green around the gills and Lawrence slumped, clearly having no doubt that Dambroke or, for that matter, Lord Thomas or Varling wielded sufficient power to "arrange" his impressment, should the notion seem auspicious.

"Where will I go? How will I live?"

But Colby had had enough. "No business of ours, now, is it? You be grateful to get away in one piece, my lad. Abducting heiresses ain't no small thing, you know." He glanced at Dambroke. "Be dawn before we get back, my lord. Do we use his carriage or take Lady Tiffany and the lad up with us?"

Dambroke cast an eye over the exhausted pair and

opted after a bare moment's thought for the carriage. "Tripler will be wanting his cattle, in any case. Team at the Running Bull yours, Lawrence?"

Lawrence shook his head. "Hired cattle," he muttered. "Rig, too." He offered no protest to the earl's decision. The starch seemed to have gone out of him entirely and he stayed where he was, nursing his injured hand. Since he had used his neckbloth to bind it, he was disheveled as well as defeated. Duff and Uncle Jig continued to eye the others warily, but neither offered comment.

Colby and Caston went to bring the horses to the door, and Teddy remained sleepily in his place; but Tiffany stood up at last, moving her wrists and fingers experimentally. The blanket slid off one shoulder and she made a startled grab for it, but Captain Varling took it from her firmly.

Catheryn and Dambroke stared at the costume thus revealed in all its splendor. Tiffany had chosen to appear at the ball as Athena and, despite her ordeal, Catheryn thought she looked magnificent. Her costume was a classical, sleeveless chiton of white silk, banded beneath the breasts and around the ribs with gold cording. The simple gown was caught at one shoulder with a jeweled clasp, and she wore a gold band around her slender throat with matching bracelets high on each arm. Her raven hair was pulled back and swept up to fall in light ringlets, laced with gold thread, from the crown of her head to her neck. Gold corded sandals completed a costume that, though a bit daring perhaps, was hardly indecent and thoroughly becoming.

"I've an extra cloak tied to my saddle, lass," Varling said gently, breaking the spell. "I'll fetch it." Tiffany smiled gratefully and then cast an apprehensive glance at her brother. Hearing her quickly indrawn breath, Varling paused and followed her glance. Catheryn knew from the look on Dambroke's face that Tiffany would face an unpleasant interview before she was much older. She didn't know whether the costume or something else was responsible, but she was not surprised to see Varling hesitate with a puzzled look at his friend. "Dickon?" The earl turned his gaze upon him without altering his grim expression. "Lord, man, you look like a thundercloud." Varling spoke with forced cheer. He paused, tugging unconsciously at a sidewhisker, as he looked first at Tiffany, then Catheryn, then back at Dambroke. "This isn't the way I'd planned it, believe me, but I promised Maggie I'd keep you from eating them . . . well, Tiff and Catheryn—Miss Westering—and I suppose she meant Teddy, too, and. . . ." He floundered.

After a pregnant pause, Varling regrouped his forces and began again. "I'm doing this badly, I know, but if I'm to have any right to defend her . . . that is, them . . . that is, to debate the matter uppermost in your mind, my lord. . . ." He floundered more, stumbling over his words in a most uncharacteristic fashion, as Dambroke's continued silence seemed to make it more and more difficult for him to explain himself. The others simply stared at him. "I want . . . that is, I'd be honored . . . oh, damn it, Dickon! I want to marry Tiffany! If you approve, of course, and if she will have me, that is," he added with a near panic-stricken look at his beloved. She was staring like the others and with her mouth open in a most unladylike way, but the light in her eyes put to rest whatever doubt anyone may have had on the subject.

The earl frowned. "You want to what?"

"Marry her. Take her to wife. Make her Lady Tiffany Varling. Someday Lady Stanthorpe, of course, but much later I hope. Oh, Dickon, I know I'm out of line. This is neither the time nor the place. You're thinking that much, certainly, and you're right! But I want her, my lord. I can handle her—keep her out of mischief, that is," he corrected hastily with a sidelong look at Tiffany. "She minds me, Dickon. I don't know why, but she does." Catheryn stifled an involuntary chuckle, but her ladyship merely held her breath. Colby and Caston, choosing that moment to return, remained silent, sensing dramatics.

"Why now, Tony?" Dambroke drawled, his eye on Catheryn. She knew he had not missed her chuckle.

"Because you look like the very devil, my lord, like you want to crack their heads together, hers and Miss Westering's. I want the right to defend her. I-I love her." His voice trailed off self-consciously when he became aware of the general interest of his audience. In the ensuing pause, Duff was heard to confide to Uncle Jig that the big cove was right, sure enough.

"Good as a play they are."

Dambroke glanced at them. "You are right about one thing, Tony. This is not the time or place to discuss the matter." The tension in the room was abated somewhat during the captain's odd proposal, but it began to deepen again when Dambroke eyed first one set of culprits, then the other. He ignored the three on the bench after that brief glance and turned back to Varling. "Whatever you think, I have a good many questions to ask each of them about this night's work, and I will want straight answers, I promise you. But Teddy is nearly asleep and ought to be got home as soon as possible. He and I already have an appointment to discuss certain other matters. This episode can merely be included." A small squirm on the settle betrayed that, despite closed eyes, Teddy was still awake and listening. Dambroke turned his attention to the ladies.

"As for Tiffany. . . ." She stiffened, watching him intently. "Though I naturally have a question or two to put to her privately, I doubt she will be in dire enough straits to require your defense, whatever your future plans may be." Varling and Tiffany looked at each other, hope springing to their eyes. "Your protection," Dambroke went on grimly, "might better be offered to Miss Westering. Her actions tonight compounded by threefold any error made by either Tiffany or Teddy, not to mention the fact that she put herself in grave danger. I shall have a good deal to say to her presently, I assure you, and there are several questions I intend to ask that I daresay she would as lief not hear at all."

Catheryn was certain he was right. She had enjoyed the little scene between Varling and the earl quite as much as Duff had, but now she found herself the uncomfortable cynosure of all eyes. A guilty thought that much of this evening's activity would have been avoided had she gone to Dambroke in the first place, instead of attempting to protect Teddy from his wrath, only made matters worse. She was tired. She could feel blood flooding her cheeks and, finally, she took refuge in dignity.

"I'm certain you will have much to say, my lord, but I

pray you will wait until we have all had some sleep and that you will choose a more private place." Her voice trembled slightly, though she fought to stay calm. "As to your questions, you may ask them whenever you like. If they are pertinent, I shall answer them willingly, of course, but you have no right to cross-question me, you know."

It was almost as though she had pushed a button of some sort. She knew he had been keeping a tight rein on himself and that he, too, was tired, but she was as astonished as everyone else when his quick temper snapped. "So you'll be the judge of whether my questions are pertinent, will you? And refuse to answer them if they are not, I suppose!" He advanced upon her in a manner much more threatening than any displayed earlier by Lawrence. "You'd question my rights, Catheryn? Well. . . ." He seized her shoulders, shaking her, his grip bruising the tender skin. "By God, my girl, I won't have it! You'll answer whatever I choose to ask or rue the day! Just remember that once we're married I'll have the right to cross-question you any time the mood strikes me. For that matter, I'll damned well have the right to beat you soundly if I don't like your answers! How will you like that, my girl!"

A sudden and deathlike silence fell upon the taproom. Varling and Caston, both looking as though they thought Catheryn truly would need their protection, had moved a step or two in her direction when Dambroke began to shake her. Now they stopped, shocked to stillness. Tiffany's hand flew to her mouth, and Teddy came wide awake. Lord Thomas grinned with unholy glee, while the three men on the bench merely looked at each other in bewilderment. Dambroke seemed to realize immediately that, as a proposal of marriage, his words left a great deal to be desired. He dropped his hands helplessly and, for the moment, was speechless.

Catheryn's face had gone white. As soon as the earl released her and without looking at him she turned away, fighting to control emotions that threatened to overwhelm her. "How dare you, my lord!" Her voice was low-pitched but controlled, and the scorn in it carried to everyone in the room. "How dare you mock such feelings as the captain has just displayed! Have you no regard for love, for gentleness? How dare you treat me so! Your behavior is contemptible." Her breath was coming heavily, nearly in sobs, and her hands were clenched fists against her skirts. That he could have spoken to her in such a way and with such an audience!

"Catheryn, please. It was my damnable temper." He was clearly appalled at what he had said. His voice was gruff, and she felt a gentle hand upon her shoulder. "I never meant. . . ."

Control evaporating, she wheeled on him in sudden fury and he staggered back, reeling from a slap delivered with the full force of her hand.

"Oh, I know you never meant it, my lord!" she blazed, barely conscious of what she said. "None of it but perhaps the wish to beat me! I know you were angry. Angry with me for meddling; but if I hadn't meddled you'd not have found them so quickly. And without Teddy's quick wits," she continued hotly, "you might not have found Tiffany at all till it was too late. But once again your stupid authority had been sidestepped and you can think of nothing else. There is nothing further to say to the purpose. Good night to you, sir!" And without another word, she stormed past an open-mouthed Colby and out of the taproom. No one tried to stop her.

XX

Driven by indignant fury, Catheryn reached the Great North Road before the enormity of her actions overcame her. Tears began to stream down her face, and Psyche slowed unheeded to a walk. How could she have done such a thing! Dambroke had embarrassed her, to be sure, but what she had done was much worse. To slap him in front of them all and then rail at him like a Billingsgate fishwife! His pride would surely never let him forgive her. She turned, almost with relief, at the sound of pursuing hoofbeats, but it was only Edmund Caston. He rode up beside her.

"Don't say anything, Edmund," she begged, eyeing him warily through her tears. "If you scold me I shall cry, and if you sympathize, I shall have the vapors, so say nothing. Thank you for coming, however." Amazingly, he acceded to her wishes and, when she sniffled, silently handed her a large handkerchief from his waistcoat pocket. She thanked him again and, oddly comforted by his presence, urged the mare to a faster pace.

Maggie was waiting when they returned, but either a sign from Edmund or Catheryn's own expression kept her from asking any disconcerting questions. Once she heard the rescue had been a success, she hustled Catheryn upstairs, chattering of her own night's adventure while tucking her charge into bed.

"Tony nearly throttled that foppish worm, Lucas Markham, thinking he'd know where Tiff had been taken. He did know about an uncle near Stevenage, but that was all." With that little bit of information the men had gone to their various abodes to change to riding dress. Maggie had gained escort by pleading fatigue and done likewise. She then followed her brother to the rendezvous point and continued to follow well behind the men until they were too far from London to send her back. "Lord, but Tony was livid! He scolded all the way from Barnet, and I nearly died when Mr. Caston offered to take me home, but they decided he might be needed. Then Lord Thomas said I had spunk, so Tony turned on him for a short time. Said if that was how he means to go on, he will live under the cat's paw for certain." Maggie grinned complacently, and Catheryn stared at her.

"They have accepted his suit, then!" Maggie nodded. "Oh, that's wonderful. I know you will be very happy." She tried to sound excited, but her heart wasn't in it.

Maggie didn't seem to mind, however, and continued with her tale. They had found Dambroke on the verge of going to bed and relayed the news of the abduction, whereupon he had immediately sent for fresh mounts and Maggie had demanded to be included. "I thought I had as much right as anyone to help rescue Tiff," she said, "but Tony objected rather rudely, and then that boy Nat came along and told us about Teddy and you. I insisted then, and I think Tom would have supported me, but Dambroke. . . ." She broke off with an odd look at Catheryn, then finished lamely, "Well, he was pretty angry, I guess."

Catheryn wondered what he had said and, remembering Varling's words about a promise to Maggie, she concluded that he must have made his feelings about her involvement rather plain. When Maggie had gone, she lay back against the pillows and let the tears come again. She could still visualize the earl's face after she had slapped him. Except for the fiery imprint of her hand, it had been chalk-white with anger and shock. She could not remember ever having been in such a rage with anyone and wondered what on earth had come over her to cause her to fly out so at the man she loved. For now that it was probably too late, now that he would probably never forgive her, her defenses were down and she could confront the feelings she had so long denied. She loved him and had done so from the moment she had first laid eyes upon him. She should have realized it long ago, she told herself, but certainly since the night of the countess's ball. Else why had she not slapped him then when surely he had asked for it, rather than tonight when. . . . Exhaustion overcame her midthought and she slept.

When she awoke, the sun was high and Mary was briskly opening curtains and wielding a feather duster. "Didn't think you'd wish to sleep the day away, Miss Catheryn. Miss Lucy's ordered a lovely late breakfast, and Lady Margaret said I was to get you up first and then see to the Lady Tiffany."

"What time is it, Mary?"

"Gone eleven, miss. Near everyone else is up but you and her ladyship. Lord Thomas and Mr. Caston left for town over an hour ago to take the news to my lady. And Master Teddy is with Mr. MacClaren doing his lessons. Which dress will you wear, miss?"

"The white spotted muslin with the blue sash," Catheryn replied, turning to practical matters in order to stem the flood of memory from the previous night. As it was, thoughts kept intruding, and she could feel her cheeks burning when she turned to let Mary do up the frock's tiny satin-covered buttons. When she finished, Catheryn slipped her stockinged feet into blue kid slippers and set off to the breakfast parlor, where she found Maggie chatting with her brother and Miss Lucy over cups of chocolate.

The three looked a little conscious when she entered, and she wondered if they had been discussing her. Feeling the color creep to her cheeks again, she firmly put the disquieting thought aside and accepted Captain Varling's offer to help her to some Yorkshire ham. She had hoped to avoid all the gentlemen, but he certainly was the least threatening to her peace of mind. Once she was seated with a heaping plate and had begun to eat, she found it much easier to take part in the conversation, and by the time Tiffany entered, she had recovered her poise; consequently, the fact that her ladyship was accompanied by the earl was only slightly disconcerting.

Pointedly wishing Tiffany good day, she avoided Dambroke's eye, but for the next half hour, though he barely spoke a word, she was extraordinarily aware of his presence. If subsequent discussion among the others was sometimes stilted and formal, and if certain subjects were strictly avoided, it was surely due to the presence of the servants. They soon departed, however, and the conversation still had a forced quality; so Catheryn, beginning to peel a peach, was not surprised when the captain suggested that Tiffany might like to stroll with him through the gardens and down to the lake. After they had gone, however, she was dismayed when Miss Lucy turned to Maggie and brightly offered to show her a shirt pattern she had asked about.

Catheryn stared pleadingly at the other girl, hoping she would delay a few moments longer, but Maggie, barely concealing a grin, jumped to her feet and followed the old lady out of the room. Catheryn shot an accusing look at the half-peeled peach. Short of flinging it onto the table and fleeing, there was nothing to be done except face Dambroke *tête à tête*. Uncertain whether to damn the others for their conspiracy or thank them for arranging that the matter would soon be done, she cut a slice and began to nibble self-consciously, not looking at him, waiting for him to begin. Silence reigned for a moment or two. Then the earl cleared his throat and pushed his cup away, but just as he seemed about to speak, the door from the morning room popped open and a tousled brown head came into view around it.

"What the devil do you want!"

Manfully meeting the earl's glower, Teddy replied hastily, "I don't. I mean, Mr. MacClaren sent me. I didn't really expect you would be here. I had breakfast hours ago. If you don't want me, I could just go away again." He seemed only too anxious to do so, but Dambroke, still glaring, demanded to know why MacClaren had sent him. Since Teddy was apparently reluctant to explain, Catheryn took advantage of what seemed to be a reprieve and pushed back her chair.

"I'm sure your business is of a private nature," she said lightly, "so I'll leave you to discuss it alone." The suggestion was strongly rejected by both brothers, the earl muttering that the devil she would and Teddy objecting in dismay.

"Oh no! That is to say," he added, collecting himself again, "it's not at all obligatory for you to leave. In fact, if you please, I wish you will stay."

She looked at him searchingly, remembering as she did that she was not the only one in difficulty with Dambroke. "Very well, Teddy. I'll stay." She glanced at the earl as Teddy shut the door. Still visibly annoyed, Dambroke's attention was focused on the boy. Catheryn began to relax, thinking that, for once, he was a little slow on the uptake. Then she saw light dawning. His eyes narrowed.

"Why look here if you were certain I'd be elsewhere, young man?" There being no acceptable answer to the question, Teddy held his tongue. One foot shifted on the carpet. "Perhaps you did not wish to find me at all," the earl mused, rubbing it in. He slid his chair back, tilting it onto its hind legs, and folded his arms across his chest. "Well, Edward?"

Despite the relaxed pose, Dambroke looked formidable, but Teddy, having found him whether he wanted him or not, seemed suddenly determined to have it over and done with as soon as possible. He sighed. "I didn't. Want to find you, that is. I told Mr. MacClaren about the rescue. I wasn't puffing off or anything," he hastened to assure them, "only telling him. Anyways, he asked a lot of questions about how I came to be at the Running Bull at the right time." He paused but hurried on when Dambroke did not speak. "I . . . I told him about Straley and the snares, about . . . well, you know, 'bout everything."

"And?" prompted his brother.

The boy's hitherto steady gaze faltered. "He said I was to find you at once and have the talk you said we were to have this morning."

"Ah, yes, our talk."

"Mr. MacClaren said there would likely be a good bit more to discuss now," Teddy added, with a dismal air of opening the budget completely. "Only everyone slept late, so . . . so we didn't have it yet," he finished in a rush.

"MacClaren's right." Dambroke's chair came back to its proper stance with a dull thud. "I suppose we may as well do it now. If Miss Westering will excuse us?"

Catheryn couldn't help herself. No matter what he thought of her meddling, she had to make a last attempt. "My lord. . . ." Dambroke shook his head, though she was surpised to see his eyes soften.

"I must deal with this in my own way, Catheryn. The boy has been guilty of disobedience and outright defiance. I am grateful for his quick thinking last night and

212

agree that it was undoubtedly responsible for Tiffany's rescue, but I cannot condone the rest. There is especially the matter of the gun."

There was nothing more to say. At least he had spoken to her. And he had not called her Miss Westering again. She sat for some moments after they had gone and then, not wanting to face anyone else, wandered down to the library where she curled up in her favorite chair, tucking her feet up under her. Her thoughts were not as muddled as they had been, but they were still far from clear. She sighed and, within minutes, had dozed off.

She was awakened by the sound of the latch clicking into place on the alcove door and looked up, stretching unconsciously. Dambroke stood just inside the door. She stared at him, caught off guard, and her heart began to pound. "So here you are. I've nearly turned the house upside down looking for you, my girl."

She said the first thing that came to mind. "I am not your girl."

"So it would seem." He stepped closer. "I shall not go away till you explain just why you are not, you know." She was silent and found she couldn't think properly at all. Her silly heart was banging against her ribs so hard she thought he must be able to hear it. Having been certain he would demand an explanation of an entirely different sort, she now didn't know what to think. "This really is a dreary place in daytime," he observed, looking around the room.

"I do not find it so," she hazarded, keeping a wary eye on him.

"Nonsense. You only mean to disagree with anything I say. I wish you will come into the study." He seemed hesitant, unlike his normal self, and it made her uncomfortable. It was easier to deal with him when he came the earl over her.

"Why the study, sir? So that you may make good your threat and beat me, too?"

"Don't be absurd. It's so gloomy in here that it makes me feel this discussion is slightly improper."

"Well, it is, and you may leave with my good will." Her voice took on a note of sharpness, purposely goading him.

"Catheryn." The note of warning was nearly comforting and the two steps he took toward her even more so. But then he hesitated again. "Damn. I'm only making more of a mull of it."

"Are you, my lord?" Her eyes began to twinkle in spite of herself and she felt a warmth spreading through her. Evidently her expression encouraged him, for he took another step toward her. Why was she trembling? He sat on the footstool at her feet and was silent, searching for the right words.

"I . . . I must apologize for my behavior last night, Catheryn. I will be sorry for it always, for having embarrassed you in front of everyone, particularly Lawrence and his lot. On my own behalf, I can only plead the strain of the past fortnight and add that I was very badly frightened to walk in and find you facing that damned pistol. Nevertheless, there is no excuse for me. May I hope that in time you will find it in your heart to forgive me?" The expression on his face when he looked up at last was so anxious that Miss Westering was betrayed into one of her low chuckles. Dambroke stared in amazement.

"Oh, my lord, you do apologize so beautifully. Of course, I hoped to see you actually upon your knees, but. . . ."

She was not allowed to continue. He jumped to his feet, looming over her, and reached to take her hands. "Come out of that chair, baggage. I cannot propose in form to a lady who remains curled up like a damned kitten."

Daintily, she untucked her feet, pushing her skirt down as she straightened her legs, but she remained seated and paid no heed to his outstretched hand. "Propose, my lord?" She looked up shyly. "I was afraid you were furious, that you would never speak to me again. What I did——"

"Hush," he said gently. She did not resist when he pulled her to her feet and lifted her chin, forcing her to look at him. "You need not apologize to me, little one. The boot is on the other foot entirely, for I deserved it." He stroked the side of her cheek. "Catheryn, my love. No, don't close your eyes. Look at me. That's better. Now, listen carefully. I love you. I know I failed to mention that bit before I blundered into my stupid speech last night, but I mention it now. I have loved you for quite a long time and have feared to put it to the test. Your attitude toward me has been so casual, almost sisterly. That night in the garden, I was nearly afraid I had ruined everything. And the next day in the library, I still wasn't sure. Then I scarcely saw you at all for three days and Monday came home to find you gone. I didn't realize how much I loved you until you brought up the fact that you might be leaving soon, and then to have it happen so suddenly! I nearly went crazy in London without you. I was so worried that you would blame me for Teddy's accident. You cannot imagine my relief when we heard he was safe!"

"Tiffany wrote that you were like a bear with a sore head," Catheryn observed sweetly.

"Did she? I probably was. I'm sure I made Mama's life miserable. I was so frustrated at having to stay in town when I wanted only to be here. And then to have to put up with your aunt's remarks . . . well, perhaps you can understand how I managed to work myself into such a snit. By the time I did arrive I was furious. Even so, I didn't realize how furious until you walked into the study looking so lovely and calm. You may have called the shot accurately when you accused me of having too high a regard for my own authority. On the other hand, I wanted to take you in my arms and tell you how much I had missed you, but I was afraid to do that, so perhaps I lost my temper instead. Then you lost yours as well, and I was terrified you would make good your threat to return to town and set up your own house. I've expected daily to hear that you were ready to leave."

"And I've been afraid you would send me away," she muttered. "And after last night——"

"Damn last night," he said. "I want very much for you to become my wife, Catheryn." He seemed hesitant again. "Is it possible, do you think?"

"What would your family say, sir?"

"I don't give a damn what they say," he replied with a searching look. "But if it matters to you, my mother will be delighted and the brat overjoyed. I didn't beat him, you know."

"I suppose that's a point in your favor." She gave herself a mental hug and began to enjoy the situation. "Why did you not, my lord?"

"Because, little witch, I thought it would please you if I restrained myself."

"Well, it does," she admitted, "though I suppose you tore a strip off him and threatened murder the next time he whispers out of turn." Dambroke only shrugged. "Well, he did ask for it, I expect. Will Tiffany approve, do you think?"

"Probably, but it doesn't matter. She's Tony's worry now. Poor Tony. I don't envy him."

"No, why should you? He manages her far better than you do, sir." She tempered her words with a smile, however, and he grinned at her.

"He does, does he?"

"Yes, sir. Besides, you have said you wish to be saddled with me, and I am not precisely conformable, you know."

"I shall manage," he said with mock severity.

She appeared to give the matter serious thought. "I suppose you mean you will beat me," she mused, "however, I am encouraged by the fact that you have never beaten your sister, no matter how——" Suddenly, she was being firmly shaken.

"Enough, Catheryn!" He stopped shaking her and looked down in near exasperation. "Have you done with all your foolishness? Say, 'yes, my lord.'"

"Yes, my lord." Her cheeks were rosy.

"Good! That method answered very nicely. We shall put it to a second test. Do you love me? Say 'yes, my lord.'" Her blushes betrayed her. She tried to pull away, but he held her, gently but firmly. "Answer me, little one."

"You have not spoken of my fortune, sir," she said demurely. "Will it annoy you if Sir Horace refuses to relinquish before I——" Again she was not allowed to continue. Instead, she found herself crushed against his broad chest in an enveloping hug.

"Naughty wench," he murmured against her curls. "What do you deserve for this behavior?" When her only answer was the irrepressible chuckle, he held her away with another shake. "I believe you are incorrigible. Will you or will you not marry me?"

"I will, my lord." He went perfectly still, and she felt her own knees begin to tremble. It took a moment for the facts to sink in. He was truly in love with her, and she had just agreed to become his wife. Soon she would be able to tell him about Dr. Keate, and maybe Teddy would be back at Eton by Michaelmas. She raised glowing eyes to his. "Oh, Richard, of course I will! I do love you so much, my lord!" And with a contented sigh she allowed herself to be gathered once again into his arms.

A moment later, he gently lifted her chin. This time, however, his kiss was no mere brush of lips as it had been the night of the countess's ball, but a soul-claiming intimation of things to come. Catheryn responded with enthusiasm, thinking briefly that if the feelings he stirred within her were wicked or even wanton, they were also incredibly delightful. Indeed, joy spread through her with a warmth that seemed to make her very skin tingle. It was perfectly wonderful!

Suddenly, the East Hall door flew open with a bang that startled them both, and Miss Lucy strode in. "Here you are, Catheryn. But what are you doing! Very improper, my dears. Very improper indeed!"

"Cousin Lucy," Dambroke said smoothly, retaining his hold on Catheryn, "you shall be the first to congratulate me. Catheryn has agreed to become my wife."

"Well, thank Heaven!" replied the old lady roundly. "Now, perhaps I shall be allowed a decent night's sleep!" And, turning on her heel, she shut the door firmly behind her, leaving them to their very agreeable business.

ABOUT THE AUTHOR

A fourth-generation Californian, Amanda Scott was born and raised in Salinas and graduated with a degree in history from Mills College in Oakland. She did graduate work at the University of North Carolina at Chapel Hill, specializing in British history, before obtaining her MA from San Jose State University. She lives with her husband and young son in Sacramento. Her hobbies include camping, backpacking, and gourmet cooking.